He Went With Hannibal

Publisher's Note

He Went With Hannibal was written over 50 years ago and tells the story of a young man accompanying Hannibal on his adventures around the world.

An excellent storyteller, Louise Andrews Kent provides the reader with the opportunity to experience a different time and place through the eyes of the main character, including the social customs, religious beliefs, and racial relations. Taking place over 2200 years ago, many parts of life are foreign and sometimes offensive to us now, including specific customs, practices, beliefs, and words. To maintain and provide historical accuracy and to allow a true representation of this time period the words used and the customs and attitudes described have not been removed or edited.

This edition published 2022
by Living Book Press

ISBN: 978-1-922919-07-6 (hardcover)
         978-1-922919-06-9 (softcover)

He Went With
Hannibal

Louise Andrews Kent

ILLUSTRATED BY
Witold T. Mars

Living Book Press

THE *He Went With...* SERIES

by

LOUISE ANDREWS KENT

Hannibal

Marco Polo

Christopher Columbus

Vasco da Gama

Magellan

Drake

Champlain

John Paul Jones

For more information about these, and other great books visit
www.livingbookpress.com/hewentwith/

CONTENTS

1.	War of the Leopard Skin	1
2.	Man on an Elephant	12
3.	New Carthage	23
4.	Folds of a Toga	42
5.	Wide River	62
6.	Only Mountains	77
7.	First Meeting	98
8.	Army in the Clouds	111
9.	Galloping Torches	127
10.	Wind, Sand, and Sun	140
11.	Ships Sail the Land	156
12.	Giant Claws	176
13.	A Slave Is Sold	185
14.	Grapevine	195
15.	At the Gates	208
16.	Freedom	223
17.	Gully at Trebbia	240
18.	Artemis or Athena	251
19.	Royal Dinner	262
20.	Sophonisba	270
21.	Zama	277
22.	Peace in Carthage	286
23.	Last Victory	294
	Author's Note	303

DATES

IT IS difficult for us to think back two thousand years and get a clear idea of the calendars of the period. We do not know the Carthaginian. The Roman dates are figured from the founding of the city by Romulus. Ours center around the birth of Christ. By relating them to the Roman dates, we get the following table for the chief events in the life of Hannibal.

247 B.C.	Hannibal, oldest son of Hamilcar Barca, born
238 B.C.	Hamilcar and his three sons leave Carthage for Spain
221 B.C.	Hannibal made commander of army in Spain
219 B.C.	He besieges Saguntum
218 B.C.	Crosses Alps to Italy
218 B.C.	Defeats Romans at Ticino and Trebbia
217 B.C.	Battle of Trasimeno
217 B.C.	Escape at Cales
216 B.C.	Battle of Cannal
216 B.C.	Capua joins Hannibal
212 B.C.	He captures Tarentum
212 B.C.	Syracuse defended by Archimedes
211 B.C.	Hannibal at the gates of Rome
211 B.C.	Capua surrenders to Rome
209 B.C.	Tarentum captured by Rome
209 B.C.	New Carthage captured by Scipio
207 B.C.	Death of Hasdrubal Barca
206 B.C.	Meeting of Syphax and Scipio
205 B.C.	Scipio crosses to Africa
203 B.C.	Hannibal summoned to Carthage
202 B.C.	Battle of Zama
202-195 B.C.	Hannibal a statesman of Carthage
195 B.C.	Hannibal in Tyre, Syria
195-183 B.C.	Hannibal a fugitive from Roman vengeance
183 B.C.	Death of Scipio Africanus
183 B.C.	Death of Hannibal

CHAPTER 1

WAR OF THE LEOPARD SKIN

BRECON WAS almost thirteen years old when he was sent as a hostage to Hannibal.

"Remember that when Orion rises behind the White Cliff," his grandmother said, "and you see his belt and his sword of stars, you will be thirteen. Almost a man."

Brecon's grandmother knew things about people's ages and the stars. She knew how to pickle fish and what herbs to mix with mud to prevent baldness. She was a tall old woman with thick black eyebrows meeting over surprisingly bright blue eyes. Her eyebrows made her look as if she were scowling but when her eyes flashed blue, she was really smiling. Brecon knew.

"And remember, only you can wear the leopard skin," she added proudly. "You are the Chief's only son."

She had a comb made of the shell of a tortoise. Few people in their part of Spain had such a treasure. Brecon wished his grandmother did not have one. He tried to slip away while she was hunting for it. They were in the cave back of their stone house, the cave with the paintings on the wall. He had almost passed the picture of the buffalo when a skinny white arm shot out from under her black cloak and long fingers grabbed him by his tousled red hair.

"No grandson of mine goes as hostage to the Lord Hannibal Barca with snarls in his hair," she said. "Hold still."

Brecon squirmed. He felt every hair of his head being yanked. "You are killing me," he moaned. "I'll be bald. Thistles—you scratch me with thistles! You sting me like a nest of wasps!"

His grandmother went on combing and said, "Did I hear you say you had washed your neck?"

At last his sufferings were over, though his neck was so clean it felt cold and his new clothes were prickly. His grandmother had spun, dyed, and woven the woollen cloth for his jacket and loose trousers. The pattern was a plaid of brown and green with a red line across it here and there. Over one shoulder she put the leopard skin. Brecon was not tall, and the leopard had been a large animal.

"It's too big for me," he said, stumbling over the tail, which had somehow got between his feet.

"You must fight anyone who says so," his grandmother said.

Brecon thought there had been enough fighting already. When his grandfather died, a cousin, leader of another tribe, had claimed the leopard skin. Dafyd, Brecon's father, had led his tribe into battle. They were victorious and the men had brought the leopard skin home and had put it in the cave with his father's sword and shield. His father never came. They had buried him in the valley beyond the White Cliff. He had won the battle, but while he was sleeping on the leopard skin he had been treacherously stabbed. The reddish-brown spot, black now and bigger than many leopard spots together, was his blood.

This was not the end of the War of the Leopard Skin. There

had been vengeance and more vengeance. Other tribes had joined in the fighting. Once, during a battle, men had seized Brecon and carried him off. His own men had come quickly to the enemy's camp. They found Brecon kicking the shins of an enormous man called Prince Leon. They had knocked the Prince down and had carried Brecon home again. His grandmother was so pleased that she had told Pablo, the smith, to make Brecon some small gold armbands out of a large one of his father's and she had given him his mother's gold chain. He did not remember his mother. She had died when he was born.

Pablo was a smith who could do anything with metal. He could shoe a horse, make a sword or a trumpet or a silver cup. He let Brecon make a cup for his grandmother while he himself worked on the gold armbands. Brecon did well, Pablo said.

"You have the secret," he said. "To work iron, you have to be iron. To work silver, you must be silver. With silver, patience is better than speed."

The cup was finished the day that the news came that peace was made between the tribes. Lord Hannibal Barca had made the peace. He had asked for Brecon as one of the hostages who were to be sent to him.

"What does a hostage mean?" Brecon had asked.

"That if our tribe makes war you will be killed or sold as a slave," his grandmother said. "I will see that they keep the peace," she added, and Brecon felt quite sure she would.

She also said that since Brecon was a cousin of Hannibal's wife, the Lady Imilce, he would be among friends. She sent some of her special pickled fish and some of her worst-tasting medicines and a blanket of her own weaving to Hannibal.

So now, when Hannibal's men came, Brecon was ready. He rode his little chestnut mare called Starlight. He rode her without either saddle or bridle but she had a saddlecloth of the brown and green plaid, like his jacket. Fastened to his belt was a short two-edged sword Pablo had made. Inlaid in silver on the bronze sheath was the pattern of Orion's stars.

Some of the hostages were crying, but not Brecon. He thanked his grandmother again for the sword.

"Remember you are the Chief," she said again in her deep voice. "The comb is in your saddlebag. Use it."

"Yes, Grandmother."

"Keep count of the moons. You have the parchment."

"Yes, Grandmother."

She had taught him how to keep track of time and she had given him a precious piece of parchment and a pen made from an eagle's feather. Every time the moon was a thin new crescent, he must draw it on the parchment, she had said. Then when it was half a silver coin he must draw it again. In seven days it would rise like a shield of gold. In seven days more he would

see the other half of the silver coin. Another seven days and, before dawn, he would see the last thin curved fingernail of brightness.

There would be thirteen new moons, she told him.

"And what else?" she asked.

"An extra day, Grandmother."

"How old will you be then?"

"Fourteen, Grandmother."

"Right. You have my leave to go now. Behave as well as you look."

"Yes, Grandmother."

She made a twisting sign that was a blessing, he knew. He bent his head till it almost touched Starlight's chestnut mane. When he looked up again she had gone into the cave. She kept her loom there, and for a minute or two he could hear the sound of weaving. Then he was riding beside one of the other hostages down the hill. The jingling of bridles, the creak of saddles, and the thud of horses' hoofs was all he heard.

He rode next to a fat, pink-faced boy with hair like yellow wool. Alain was his name. Brecon had seen him before. Alain was the son of Prince Leon, whose shins Brecon had once kicked. Alain had splendid weapons and a big black warhorse. He had silver stirrups and a saddle trimmed with silver. His horse's headband and bridle were as bright with gold as a lady's necklace.

"Who's that little man who calls himself the leader?" Alain asked Brecon.

"My grandmother said it was Lord Carthalo."

"He doesn't look like a leader."

"How should a leader look?" Brecon asked.

"Why, tall, of course, with arms like branches of a great

oak. Fair-haired, nose like an eagle's beak. White teeth like a lion's. A mustache like a curtain of gold. He should have a voice like a trumpet and be dressed in purple and gold," Alain said.

Carthalo certainly did not fit this description. He was neither tall nor short, fat nor thin. His hair was no special color. His eyelids drooped over eyes that were perhaps gray, perhaps hazel. His nose was not at all like an eagle's beak. His teeth were white but not suitable for a lion. His upper lip had been shaved but not lately. His beard was roughly clipped, apparently with a dull pair of scissors. As for his voice, it would not, like a trumpet, rouse anyone from a sound sleep at dawn.

Yet, Brecon noticed, though Carthalo's orders were softly spoken, his men obeyed them quickly and without question.

"My father's shepherds wear better cloaks," Alain added.

Carthalo's cloak had once been black. It had been wet so many times, slept on, wet or dry, so often that it was now blackish brown.

"I think he'd make a good shepherd," Brecon said. "Keep the sheep together. Keep wolves away. Know all the dangers."

"Dangers! What are you afraid of?" Alain asked with his whining laugh. "Of me? You'd better be."

"No, not of you," Brecon said.

"Want to fight?"

"Not especially. Certainly not just now."

"We'll wrestle at Hannibal's camp. I'll throw you down, crush every rib you have. You know I can, don't you?"

"You certainly weigh more than I do," Brecon said, "but perhaps we would not be wrestling. I have a sword."

He drew it out so suddenly that it flashed in the clear blue air. Alain's horse reared.

"Put that thing away, you fool," he shouted. "Can't you see you frighten my horse?"

"Certainly," Brecon said, sheathing the sword.

The whole thing had taken only a minute but Carthalo had noticed it. He waved his men and the other hostages ahead, stopped his old brown horse beside the trail, and waited till Alain and Brecon came up with him.

He looked at them without speaking for a moment and then said to Alain, "Has there been trouble between you and the young Chief, Prince?"

"Chief indeed! Chief of the Leopard Skin with a little boy's sword. He's a coward. Won't fight. Make him get off that skinny horse, and drop that carving knife, and I'll break his ribs and knock his teeth out." Alain's pink face was red. His voice ran up into a squeak.

"You wish to accept this invitation?" Carthalo asked Brecon.

"No, my lord," Brecon said. "It was my fault, the disturbance. I should not have pulled out the sword. I ask your pardon. And Alain's."

"So now he apologizes. I said he wouldn't fight," Alain said.

"You don't enjoy fighting?" Carthalo asked Brecon.

"When I'm older I might learn to fight in a good cause."

"What is your idea of a good cause?"

"Why, to defend my land and the people of my tribe from harm."

"Ha!" Alain broke in. "The dirty little coward means his grandmother. The old witch. Everyone knows she's a witch."

Carthalo turned to Alain. His voice was not loud but it had a tone that made Alain's red face turn pale.

"If I hear more of such talk, I must report it to my Lord Hannibal. You are hostages, pledges that peace has been made between your tribes. The penalty of breaking the peace is one I prefer not to speak of," Carthalo said. He turned to one of the rear guard waiting on the trail. "Escort Prince Alain. You, Sir Brecon, may come with me."

The journey took many days. It was the time beech leaves turn bronze and gold. The sky was a clear cloudless blue. At night, as Brecon lay curled up on his cloak with his leopard skin over him, stars were gold sparks in a silvery-green sky. Sometimes he woke and saw the Pleiades twinkling, the red glow of Sirius, the bright flash of Orion's sword.

He and Alain were never close enough to quarrel for the rest of the journey. When the track was narrow, Brecon rode behind Carthalo. When it was wide, the leader would wave one of the hostages, often Brecon, to ride beside him. The Carthaginian was easy to talk to. Brecon found himself telling Carthalo things he had never told anyone else.

Once Carthalo said, "You are young to be the chief of a tribe." And Brecon answered, "No boy thirteen years old can really be a chief. I am only a toy chief."

"There must be a real chief—who is it?"

Brecon laughed and said, "Why, my grandmother, of course. She always tells whoever is called the chief what to do. First my grandfather, next my father, then me. If I do not go back, it will be my Uncle Carlo, I think."

"You wish to go back?"

"Someday. But I'd like to see the world—Italy and Greece and Carthage. Will you tell me about Carthage, my lord?"

So Carthalo told about Carthage: about the arm of land that circled the harbor, about the quays where ships brought elephants and silver and purple cloth or carried away peacocks and glass and the skins of lions.

"Or leopards," Carthalo added, the crease in his cheek deepening into a smile.

He told about the Byrsa, the hill high above the city. There was a great temple on top of it. Nearby were palaces and, along the streets below, factories six stories tall. On one floor men might be making swords. Below, glass masks might be made, or wigs of red hair for ladies who were tired of brown. He told about palaces where the floors were pink cement, veined and polished to look like marble. There was the inner harbor where you tied up your galley to a ring in a white marble wall.

It was a hidden harbor, Carthalo said, a circle with an island in the middle of it. There was a high tower on the island from which the admiral could see all the ships in both harbors.

No, he said when Brecon asked him, it was not true that ships of Carthage were rowed with oars of solid silver.

"Alain said so but I told him they'd be too heavy," Brecon said, and Carthalo made the quiet chuckling sound that was as near laughing as he ever seemed to come.

The track soon narrowed and Brecon dropped behind. It was not until the last day of the journey that he asked about Hannibal.

"What do you know about him?" Carthalo asked.

"Just what Alain was telling everyone at supper last night."

"What was that?"

"He says Hannibal is an enormous man with eyes like a cruel snake's. That he dresses in purple and gold and wears a jeweled crown. He sleeps on a gold couch stuffed with the down of a thousand geese. He rides an elephant in a gold and ivory tower and prods the elephant with a gold spear. Rich food is brought to him from all over the world. He calls himself King of Spain and has your tongue cut out if you won't call him so.

He swore when he was nine years old to hate Rome, and every day since he has been planning to burn every Roman alive and be king of the world."

"Do you believe him?" Carthalo asked.

"No."

"Why not?"

"I do not think a man like you would be his follower," Brecon said.

"I thank you," said Carthalo. He rode on in silence for a moment and then added, "When I was your age, I followed Hannibal's father, Hamilcar Barca, wherever he went. He was wise, brave, and just. He loved Carthage. The Council and the Shofets—they are the rulers of Carthage—made him their general. His trade was fighting, but when he made treaties he kept his word. The Romans did not. There should be room along the Mediterranean Sea for both Carthage and Rome. Carthage wants to trade with people. Rome wants to rule them. She threatened Carthage, so the city sent Hamilcar here to Spain to set up new trading posts. There is Gades on the Atlantic and New Carthage south of the Ebro. Hamilcar brought Hannibal to Spain when he was nine years old. Hannibal did make a vow. I heard him. Shall I tell you about it?"

"Please."

"Before we left Carthage, Hamilcar and his officers met in the temple. At the altar Hamilcar prayed and offered a lamb as a sacrifice. Hannibal remembers the day well. This is how I have heard him tell about it. He said, 'My father had a cup in his hand. He poured a libation to Melkart. I was standing near the altar. My father asked all the others to draw back a little way. Then he called me over to him and asked me very gently if I wished to go with him on his journey. Like a boy, I quickly said yes, even begged to go. He took me by one hand, led me to the altar, told me to put my other hand on the sacrificed lamb. He asked me to swear never to be a friend to Rome. I did so."

"When a city becomes a friend of Rome," Carthalo went on, "its spirit is soon broken. Hamilcar Barca—Barca means 'thunderbolt'—fought until he died to keep the spirit alive. Now this is the work of his sons, Hannibal, Hasdrubal, and Mago. As to the foolishness about jeweled crowns and couches of down—Hannibal dresses like any soldier of Spain, in a black cloak and a headcloth of black wool. He often sleeps on the cloak near his sentries. Or on a lion's skin. Or on bare ground. If there is an icy stream to swim, he is the first in the water. Where the greatest danger to his men is—there is Hannibal. He eats what his men eat—a little porridge, a little cheese. If anyone goes hungry, it is Hannibal."

"And he's not a giant?" Brecon asked.

"A little taller than you and I," Carthalo said, smiling.

"I think I'll know him when I see him," Brecon said.

CHAPTER 2

MAN ON AN ELEPHANT

THEY PASSED the White Castle, a citadel in the mountains. Carthalo told Brecon that Hannibal's wife, Imilce, came from there.

"Yes, my lord," Brecon said. "She was a cousin of my father's. My grandmother sent her a message."

He was glad Carthalo did not ask what the message was. It began with fine words of courtesy and it ended by asking Imilce to be sure that Brecon combed his hair.

He must find the comb, he thought, and asked aloud, "When shall I see her?"

"Not soon," Carthalo said. "She is at New Carthage. We'll sail there after we have seen Hannibal. His camp is near this river we are following."

The country had changed. The high brown pastures, the mines where men dug silver, the high bare mountains were far away now. Here were rich fields where wheat had been cut and green pastures were full of grazing cattle and horses. Grapes grew here. At one small village was a table with a great silver bowl of wine on it. Men picked up silver cups and drank the wine from them. There was dancing in the street and the sound of flutes.

"They sound like nightingales," Rhodri, the youngest of the hostages said.

"Yes, much prettier than bagpipes," Brecon said, but they both were homesick for the scream of the pipes.

Now they were following a green path beside a wide smoothly flowing river. Suddenly Brecon said he heard trumpets.

"What kind?" Carthalo asked smiling.

"Not bagpipes," Brecon said. "Bigger."

"Nine feet tall," Carthalo said, and, seeing Brecon looking puzzled, he added, "elephants."

"Elephants! Shall I see one—today?"

"Ride one, perhaps. See, through the oaks there, where the dust is blowing. That's from their feet."

The camp was on a big open field near the river. Dust rose so thickly from it that the charging elephants and horses were only shadows.

Rhodri asked timidly, "Is it a battle, my Lord Carthalo?"

"No, Rhodri," Carthalo said kindly. "They are only practicing. We'll wait here at the gate and watch. See those shields on the wall? Here come the Numidians to throw javelins at them."

Beautiful horses, slender, quick, moving faster than a swift waterfall, streamed past them. The riders used neither saddles nor bridles. Each man seemed part of his horse. Suddenly the whole troop wheeled. The air hummed strangely as javelins sped toward the targets, each landing with a splintering crash.

"The best horsemen in the world," Carthalo said, "but your men of Spain—Celts and Iberians—are next best, and growing better. Come, we must find my Lord Hannibal before the elephants charge again."

The guards at the gate waved them on and the little troop moved down the field in what—before the Numidians passed— would have seemed like pretty good order. They dismounted near a platform with many handsomely dressed men standing on it. Grooms led the hostages' horses away. Brecon found himself at the end of the line, with Alain on his right. Carthalo was in front of them facing the platform. The soldiers were behind.

Alain said, "So Chief Brecon of the dusty old leopard skin honors me with his presence. I'm honored. Hannibal's honored. See—there he is in purple and gold."

"Silence," Carthalo said without turning his head.

There was a very tall man in purple and gold on the platform. The men around him were richly dressed. They wore swords like Brecon's, short curved swords sharpened on both edges. They wore plumes in their helmets. Some of them had shoes of scarlet leather. The tall man's shoes were purple. They were talking and laughing. No one noticed Carthalo's party. Except one.

He rode up to the platform, appearing so suddenly out of the dust cloud that even Carthalo, who had just turned to speak to the hostages, did not know he had come. That is, he did not know it until he saw Brecon's face.

Brecon was looking up, far above the heads of the tallest men. It was a question which he had opened wider, his mouth or his eyes. He had turned pale. His red hair looked redder than ever. He had seen his first elephant.

Probably, he decided quickly, it was like other elephants. It was large, leathery, wrinkled, and dusty, with big ears, small eyes, and big soft feet. It had a trunk like an old snake and a tail that matched the trunk fairly well. It swayed all the time from side to side.

Carthalo said, "Are you looking at the elephant, Brecon?"

Brecon gave a slight gasp.

"No. No, my lord. Not now. At the man," he said.

The man had on a dusty black cloak. His boots, dusty too, were of brown Spanish leather. Instead of a whip he had a small oak branch with a few dry leaves on it. He made the elephant turn right or left by touching one of her big flapping ears gently with the stick. Brecon noticed that the man's curly brown hair did not look as if it had been combed lately. He liked the hair, the finely arched nose, and the large brown eyes—eyes full of kindness as he looked down and smiled at Carthalo and the hostages.

"Gentlemen," he said to the men on the platform. "We have visitors."

He did not speak loudly but he might as well have blown a trumpet. Every man turned toward him. As they did so, Brecon thought, each changed a little. Each was still himself but part of him was also Hannibal. Because, of course, this was Hannibal. Even Alain knew it now and was kneeling on his plump knees.

"You may rise, Prince," Carthalo said. He began to say the names of the men the hostages were facing—my Lord Hannibal Barca, his brothers my Lord Hasdrubal Barca and my Lord Mago Barca, and the General my Lord Hasdrubal, son of Gisgo...

Brecon tried to hear the names but they were strange. The owners came from many countries—Greece, Egypt, Libya, Numidia—as well as from Spain.

Well, he thought, looking at a short man in a pointed black cap covered with gold stars, I must listen and learn.

Now Carthalo said the names of the hostages, the names of their fathers, their tribes, their villages. As he heard each name, Hannibal fixed his bright eyes on the boy, learned him, Brecon thought, so he would never forget him, smiled kindly down at him. He bowed as the boy bowed, then turned his eyes on the next one.

Brecon was at the end of the line. At last he heard Carthalo say, "Sir Brecon of the Leopard Skin, son of Dafyd."

He felt, rather than saw, Hannibal's eyes meet his own. He saw Hannibal touch the elephant lightly with the oak switch, then bend forward and say something. Then a dark mountain cut off the light. Brecon stood firm. Suddenly the wrinkled dry trunk twisted around his waist. He was swung high in the air. He heard men laughing below him, found himself on the elephant's neck facing Hannibal.

"Welcome, cousin," Hannibal said. "Shall we ride?"

Once Brecon had felt an earthquake. Riding an elephant was rather like it, he thought. Especially backward.

When they were half around the field, Hannibal said, "Your cousin, Imilce, will be glad to see you in New Carthage."

Words were jounced out of Brecon.

"I shall be—glad to see—her. I was—quite young when she—went away. Seven—I think. I thought she was—very beautiful."

"She still is," Hannibal said. "I wish I could go with you and see her. And Hamilcar. That's my son's name. I cannot leave here yet, but I hope it will not be long now."

Spanish cavalry dashed past and flung javelins against the targets.

"Not quite so swift as Numidians," Hannibal said, "because they use bridles so they have only one hand for throwing. But they are fine cavalry. Would you like to be a horseman? Fight in my army?"

"My lord—"

"Call me cousin," Hannibal said.

"My cousin—I don't like—fighting."

"That's what Carthalo said."

"He spoke of me? But—when?"

"He wrote me a letter about you. He wants you himself." Hannibal shoved a hand into a dingy leather pouch he had strapped to his belt. "Here—read it."

"I—can't read, my lord—cousin, I mean. I never saw a letter before. And I can write only a little," Brecon said.

"But not read?" Hannibal asked with his twinkling smile. Brecon pulled out his parchment.

"My grandmother taught me to make marks that show how the moon grows big and small again. When I have done it thirteen times—and added a day—I shall be fourteen years old."

"Why, you have made marks with a pen and can tell what they mean. You'll soon learn to read and write. You'll have to—if you work with Carthalo. Would you like to?"

"What does he do?"

Hannibal said that Carthalo found out things for him, carried messages, looked into the minds of men who were far away.

"I need more than one pair of eyes and ears. I need men I can trust who will tell me things I must know. Like when the moon will be full, how many shiploads of grain Sicily is sending to Rome, who commands Rome's legions, how they fight, how they think."

"Whether they are brave?" Brecon asked.

"Most Romans are brave," Hannibal said. "So are Gauls and Iberians and Numidians. But someone has to know how to use their courage. Thinking is sometimes harder work than hitting someone over the head with a large club. Carthalo is not too lazy to think."

"I would like to work for him—and for you, cousin," Brecon said.

Each of the hostages rode with Hannibal on the elephant. They all promised to help him. Most of them kept that promise, always.

They stayed three days in the camp, watching elephant and cavalry charges, seeing lines of foot-soldiers change swiftly from one formation to another, listening to songs around the campfires. There were stories too. Many of them were about Hercules. Some of the soldiers thought—or at least said—that Hannibal was really Hercules. Also that Hasdrubal Barca, only a little younger than Hannibal and much like him in looks, was Hercules' twin brother. They said that Mago Barca, the youngest brother, who rode like a Numidian on a white horse and wore a crimson cloak, was a god and lived only on golden apples.

Brecon, who had seen Mago eating roast lamb and pickled fish and fresh figs, knew this was not true. Mago did like oranges, and several times had tossed one to Brecon shouting, "Catch, cousin!" Brecon thought they were the best fruit in the world. The Numidians said they were sour things and dates were better. The Libyans agreed. Alain shouted at a rather small Numidian that grapes were the only fruit fit to eat. He was gobbling a large bunch and had not offered any to the soldiers. The Numidian, most unfairly, hit Alain in the stomach. Alain fell down—and the grapes were mashed in the dust. He got up and knocked Brecon down—he said Brecon was laughing at him. It is possible that he was right. Anyway, both were dusty and both had black eyes when they started for New Carthage.

Hannibal gave Brecon a leather sack to carry and guard. It contained presents for his wife and son. There were also things for Saafanbaal and Athena, two girls who lived in Imilce's palace. Saafanbaal was the daughter of the General Hasdrubal Gisgo, the big handsome man who always dressed in purple and gold. Athena was a little Greek girl whose parents had been lost at sea. Hannibal had rescued her from a pirate ship with other Greeks who became part of Imilce's household.

Both girls were about seven years old, Hasdrubal Gisgo said. He gave Brecon two bundles wrapped in soft woollen cloth to take to them.

"Dolls," he said. "Right things for girls that age, eh? Tell Saafanbaal to be a good girl, to do what my Lady Imilce tells her. Hope she's learning to spin, weave, all that sort of thing," he added. "Nothing like spinning to keep girls out of mischief. Sewing is good too. And cooking. Singing, reading books, playing the lute may be all very well. But they are not solid. See what I mean?"

Hasdrubal Gisgo was solid anyway, Brecon thought. Even an elephant would find him hard to carry. He looked very handsome in his purple and gold and his fine bronze helmet. He had a curly black beard. It could be spun, Brecon thought, and woven into something useful. Or used to stuff a pillow.

Brecon wondered whether spinning would really keep a girl out of mischief. He felt rather sorry for Saafanbaal if she had to spin instead of playing the lute. Seven years of age was rather young to get into much mischief. If Gisgo's daughter was like him, she was probably a good serious fat little girl, he thought, and forgot all about her. Their galley was ready. The rowers were at their oars. The last sacks of food were being carried on board. Another ship, which carried their horses, was already dropping swiftly downstream.

The voyage did not seem long to Brecon. He learned to row and took his turn at an oar. When the ship was anchored, he listened to the sailors tell about different ports they had seen. These men were not slaves chained to the oars as men were in Roman galleys. These were freeborn Carthaginians who sailed the sea because it was the life they liked. The only air fit to breathe was at sea, they said. They pitied soldiers who had to march in mud and dust. And to work in a noisy factory seven stories high! What sort of life was that? Why not live in a prison? And farming! Break your back growing food for a cow, and when you milk her she kicks the pail over and kicks you in the shin.

"Did you ever see any one stupider than a goose?" one sailor asked.

"Yes—the man who owns one," said another.

At this show of wit all his mates laughed loud and clapped him on the back.

They respected merchants and shipowners. After all, they were all merchants themselves. Each had his own little trading venture—a few glass beads, a little purple cloth, a box of spices. Each hoped to command his own ship someday.

They told Brecon how ships from Carthage sailed down along the west coast of Africa and anchored off certain trading beaches. Sailors piled goods on the beach. The big pile belonged to the ship, small piles to the sailors. Then you went back to the ship and waited. Natives would come bringing their goods, skins of lions and leopards, feathers, ivory, sometimes wedges of gold. They would put down what they would give next to each pile and go away. Then you would go ashore again. If you were satisfied with the trade, you picked up the things they had left. If not, you touched nothing and went away. They usually came back and added more. This might happen several times. When you were satisfied, you shoved off and went back to the ship.

Brecon had a hard time at first understanding the sailors' talk, but as the days went on he found himself speaking in their strange mixture of tongues. They used Celtic and Iberian words and words from Greece, Egypt, Sicily, even from Italy. They spoke too in their own language, which they called Phoenician and which the Romans, they said, found easier to call Punic.

During clear calm days while the oars of the galley made white fountains in the dark blue sea, Brecon was learning to speak Greek and to read it too. Sosillos, a Greek who had taught Greek to Hannibal, would scatter sand on a table and write words in the sand for Brecon to read. If he did well, Sosillos would tell him a story from the Odyssey. He would half speak, half chant the lines over and over again. After a while the words began to be written in Brecon's memory. They were not like words written in sand that could be brushed away. It was more as if they had been carved in marble. For the rest of his life they would bring back not only the wanderings of Odysseus but this first voyage of his own.

The rhythm of Homer's words would be mixed with the beat of oars, water bubbling past the ship, dolphins leaping in the waves. He would breathe clean air, feel the sun hot on his cheek, and hear Alain's voice say, "Now Sir Brecon of the Leopard Skin is freckled like a leopard—or a toad."

Rhodri would clench his small fists and squeak out, "Don't you dare say that!" but Brecon would only laugh. Alain with his thick pink nose peeling did not trouble him much, until one day when Alain twisted Rhodri's arm badly. Brecon was angry then and fought with Alain. Synhalus, Hannibal's Egyptian physician, and Carthalo separated them. Synhalus bandaged a cut over Brecon's right eye and gently felt Rhodri's arm, turning it first one way and then the other. He had wonderful strong square hands. They seemed to know all about whatever they touched. He rubbed a little ointment on Rhodri's arm, said it would soon be well—and it was. Brecon thought it was more the touch of the Egyptian's hands than the ointment that cured it.

Synhalus also applied medicine another way. He took one of Alain's hands in his and in a few moments, almost without motion, had Alain crying and begging for mercy.

"That hurts you?" he asked softly. "Why, I had only just begun. Touch the little boy again and I might have to finish."

For the rest of the voyage there was no more trouble. It had begun to seem endless when, just at sunset one evening, Carthalo said quietly, "There it is, New Carthage."

CHAPTER 3

NEW CARTHAGE

BEHIND THEM the sky was flaming in crimson and gold. The blazing shield of the sun was slipping down quickly into a cloud of deep purple. The light turned the walls of the city to a coppery rose color. An arm of land shut in a green lagoon. The water was so still that there seemed to be two cities: one of red copper above, one of green copper in the water below.

Then the sun plunged into the purple cloud and the city of copper was only brown and gray stone. They could see a narrow street twisting uphill from the quay. A train of mules was climbing it. There were casks of wine on their backs and boughs of cedar on the casks to keep the wine cool.

Carthalo climbed the same street after their galley was safely at the quay. The hostages followed, carrying their bundles.

"Like slaves," Alain grumbled.

He did not have far to go. He and another hostage were left at a house just within the city wall at the foot of the hill. Two more stayed at a house halfway up, two others nearer the top of the hill. Brecon and Rhodri climbed on after the others had all vanished through dark doorways.

Carthalo, who had stopped to introduce the last pair to their hosts, said to Brecon, "Walk on. Toward the lights."

The lights were blazing torches. Sosillos and Synhalus were already at the door.

"We will go in," Sosillos said.

On the polished pink floor two girls were playing a game with small pieces of bone. They were tossing the bones into the air and catching them on the backs of their hands. One girl had plump dimpled hands, dimples in her cheeks, light brown hair, and eyes that were round circles of blue in a pink face.

The other girl was thin as a snake. She moved as silently and gracefully as a snake. She had long narrow eyes as green as the lagoon. Her face might have been carved out of ivory. Her hair might have been carved too, only out of ebony. Both girls stopped their game and stared at the visitors. It was the roly-poly one who got up and trotted across the room to where someone was sitting.

The window faced west. It was a dark blue oblong against the fading sky. A woman with a small boy on her lap was looking out toward the sea and singing softly. Brecon only half heard the song. He recognized it—it was one his grandmother used to sing to him—but he was watching the girl playing with the knucklebones. She was tossing them from one hand to the other and looking at Brecon out of those strange green eyes.

He thought, she must see every one of my freckles.

Then she looked down at his feet and he looked down too at his old water-stained boots. As he shuffled his feet uneasily, he wished his boots were made of purple leather. He remembered that he had not combed his hair.

Then he thought, Gisgo said she was seven and sent her a doll. She must be nine at least. But why should I care what a nine-year-old girl thinks of my shoes?

A gentle voice said, "Sosillos! Synhalus! Welcome! And this must be Brecon, my cousin—grown to be a man, almost. Welcome to New Carthage! And is this Rhodri? I used to roast chestnuts with your mother, Rhodri—you are welcome too."

This must be Hannibal's wife. They both made their best bows.

The Lady Imilce was beautiful still, especially when she smiled, but she was thinner and older than Brecon remembered. The baby, Hannibal's son, was too heavy for her to carry. She handed him over to a nurse, who took him away to bed. He howled so that no one could hear anything else. Then Carthalo came in.

Imilce hurried across the room saying, "Welcome, Carthalo! What of my lord? I was watching—I always sit at the west window, you know, and watch the sunset. I saw the ship. I thought he might be on it. Will he come soon?"

"Soon, I hope," Carthalo said. "There is a letter that will tell more than I can."

She looked quite young again, Brecon thought, as she stood reading the letter in the light of the largest lamp.

The plump little girl ran up to Carthalo.

"Athena, my favorite goddess!" he said and added, turning to the boys, "She came all the way from Greece. These are Brecon and Rhodri from the other end of the world, from Spain, Athena."

The other girl was on her feet now. She was running those strange green eyes of hers over Carthalo's face and over his shabby brown cloak. Brecon admired Carthalo more than ever because he did not shuffle his feet when she looked scornfully at his old brown boots.

"This is Saafanbaal, daughter of Hasdrubal Gisgo," Carthalo said.

"But I call her Sophonisba," Athena said. "I named her myself, because it's easier for my tongue to say. Everyone calls her that now."

Sophonisba paid no attention to the boys or to Athena.

"What did you bring me? What did my father send me, Carthalo?" she asked.

She spoke in a soft sweet voice, rather like the notes of a shepherd's flute, Brecon thought.

He handed the leather sack to Carthalo, who reached into it and took out the bundles containing the dolls. The girls unwrapped them. The dolls were dressed alike in purple and fine linen. Their heads were made of glass. They had bright scarlet mouths, big black eyes, and black hair rather like Sophonisba's.

Athena clasped hers to her saying: "Oh, she's beautiful, beautiful! She is like my beautiful Sophonisba. I shall call her Sophie."

Sophonisba hardly looked at hers. Her voice no longer sounded like a flute. More like a bagpipe, Brecon thought, or an angry mule.

"A doll! He sent me a doll! I haven't played with dolls since I was six. This must be a joke, Carthalo. What did he really send?"

"What did you expect?"

"Why, a jar of perfume from Arabia. An emerald from India. Or a box of carved ivory with rubies for my ears in it. Or at least a few pearls. But a doll!"

She threw the doll across the room. The glass head shattered against a marble pillar. Athena was standing near it. A splinter of glass struck her forehead. Blood trickled down her face. She did not make a sound. All the noise was made by Sophonisba, who screamed, "Oh, I have hurt her! My treasure, my precious Athena, my little goddess, my owl, my wise serpent, my olive tree! I kiss your feet!" She did so, shedding tears on them. "Forgive Saafanbaal! Forgive your Sophie!"

Athena said, "It was an accident, Sophie. It's all right."

Synhalus, who had left the room, came back again. He held the edges of the cut together but blood still pumped out of it.

He said to Brecon, "Lay her on the bench. I must take a stitch there. Hold the edges together—yes, that's right—while I get my needle."

By now the room was full of people. Imilce was on her knees beside Athena, wiping the blood off her face with a scarf of white linen. Slaves were on their knees hunting for splinters of broken glass. Little Hamilcar's nurse, not wishing to miss anything, brought him back and his roars were added to the general confusion. Synhalus came striding back. He had to cut away some of Athena's hair before he sewed up the cut. More lamps were brought.

Athena looked pale in their light but she did not cry, even when Synhalus sewed up the wound. He said magic spells loudly while he worked. The bandage was soon in place. Blood no longer stained it but he still had work to do. Slaves, who had cut their fingers on bits of glass, groaned and asked for bandages and spells. Sophonisba fainted in Brecon's arms just as he finished helping Synhalus.

"What shall I do with her?" Brecon asked.

"Put her down on the floor and pour a bucket of water over her," Synhalus said.

Sophonisba revived just as the water arrived. The steward made the slaves mop the floor with it instead. He soon reported that every splinter of glass was found. Brecon wondered how he could tell. The steward later announced that every drop of blood was washed up.

"There must have been at least eleven," Carthalo said. "I've seen battles where ten thousand men were fighting where there was less fuss."

By this time Sophonisba had recovered.

"What did the Lord Hannibal send me?" she asked Carthalo in her softest, sweetest voice.

"Oh, probably another doll," Carthalo said. "Ask Brecon for it. He knows where the bag is."

Sophonisba turned her best smile on Brecon saying, "It's not a doll, is it, Brecon? Prince Brecon, Brecon of the Leopard Skin. Where is it? What is it?"

She patted his arm.

She's like a kitten, purrs, pats one minute, scratches the next, he thought, and said, "I'm not a prince and I don't know what he sent. I will give the bundle he gave me for my cousin to her. She will know which is your present, no doubt."

Sophonisba scowled at him, said, "Oh, very well, freckle face," and went running across to Imilce, announcing, "Prince Brecon has a bagful of treasures from my Lord Hannibal."

More noise followed while a table was brought. Brecon handed the bag to his cousin, who spread out the things it contained. There was a toy lamb for Hamilcar, another doll for Athena, perfume and a necklace of pearls for Imilce. There was also something for her wrapped in linen, something round and flat. She looked at it hastily, turned pink and wrapped it up again before Sophonisba, who had sidled up to her, could see it. Just then Imilce found Sophonisba's present. It was a box of carved ivory. In it was a bracelet, a gold snake with emerald eyes.

Sophonisba put it on her wrist and went dancing around the room and showing it to everyone saying, "Just what I wanted—he knew just what I wanted."

She said so, shoving it under Brecon's nose.

"How lucky!" he said. "Now you won't throw it and put someone's eye out."

"I hate you," Sophonisba said. "I hate red hair and freckles."

"Good," said Brecon.

"All you look at is Imilce. I suppose she was pretty once. But she's old. Why she must be twenty-five!"

"You may be twenty-five yourself someday. Unless someone chokes you first."

Sophonisba thought this over. There seemed to be a certain amount of truth in it.

"I shall use magic lotions on my face. My age will be a mystery. I shall not sit looking out a window, crying for a man who does not care a thing about me."

"But he does care," Brecon exclaimed. "He showed me what he wrote—and her present."

"Those pearls! A fat old lady down the hill has bigger ones."

"Not the pearls. It's a flat circle of polished silver—the real present. It's framed in gold. In the letter he said, 'Look deep into what I send. You will see what I most long to see.'"

"Oh—a mirror. I knew I'd get it out of you," Sophonisba said calmly. "Boys are so stupid—almost as stupid as men."

Brecon wished he had bitten his tongue out.

Sophonisba said in Spanish, "Even your ears are red now." Then she added in Greek something Brecon understood because Carthalo had taught it to him. "Don't make an elephant out of a fly," she said. "I'd have found out anyway. She'll show it to me. I always get what I want."

No doubt she does, Brecon thought.

He yawned. The room seemed to be spinning like a ship in a whirlpool. There was a story about Odysseus and a whirlpool, he remembered. He tried to say it to himself but all he said before sleep came was, "When will he come? When will my lord come?"

It was more than a year before Hannibal came.

Brecon had not been homesick on the voyage but he was in New Carthage. It was like an ache in his bones that never quite stopped. Two things helped him. One was that Rhodri was more miserable than he was himself. Rhodri was cheerful enough in the daytime, but at night he used to cry himself to sleep unless Brecon told him stories. Even then Brecon would wake in the night sometimes and hear Rhodri's half-choked sobs.

The other thing that helped was Athena. She worried about Rhodri and she would say seriously to Brecon, "We must give Rhodri something good to eat. I will ask the cook to make some little ground almond cakes," or "Would Rhodri feel better if he had a kitten? Or a puppy?" or "I must teach Rhodri to play knucklebones. Come, please. He'll like it better if you are there."

By the time Orion's belt showed over the mountains that autumn, Brecon had grown three inches. He could wear the leopard skin without the tail dragging on the ground. He spoke Greek well now and knew much of the Odyssey by heart. He worked with numbers on the sand table every day with Sosillos. He still kept the record of the moon's changes on the parchment his grandmother had given him.

Sosillos said that both Greeks and Romans kept track of time by what were called calendars. So did Carthage, but the world had got into the habit of using Roman dates. According to the Romans, time began with the founding of Rome. Brecon did not, Sosillos said, need to learn Roman history. It was made up of stories that only Romans would believe. What he must remember was that a little town on some hills near the river Tiber, not even a seaport, now ruled most of Italy and Sicily, and part of Gaul, and now meant to rule the world. Especially Carthage.

Carthage, he said, had never tried to rule the world. She wanted to trade wherever her ships could sail. Fighting was a Roman, not a Carthaginian habit, but Carthage would always fight for the right to trade freely on land and on sea. For these rights she fought the Romans in what they called the Punic War. They had won it after many years.

"There may be another war sooner than anyone thinks," Carthalo told Brecon and Sosillos.

He slipped in and out of New Carthage many times during that year. Sometimes he went in a galley, sometimes he rode a horse. Once he went off on an elephant for an afternoon ride. He did not come back for two months.

This time, he told Brecon, he had crossed the Alps into Italy and had seen Rome. He had made friends with tribes of Gauls who hated Rome.

"Has an elephant crossed the Alps?" Brecon asked.

"Not yet," Carthalo said, the crease in his cheek deepening.

Carthalo worked on maps with Brecon for the next few weeks. They worked in a room where Hannibal's rolls of papyrus and parchment were kept. On one wall hung a sheet of polished silver with all the shores and islands of the Middle Sea engraved on it. Carthalo made Brecon learn how it looked so he could stand with his back to it and draw the map on the sand table from the Pillars of Hercules to the shores of Sicily.

Among the parchment rolls were charts that showed Greece and Egypt and ancient Tyre. Rivers and harbors, dangerous shoals, hidden rocks, currents and whirlpools were marked on the charts. One chart showed distant islands in the stormy Atlantic. Tin was mined there, Carthalo said. Another showed the great bulge of West Africa. Places were marked on it where natives brought wedges of gold in exchange for glass, for purple cloth, for dolls like the one Sophonisba had broken.

Carthalo would ask Brecon questions about these faraway places and Brecon would try to answer as if he were steering a ship or walking through the streets of some great city.

Once he said to Carthalo, "I could copy the charts, carry them with me."

"Yes," Carthalo said, "but they could be stolen from you after you had been knocked on the head. These were Phoenician secrets for a thousand years. Now they are better known, but still—if you carry them in your head, no one can steal them. Messages, too, are better learned than written. No one can read a message that's in your mind."

Brecon did not spend all his time studying charts. With the hostages and with other boys of New Carthage he learned to throw spears and javelins from the backs of running horses, to take long marches with little food, to make signals with smoke. Brecon was also learning to wrestle, not outdoors in the big training field but in Hannibal's library. Carthalo, from one of his trips to Sicily, had brought back a Greek wrestler.

"I would teach him the holds myself if I had time," Carthalo said, "but he must practice every day, and the wrestling on that training field!" He spread out his hands in a gesture of contempt, thumbs down.

"It's nothing," Sosillos agreed. "The trainer learned his wrestling in Rome. The Romans think all the heaviest things are best—shields, lances, horses, wrestlers. We will put down a thick mat in the library. Brecon shall work there for an hour every day between his geography and his arithmetic. By the time Hannibal comes I hope we can show him how a wrestler should be taught."

It did not occur to either Carthalo or Sosillos—or even to Brecon—that he might not enjoy being thrown around every day by a cross-eyed Greek wrestler. Stephan was the man's name. He was a small wiry man who had wrestled in Greece, Sicily, and even in Rome. He was a slave there and had won his freedom by defeating a giant Gaul in a show given to celebrate a Roman victory. There were lions and tigers fighting each other and dancing elephants in the show too.

"He could have crushed me," Stephan said, "but I remembered Archimedes."

"Who? You mean the mathematician? How did that help?" asked Brecon.

"Because he said to me, 'Stephan, you can make a lever of your body and move more than your own weight. If I had a lever long enough and a place to stand, I could move the world.' So when things were right—they have to be just right—well, I didn't move the world, but I moved that Gaul. Like this—"

Things did not come just right for Brecon. He was black and blue in many places but he kept trying.

Athena and Rhodri liked to go to the training ground and watch the horses and elephants, the javelin throwing and the wrestling.

"Alain is a great wrestler," Rhodri told Brecon. "He throws everyone. Come and watch."

"I'm sorry, Rhodri, I can't come now. I have to work," Brecon said.

"Sandy Brecon," Sophonisba said. "Always at the sand table. You must be stupid to have to study so much. Your master beats you often, I know. I've heard him thumping and you groaning. Why do you let him beat you? He's only a slave. Beat him yourself—you're big enough. Prince Alain would never let anyone beat him."

She gave Brecon a look out of her green eyes that reminded him of a cat watching for a mouse.

He said, "Oh, I have a lot to learn. Arithmetic is a hard subject for an ignorant boy out of the mountains."

This statement was, of course, true. It pleased Sophonisba and she went off with the others to the training ground. Brecon wished she had not heard him groaning.

"She won't again," he decided. To his surprise there still were groans, but they were Stephan's.

Brecon said to Sosillos, "Stephan made a great noise when he wrestled with me today," and Sosillos said, "Good. You are making him work. Groans are the praise of the wrestler."

"I'll never throw him," Brecon said.

"Probably not. But some dark night when you need strength— who knows?"

Sophonisba talked a great deal about Alain. He was the only handsome hostage, she said. Had Brecon seen Alain's new horse? It was a real dappled-gray Spanish war horse. His family had sent it. Of course Alain must have a proper horse.

"Because," Sophonisba said, "Alain's tribe is one of the most important in all Spain. When will your family send you something fit to ride? But I suppose they won't. Alain said your tribe was not important, that you were just sent as a hostage because you were a poor relation of Imilce's."

Brecon felt the blood rushing into his cheeks.

"A horse is supposed to last more than a year," he said as calmly as he could, but he could not help adding, "I'll race Alain on Starlight any day and beat him."

"And in dart throwing and wrestling too, I suppose," Sophonisba said, laughing. "I suppose you learn how by studying those old maps."

"Oh, I visit the training ground sometimes," Brecon said.

"I know. You ride like a centaur, no saddle, no bridle. Rhodri said so. Be there tomorrow, Brecon. I want to watch you. I've never seen a centaur."

Brecon said, "If I'm a centaur you're an Amazon."

He had forgotten that in fights between centaurs and Amazons, it was usually the Amazons who won.

The training ground, the arena, was a flat sandy circle with rocky hillsides sloping up around it. On the fourth side, toward the sea, rocks had been roughly piled to make a wall. There was a wide gate in the wall. It was made of logs with the bark still on and was wide enough for an elephant to pass through.

This sunny spring afternoon Sophonisba was sitting on the gate with Rhodri and Athena when Brecon came to the training ground. Alain was riding toward the gate from inside the field. The gate had to be opened for Brecon to ride through. Rhodri and Athena climbed down cheerfully, Sophonisba impatiently.

"Why can't you ever come when everyone else does?" she asked.

"Sorry," Brecon said.

He dismounted, gave Starlight to a groom to hold, helped Athena and Rhodri back to the top of the gate, and held out his hand to Sophonisba.

"Prince Alain will help me," she said, turning her green eyes on Alain, who swung off his horse, flung the reins to a groom and came hurrying toward her. Before he reached the gate, he stumbled over a basket Athena had dropped. He fell in a large heap at Sophonisba's feet.

"Shall I help him up so he can help you?" Brecon asked.

Alain, crimson in the face, panted furiously, "Don't touch me. Don't touch her or I'll throw you over the fence. Break every bone in your body."

"Try it," Brecon said.

"Oh Prince—don't hurt him," Sophonisba shrieked. "Don't hurt Brecon. He's much smaller than you and he doesn't mean anything. He didn't trip you up or anyway he didn't mean to. Did you, Brecon?"

Alain was now standing up.

He said with great dignity, "I challenge you to a trial of strength, Sir Brecon of the Leopard Skin. I suggest a contest of three events. I will choose one—since I am the challenger. You may choose the other two. Agreed?"

"No," Brecon said, "I don't agree. You would not like my events. I might choose grooming a horse or catching jellyfish or climbing to an eagle's nest. Or wrestling. I might win and you would say it wasn't fair. Choose all three yourself. Choose like a prince."

"Very well," Alain said. "I choose casting the javelin, hurling the lance and—"

"Oh Alain, be careful, don't choose wrestling—you might be hurt," Sophonisba wailed. "I don't want you getting all dusty in your beautiful clothes. You are every inch a prince from those purple boots to the top of your helmet. Is it gold?"

"Bronze, gilded," Alain said in his peevish voice. "Gold is too soft for armor. I choose wrestling," he added to Brecon. "Of course unless you'd rather play knucklebones. I hear you're good at that."

"Wrestling then," Brecon said quietly.

"Oh, don't wrestle with him, Brecon. He'll kill you," Sophonisba screamed. "Athena, don't let him wrestle. Get him to go home."

Athena said calmly, "Brecon is not a coward. He'll meet plenty of Romans bigger than he is. He might as well practice."

"You cruel little thing—my poor Brecon! Alain, if you break even his little finger, I shall cry for weeks. You're so brave, Alain, and so strong..."

Alain was no match for Brecon with the javelins. Starlight without a bridle, with only a faded plaid saddlecloth, carried him much more swiftly than Alain's big dappled-gray war horse did Alain. Guiding Starlight only with his knees and the swing of his body, Brecon had both hands free to take a javelin from its quiver and send it whizzing toward the target. They had agreed on each throwing five javelins. All five of Brecon's splintered their targets. Only three of Alain's struck their mark.

With the lances each had three casts. These were Spanish lances, five feet long, tipped with iron. They were like big sharp needles. Thrown from a fast-moving horse, they could pierce shields of wood and leather—and even metal armor. Alain had great skill with the lance. His weight, the strength and weight of his galloping charger, all helped send the lance on its way. All three of his casts struck the shields fairly and squarely. One of

Brecon's lances fell short of the mark. The next one just touched the edge of the shield. The third one crashed into the center.

So it will depend on the wrestling, Brecon thought.

He felt his blood beating loud in his ears. He tried to remember things Stephan had taught him but he could think of nothing except that the Greek had said, "A snake can fight a lion."

But not an elephant, Brecon thought dismally.

He was stripped down to a short kilt. A cold wind was blowing now from the north. He felt himself shivering.

Sophonisba called out, "Brecon, Brecon! Everyone knows it isn't fair. He's twice your size. Please don't wrestle with him!"

Brecon looked past her to Athena.

She looked as if she might cry any minute but she called bravely, "Go on, Brecon—you'll win. I-I know you'll win," and Rhodri squeaked, "Go in and win, Brecon."

A crowd was gathering in a ring around the two boys. There were their friends who had been throwing javelins and lances. Some were on horseback, some had dismounted. Holding their horses were their slaves—dark-skinned men from Libya and Morocco, fair-haired Gauls, men from the Greek islands seized by pirates at sea. There were Greek traders from Marseilles and Saguntum, Numidian riders, black-bearded sailors from Carthage. The crowd as a whole spoke Greek, not the Greek of Homer but trade Greek with Latin, Punic, and Spanish words mixed with it.

Brecon could understand it. He heard one trader say to another, "Well, sometimes a skinny one does better than you think. I'll put a denarius on the redhead."

"Even money?" asked the other.

"No, you'll have to give two to one."

"Bets are off then—or I'll tell you what I'll do," said the second

trader. "I'll throw in a jar of my new hair dye. It covers up the gray and brings back the hair to its natural color. Color freshener, I call it. Comes in red, black, yellow, and three shades of brown. Worth more than a denarius. The ladies love it."

"All right, you old robber. Here comes the trainer to see fair play. Let's climb on those rocks so we can see over the crowd."

Brecon stopped shivering. Suddenly he felt quite calm. He thought, Well, somebody's risked his money on me. I must do my best for him—a snake can fight a lion.

Then suddenly he was on the sand with Alain on top of him, crushing him.

He thought, Alain's been using Egyptian scent, smells like a civet cat. Or a crocodile. He wriggled, twisted, was on top briefly, heard the trader yell, "Go it, redhead, good boy!" and was on his back again, his shoulders almost pinned to the ground. He heard Alain grind his teeth. He breathed in musk and sweat, felt sick and dizzy, but threw Alain off again.

The fight seemed to last for hours. The wind had dropped and the sun was hot now and shone into his eyes. Alain's weight was crushing him but he threw it off and looked down into the sand. He heard the crowd roar. Once he thought his arm would break as Alain twisted it but he freed it and heaved Alain on his side. The crowd roared again.

Why, they want me to win, Brecon thought, and then, How he's panting! Keep at it, don't let him rest... headlock... finger lock... hammerlock...

He kept at it. How many times he barely escaped from being held helpless, both shoulders pressed to the sand for the count of three, he never knew. Stephan had said, "Never give up—the right moment will come," but it was long in coming.

Then at last he thought, This is the hold. This is the moment. He heard the crowd roar again, thought dizzily, But it doesn't sound the same.

He saw feet move, felt—rather than saw—the circle moving, spreading out. A shadow cut off the sun.

Brecon thought, They don't care now whether I win; but I care. Then he seemed to hear Stephan's voice saying, "Archimedes... lever, move the world... body a lever... just right, just right..."

At last the pattern was clear. He knew what he must do. He did it. Alain's heavy body spun over his head. Alain lay there gasping. He hardly moved when Brecon pressed his shoulders to the ground. Above them the trainer swung his arm up and down like a man smashing a rock with a mallet and shouted, "One... two... three."

They were in sunshine for a moment. Then a cloud moved

across the sun again. Brecon felt something touch his shoulder. He stood up. An elephant's trunk was swinging in front of his nose.

The man in the black cloak smiled down from the elephant's neck and said, "A very pretty throw, cousin."

Hannibal had come home.

Chapter 4

FOLDS OF A TOGA

THE THROW was not fair—Alain said. The referee wasn't looking. No one was looking. He would never have been thrown if Hannibal had not come just then. He was so surprised—he said—to see Hannibal that he had let Brecon throw him. So— he said—he had really won two matches. Lances. Wrestling. Horse wasn't used to javelins yet. Anyway, javelins were for Africans. Not for a Spanish prince, whose horse ate out of a silver manger.

"There will always be plenty of Numidians for that sort of thing," he added.

To Sophonisba he said, "Of course the wrestling was unfair. Brecon had been practicing—you know he had."

"Yes," Sophonisba said. "Hadn't you?"

Alain scowled, grunted, and rode off.

Sophonisba asked Brecon to take her home on his horse's neck. "I don't want to walk. Give me a ride—you owe it to me. "Why?"

"Why? Because I fixed it so you wrestled with Alain and beat him. That's why."

"*You* fixed it?"

"Of course I did. First I made him angry with you. Then I made you ashamed not to fight him. I made him think he could beat you and that you were afraid of him and didn't know how to wrestle. You don't suppose I didn't know what all that thumping and groaning in your room was about, do you? I could have told him, couldn't I?"

Brecon thought back over the afternoon. "I suppose you did fix it," he said. "But why?"

"He treats me like a child. I, Safaanbaal, daughter of Hasdrubal Gisgo, offered to be his wife. I told him my father would give me a fine fortune. He laughed and told me to play with dolls."

"Aren't you rather young to marry?" Brecon asked. "And why choose Alain?"

Sophonisba said impatiently, "Girls in Carthage are betrothed when they are much younger than I. But I forgot, you've never been there. You just came out of a hole in the ground in Spain. I chose Alain because he's the only prince I know."

"Better wait. You might see a prince you like better," Brecon said.

"I wouldn't have Alain now if he went down on his fat knees and if his horse ate out of a gold manger." She mimicked Alain's peevish voice saying, "It wasn't fair, it wasn't fair," and added, "Let me ride Starlight. I want him to see me ride by."

Brecon said to the groom, "Help the Lady Sophonisba to the horse's back and lead Starlight home. Hold on to her mane, Sophonisba, if you think you are going to fall."

Sophonisba did not touch the mane. She rode off looking proud and happy and sitting very straight. Brecon, Athena, and Rhodri followed.

They found Hannibal tossing his son into the air and Imilce smiling at them. There was a splendid dinner, of which Hannibal ate less than anyone. Afterwards the Greek traders came to see him and he asked them questions about Marseilles and Saguntum and Roman ports that Brecon had never heard of before. Usually Carthalo or Sosillos would make notes for him. Tonight they were both away.

Hannibal said to Brecon, "I hear you can use a pen as well as wrestle. Be my writer." So Brecon sat there listening, writing down things about towns in Spain and Gaul.

Hannibal would ask who lived in a town, what they made, how they lived, how far it was from the nearest port, the nearest mountain pass. When he asked them about Saguntum, the traders told him that Rome had taken this Greek colony under her protection. They said Rome was already building a great fleet of galleys to keep Saguntum safe. Brecon wondered if they had come to New Carthage to tell Hannibal this and to frighten him.

He did not seem frightened. He said that Rome and Carthage had a treaty in which both cities promised that their soldiers would not cross the river Ebro with weapons in their hands. Saguntum was south of the Ebro. It was in the part of the world where Carthage ruled. Of course Rome would not break faith and send armed ships there.

One of the traders laughed and said, "In the Roman senate the Scipios say that Rome should build a fleet to attack Carthage from Sicily and another to attack Spain." And the other trader added, "Yes. The Scipios want war and one of the new consuls is a Scipio, but there's Quintus Fabius."

"What does he say?" Hannibal asked.

"He's a sensible man. He said, 'It is one thing to talk about war in the Senate chamber. To meet it on the field of battle is quite different.'"

"Very sensible," Hannibal said, and added that there were also two parties in Carthage. One was in favor of defending the rights of Carthage everywhere. The Hanno family, the great merchants, grudged every ounce of silver spent for war. He himself, he said, was under the orders of the Shofets and the Council of Carthage. Those orders he would follow.

The traders left, loaded with gifts. They had not learned much, Brecon thought. Within a few weeks two envoys arrived from Rome. Again Brecon acted as Hannibal's writer. The envoys were elderly men, simply dressed in yellowish, badly washed wool. They brought from the Roman senate a message asking Hannibal to keep his pledge not to cross the Ebro with an army and not to attack Saguntum, now a friend and ally of Rome.

Hannibal reminded them that Saguntum was south of the Ebro. The treaty signed by Rome and Carthage made it the business of Carthage—not of Rome—to keep peace there. Lately the Saguntines had killed Carthaginians living in the city. They had also made war against Tartessians living nearby.

"I shall follow the orders of the rulers of Carthage," he said. "It is the custom of Carthage to aid oppressed people."

The envoys, frowning solemnly, went back to their ship. They said they would sail first to Rome, then to Carthage to appeal to the Shofets and Council for peace with Rome's friend Saguntum.

Hannibal did not wait for them to reach Carthage. He already had his orders. He laid siege to Saguntum.

Brecon did not see the siege. He saw the army start to march there. Elephants, quick-stepping small oxen dragging light carts with food for the troops, mules, Numidian and Spanish horsemen, slingers from the Balearic Islands, footsoldiers from Libya with their heavy shields, spearmen from Spain, all moved along against the sky.

He was down on the quay with Carthalo. Their galley was being loaded for a voyage to Carthage. With the help of Synhalus, they were to take care of Imilce and Hamilcar on the voyage. Sophonisba, Athena, and Rhodri were going too.

"You will be safe in Carthage. There will be no war there," Hannibal told Imilce.

"Surely it will be safe here," she said. "With the lagoon and the sea wall. And Romans will not come by land."

Hannibal shook his head.

"I cannot leave men enough to guard it. The lagoon looks safe but there is a little tide in it. Very little, yet enough so that when the wind is right and the water at its lowest, men could wade through it."

"But the Romans do not know that."

"All Romans are not stupid," Hannibal said. "They might learn."

To Brecon he said, "Help Carthalo all you can. Learn to speak and understand Latin. Help your cousin. Look after Hamilcar. Come back."

Hannibal was riding Surus, the elephant Brecon had first seen. She was an Indian elephant, bigger than the others in his army.

"Lift Hamilcar up," he said to Brecon and then spoke to the elephant, which reached down and brought Hamilcar up to face his father.

The little boy laughed. "Am I going with you? I want to go with you," he said, jouncing up and down in the chair made by the twisted trunk.

"You must go with your mother and take care of her," Hannibal said. "Now goodbye, little Thunderbolt. Stand with Brecon like a good soldier. Let him go, Surus. Now give me a good salute." Hamilcar had begun to cry, but at the word "soldier" he stopped. Surus put him back in Brecon's arms. They both stood with raised hands, palms forward, until the elephant vanished around a rocky shoulder in the road.

Their ship was a fast one, five rowers to each long oar. The winds were favorable, their captain—the same man who had brought Brecon to New Carthage—one of the best. Brecon knew some of the crew.

"I am glad we are going by sea," he said to one of them.

"How else?" asked the sailor.

"Some people say it is better to go by land to the Pillars. Then across to Africa and along the coast to Carthage."

"Land," said the sailor, "is for elephants. They don't show dust. I'll say that for them."

Brecon asked if they weren't useful in battle.

"If they don't panic," the man said. "And if the enemy does. But you never know about elephants. If you'd ferried as many across the Strait as I have—why I almost lost a ship once because the elephant I had on board saw a mouse."

One sunny afternoon Synhalus said to Brecon, "You will see the Byrsa soon. Look to the east."

It was only a blue shadow at first. Then it became clearer and Brecon could see the temple shining on a hill two hundred feet above the water. On the slopes of the hill were the tallest buildings he had ever seen, six stories high, some of them. He saw villas, too, in gardens full of blossoming fruit trees. Farther off were green fields of young wheat. Then they were so close to the city that they saw only shops and factories and heard the city noises. Soon their sails were lowered. The rowers brought them first into the outer harbor, which was crowded with ships, then into the inner one, where they tied up the galley to a ring set in a wall of white marble.

It was weeks before the envoys from Rome arrived at Carthage. In the meantime news came from Hannibal. It came overland except for the crossing of the Strait at the Pillars of Hercules. A fast-riding courier would ride until he could ride no longer and then hand his message to another with a fresh horse. After the last of the Spanish couriers had crossed the Strait, another relay of galloping horsemen would carry the letter to Carthage.

Hannibal reported that the siege of Saguntum would take a long time. Their surprise attack had failed. They had no siege machinery to break the walls. The jagged rocks around the town were impossible to climb. Their forces were encamped in a half circle around the city. They would wait until it was starved out.

There were letters for Imilce, too. They ended with messages for the family. This meant Sophonisba, Athena, Brecon, and Rhodri as well as Hamilcar and Imilce. He asked what they were doing, asked them all to write, wanted to know if they had learned to swim, hoped they were all well. Brecon used to write for them all. They had learned to swim in the pool below the palace, he reported; only Sophonisba would not try. She just sat on the edge and told them how. They were all well except Rhodri. He had a fever, but Synhalus was giving him his best drugs and he seemed a little better.

Poor Rhodri! He felt better the next day. The fever had gone. Luckily Brecon was there when Rhodri tried to get out of bed.

"My legs—won't work," he said, looking white and scared.

Brecon was just in time to catch him as he fell.

Synhalus used a frightening word—paralysis—to Brecon. He did not say it to Rhodri or to Imilce.

"I need your help," he said to Brecon. "I have seen cases like this before. No one knows why or how it happens. Strong, healthy young children are usually the victims. Sometimes they get well. More often they are lame for the rest of their lives. Rubbing and exercises seem to help but I think the most important thing is to make them feel they will be able to move about even if it means braces for their legs and crutches. You have to give them courage as if you were giving them a medicine, a dose, many doses, every day."

"I'll try," Brecon said.

Synhalus showed him about the rubbing and the exercises. He worked over Rhodri much himself and after a few weeks he felt sure that strength was slowly coming back into Rhodri's legs. During the hot summer days they would take him into the pool and get him to move his legs while his weight was supported by the water. Synhalus had wooden braces and crutches made for Rhodri. He was using only the crutches when word came from Hannibal that Saguntum had fallen, that he needed Synhalus at New Carthage.

It was almost spring again when Synhalus left Carthage. He told Brecon and Rhodri that he was sure now that Rhodri would be walking without crutches when he came back. He need only take the exercises when Brecon told him to.

"Someday," he said, "you can have a bonfire and burn the crutches."

"When you and Hannibal come back," Rhodri said.

Even the party of the Hannos, the rich merchants, spoke well of Hannibal now. A great treasure of captured goods and silver came to Carthage from the ruins of Saguntum. The message that came with the treasure said that sooner or later envoys from Rome would arrive in Carthage. Hannibal advised the Shofets and Council to give the Romans no satisfaction.

They gave none.

In March five envoys from Rome arrived. Three of them belonged to the war party in the Roman city. The other two were friends of Quintus Fabius, the man who had sensibly said that

war was different in the Senate chamber and on the battlefield. The leader of the envoys was his kinsman, another Fabius.

Brecon was glad that he had learned to speak Latin from Carthalo. At the council meeting at which the Romans appeared, Brecon acted as Carthalo's secretary. The envoys spoke through an interpreter. Even before the interpreter spoke, Brecon understood what Fabius said.

"Will the Republic of Carthage now hand over Hannibal, son of Hamilcar, and all his officers to Rome?" Fabius asked.

The Council, without debate, said loudly, "No!"

Fabius went on, "Does the Republic of Carthage approve of the action of Hannibal, son of Hamilcar, in attacking Saguntum?"

The Council answered this question by asking others. "Do the Senate and the Roman people care more for the friendship of Saguntum than for their treaty with Carthage?... How long has Saguntum been an ally of Rome?... Is not Saguntum south of the Ebro?... Why then does Rome interfere between Saguntum and Carthage?"

Fabius stood up.

"These questions weary me," he said. He took one of the folds of his white toga edged with Tyrian purple in his hand and went on, "I hold, in this fold of my toga, peace or war. Choose, men of Carthage! Which will you have?"

The elder Shofet said, "With your permission, I will withdraw with my councilors and talk over what you have said."

Fabius agreed. The councilors, Carthalo among them, and the two Shofets left the room.

It was very quiet after they had gone. Brecon heard a bee buzz in and out of a window, distant sounds from the harbor, distant clanging of metal where swords for Hannibal were being forged. The breeze that brought the sounds also brought the scent of flowers, the smell of the sea and of fowls being roasted on spits over hot coals.

For the envoys, Brecon thought. I wish I had a wishbone. The councilors were coming back, handsome figures in robes of Tyrian crimson or purple, with shoulder clasps of gold in the shape of the heads of rams or lions or elephants. These black-haired, keen-faced men gave no sign whether they had chosen war or peace.

The Shofet waited until all were seated except Fabius. He still stood with the folds of his dingy toga clasped in his thick fingers.

The Shofet moved toward him, faced him, and said, "Choose, yourself!"

Fabius let the fold of his toga fall.

"Then," he said, "it shall be war."

Carthaginian voices cried, "War! War it shall be!"

Brecon wondered whether the envoys enjoyed those roasted fowls. They were stuffed with Spanish chestnuts and Carthaginian wheat, someone told him. He had stopped in the marketplace to buy presents for Rhodri and Athena and Sophonisba and Hamilcar. He was going away. When he would come back, he had no idea. Already couriers were galloping along the African coast with news for Hannibal. When darkness came a quinquereme would leave its place at the marble wall of the inner harbor and set out across the sea for northern Spain.

It was hard to say goodbye to his friends, especially to Rhodri. Sometimes, when Rhodri was too tired to use his crutches, Brecon carried Rhodri on his back.

"My roan Spanish horse," Rhodri called him. Now he asked, "What shall I do without my Spanish horse?"

Brecon said, "You don't need him. When I come back, you will run to meet me."

"I will," Rhodri said. "I will."

CHAPTER 5

WIDE RIVER

THEY HEADED FOR the mouth of the Ebro but they did not really expect to find Hannibal there.

"If I know him," Carthalo said, "he is far across it already. Let's look at a map."

They found him at last near the Pertus, a pass in the Pyrenees mountains. He had left his brother Hasdrubal in command of all the forces in Spain. His brother Mago was with Hannibal commanding a troop of cavalry. There were only a few Carthaginians among Hannibal's officers. You could tell them by their cloaks of Tyrian purple or crimson. As Brecon had learned in Carthage, there were two kinds of dye made from the shellfish called the murex. One was really a deep violet in color, one crimson with a purple tinge. The Romans called them both purple, Carthalo said, but the color they used most was the crimson. There was very little of the true violet dye. Enough for robes for a few kings and Shofets.

"And for Hasdrubal, son of Gisgo. And for Alain, of course," Brecon said, "but not for Hannibal."

Hannibal was still wearing his old Spanish cloak, once black, now the brown of dry seaweed. He did, however, have a new pair of boots. This was fortunate, Carthalo said. They would all need strong boots before their journey was over.

"He told you where we are going?" Brecon asked.

Carthalo had a sharp stick in his hand. He began to make marks in the dirt. Brecon saw the Spanish coast from New Carthage to the Pyrenees, the barrier between Spain and Gaul. He saw the Ebro, the river Rhone, and the Alps. Carthalo heaped dirt high for the Alps. They were not just a wall but a series of walls, he said. There were valleys that twisted and turned, rivers that ran between towering cliffs, mountains so high that there was always snow on them.

"There will be snow in the passes too if we don't move fast," Carthalo said. "We'll cross here. And see Italy."

He drew a twisting line through the mountains, then dropped the stick and scuffed the map away with the side of his foot.

"You mean I'll see Italy, see Rome?" Brecon asked excitedly.

"Perhaps more of both than you'll like," Carthalo replied.

"Do the soldiers know?"

Carthalo said that some of them had guessed and had refused to go. "Hannibal said that they need not go unless they wished to. More than ten thousand Iberians marched off last week to Hasdrubal Barca, who will need them. The news from Rome is that Publius Cornelius Scipio the Consul will attack Spain and that a fleet will sail against Carthage. Hannibal says the way to keep Carthage safe is to fight Rome in Italy. You and I are just in time," he said. "We start tomorrow."

Hannibal still had an army of more than thirty thousand footsoldiers and eight thousand horsemen. There were mules, packhorses, oxen and their drivers. He had thirty-seven elephants. Four days after they had crossed the Pyrenees, they reached the Rhone. So far the people of Gaul had been friendly. Envoys had crossed the Alps from Gallic tribes of northern Italy. They told Hannibal that many cities in Italy would rise against Rome. They promised that their own tribes, the Boii and the Insubres, would help with men and with food. The envoys were tall, fair-haired men with horns growing out of their helmets. They had shields with the heads of fierce animals molded on them, cloaks lined with fur, broad bracelets of gold around their wrists. They knew Carthalo, who had visited them with gifts from Hannibal earlier in the year. He acted as their interpreter. Their speech was a little like that of Brecon's own tribe. He could understand a word here and there, enough to know that they spoke fiercely of chasing the Romans out of their fields.

"The Romans drank the waters of the Po. Now our horses drink it," one said.

He himself preferred the red wine of the country around them. He drank it through his enormous yellow mustache. Brecon had seen men in his own country do the same thing.

"Why do they do that?" he had asked his grandmother.

"To strain grasshoppers out of it," she had said scornfully, "or mice—for all I know. Whatever floats around in the badly made wine of those people. Never let me catch you with such manners! Hear?"

Brecon had said, "I promise," an easy promise to give at nine years of age. Now, feeling a few hairs growing along his upper lip, he rather envied those with yellow-silk strainers.

Carthalo, who often knew what Brecon was thinking, said with a twinkle in his gray eyes, "Your mustache will be Tyrian crimson, Brecon. Much more unusual. But do train it to grow up, and keep it out of the soup."

Carthalo himself had his beard and mustache shaved at least once a week. Carthaginians had razors and barbers who were skilled in using them. Older men often wore beards but younger ones usually had shaven chins. Some coins of Carthage showed Hamilcar Barca, Hannibal's father, with a laurel wreath on his head, a mustache that pointed up to his cheekbones, but no beard. Now that Hannibal had been made head of the armies of Carthage in Spain, there were coins with his face too. He also had the laurel wreath and the upswept mustache and a nose rather like an eagle's beak, but he looked younger and thinner than his father.

Brecon had one of these coins in his pouch. He pulled it out and held it out to Carthalo saying, "Like this?"

Carthalo smiled. He said Hannibal was supposed to be Hercules on the coin.

"I know it's not much like him but it's the only picture of him I have," Brecon said.

"Would you rather be like Hannibal or like Hercules?" Carthalo asked.

"No one can be like Hannibal. Hercules was nothing to him. I'll just try to do errands for Hannibal the best I can."

"You and I both, Brecon," Carthalo said.

Brecon's first chance came when Hannibal was getting ready to cross the Rhone. News came that a Roman fleet was at the mouth of the river, that soldiers were landing and would soon march up the river against Hannibal.

Just then, on the east bank of the river, Gauls from a hostile tribe appeared, ready to attack anyone who tried to cross. Hannibal had crossed rivers with enemies on the opposite bank before. He paid the people on his own side in silver to lend him their boats. They helped him build rafts. They sold goatskins to the cavalry, who used them as packs while they swam their horses across the river.

Hannibal sent one of his officers, Hanno Bomilcar, far upstream where the Spanish cavalry could cross by a ford near an island. Brecon, perched in a tall oak tree, watched the sky to the north. When Bomilcar reached the island a black column of smoke would rise from it....At their own camping place there was already smoke rising in the still air.

"You will see Bomilcar's smoke choked down while you count twenty," Carthalo said. "They'll put a wet oxhide over it, count twenty. Then take it off and let the smoke come up again. They'll do it three times. The third time will mean they have forded the river. Whistle to me through your fingers as soon as their smoke puffs up the third time and I will answer with our smoke to show we've seen theirs."

"Shall I come down then?" Brecon asked.

"No. Stay there until you see Bomilcar's men on the opposite bank. The other side of that point. Then whistle again and come down. Our men will be starting across."

From his tree Brecon could see the Gauls across the river. Pale sunshine glittered on their shields and helmets. They shouted and blew horns and shook their long swords at Hannibal's men, who paid no attention but went on loading their rafts and packing their boats.

At the place where the water was shallowest, carpenters were building an enormous raft for the elephants. When it was finished, they covered the logs with dirt and turf to make it seem like part of the land. They put planks covered with turf between the raft and the land. The male elephants trumpeted wildly and refused to set foot on the raft. The females were easier to manage.

Brecon saw their drivers talking to them, patting their shoulders, tempting them along with chunks of bread. At last he saw Surus walk slowly onto the raft. Others followed, gingerly picking up each big soft foot and setting it carefully down again. At last one of the males followed. Just then Brecon saw black smoke in the north. It was damped down while he counted twenty, rose and fell, rose and fell, puffed up again.

Brecon whistled. Carthalo made the return smoke signal. Soon the whole camp knew that Bomilcar and his horsemen were on the way to attack the shouting Gauls. Pipes, trumpets, and war cries sounded through the camp. Brecon saw Hannibal himself swim his horse into the stream. Numidians followed close behind him. Mules brayed, oxen bellowed as rafts full of them were pushed from the shore. Big boats full of Balearic slingers were already in midstream to protect the swimming horsemen and the rafts. Their slings whirled around swiftly,

sending lead balls to break the shields of the dancing, shouting Gauls. Some of them were knocked down and fell into the water.

Now the elephant raft was unfastened from its moorings and pushed into the stream. Sunlight flashed on yellowish tusks. For a moment fierce wild trumpetings drowned all other sounds. Males not on the raft splashed into the water after it. As they swam out into the stream, the shouts of their drivers were added to the tumult of noise.

Brecon watched the wooded point of land that hid Bomilcar's horsemen from the Gauls and from Hannibal's men. At last he saw them galloping along the east bank of the river. He whistled and swung himself out of the tree, dropping from branch to branch. From the lowest one he made a nine-foot drop into a mossy hollow, squelched down into mud, pulled his feet out of it, and ran after Carthalo.

Carthalo had already shouted to the commander of the foot-soldiers that Bomilcar was coming. They were soon crossing in coracles or on rafts. Their shouts were added to the neighing, splashing, and trumpeting.

"Shall we find a boat?" Brecon asked.

Carthalo said, "Hannibal left horses for us. One of them is—guess!"

"Not Starlight!" Brecon said.

It was Starlight. She knew Brecon and whinnied joyfully, pushing her velvet chestnut muzzle against his cheek. They were still swimming the river when the first of Bomilcar's horsemen appeared. The Gauls faced around to meet the horsemen. As they did so, Numidians, footsoldiers, and slingers rushed up the bank behind them. The Gauls, caught between the two forces, turned again, facing south this time, and ran away as fast as they could go.

Carthalo and Brecon found Hannibal, calm, dripping wet, standing beside his wet horse and greeting his men as they came out of the water. His officers, who had crossed in boats, stood around him, dry and sleek in their purple or crimson cloaks; but it was at Hannibal the soldiers looked. He had for them a smile, a word of praise, a quick wave of his thin hand that was praise too, they knew.

They waved in return. Brecon never forgot those hands— square and thick-fingered or long and slender, dark brown with pink palms, pale skin sunburned to the color of a ripe olive, fingers blue with cold, hairy hands, smooth ones, hands spattered with freckles, hands with fingers missing, one hand dripping blood. It had been cut by a Gallic sword. This was one of the few wounds Brecon saw that day. He helped Synhalus sew it up, thought of the day Sophonisba smashed her doll. Wondered about her and Athena and Rhodri. The wounded man came from a part of Spain not far from Brecon's own home. They talked about it while Brecon bandaged the wound.

"It's nothing," the man said. "I've had worse bites from wolves, and no fancy sewing." He showed scars to prove it, then nodded in Hannibal's direction and added, "I don't care how many I get fighting for him. He's not one of those fat shepherds who'll send a boy out to chase off wolves and stay safe and warm in the hut themselves. He never asks you to do what he won't do himself. And if there's silver and gold or only a crust of bread rubbed with garlic, whatever he has, he shares it with you fair and square. If there's nothing, you all go without together."

Carthalo had been talking with Hannibal.

"He has an errand for you, Brecon," he said. "He will tell you what it is."

Brecon said goodbye to the Spaniard and, leading Starlight, crossed the muddy, trampled piece of ground between him and Hannibal.

It was always, when he met Hannibal, as if he had seen him only a few days before. They talked for some time. Hannibal still greeted soldiers from the river and sometimes gave an order. He asked Brecon questions about his wife Imilce, and their son, about Sophonisba, about Rhodri's illness.

"Your cousin Imilce told me in a letter about the owl," he said.

The owl was a small one that had fallen out of a nest. Brecon had heard it screeching in the garden. It had a broken wing. He had made a splint for the wing. Either in spite of the splint or because of it, the wing mended. He gave the owl to Athena and he had a cage made for it. He took one of his own gold armbands, once his father's, and made two out of it, one for Rhodri, one for Athena. On hers he engraved a picture of the owl with spread wings. He made a ring for the owl's foot and fixed his own gold chain so it could be clasped to the ring and to Athena's armband.

"It was just so she would not feel so lonely. She and Rhodri are both homesick, I'm afraid. It's hard on them both, Rhodri's being able to walk so little; but he is much better, will soon be able to give up his crutches, I hope."

"What did you make for Sophonisba?" Hannibal asked.

"Why nothing, cousin. She's not homesick, she's at home. She loves Carthage."

"I hope that explanation satisfied her," Hannibal said, smiling.

Brecon said he hoped so. He did not mention that Sophonisba had first tried to wheedle him out of his other armband and then had almost clawed his eyes out when he refused to give it to her.

Just then a party of Numidians reported for orders. Hannibal told the leader to ride south until they met some Roman cavalry.

"They will send some, I'm sure," he said, "to find out where we are. You will know them by their heavy horses and their helmets bristling with red and black plumes. Now I want them to think I am nearby. Make them follow you back to the camp. Waste all the time you can. Every hour they waste chasing you, will help us on our way to Italy. Don't have a real fight with them. Toss a javelin or two and retreat, not too fast. When they catch up with you, do it again. Keep doing it. Let them think they are playing cat and mouse with you and that you are the mice. Understand?"

The Numidian grinned broadly and nodded. This was a game he liked. Hannibal added, "Sir Brecon will ride with you. Brecon, I want a full report from you about the Romans—numbers, equipment, how they fight. Send it to me by the Numidians. They must ride after me as soon as they are sure the Romans will follow them here."

"Shall I stay here?" Brecon asked.

"Yes. See that the fires are burning. Have a good stew cooking in the kettles. Serve out wine to any Gauls who come to loot the camp. The Romans will think you are one of them, with that red hair of yours. Be their interpreter. Be sure they think I have just left. I want them to tell their commander that he can catch me if he hurries. I only want him to chase me as far as this camp, though."

He showed Brecon a map and pointed to a triangle of land between two streams.

"It's called the Island," Hannibal said. "Come to me there and tell me all you can learn about Scipio the Consul's plans."

He gave one of his quick twisting waves with his long fingers spread out. He and Carthalo started north. Brecon followed the Numidians, who were already loping easily south along the trail.

By noon next day Brecon had seen his first Roman soldier. He had always pictured a Roman as twice as big as an ordinary man and as fierce as a tiger. He had seen a tiger in a cage at Carthage. He remembered well how the tiger's eye flashed green as it restlessly paced its cage, how it switched its long tail, and how it had yawned, showing sharp yellow teeth.

This Roman did not seem at all like a tiger. He was a sturdy square-shouldered man, round-faced, with scrubby brown whiskers, no taller than Brecon himself. In the shock of the Numidian attack he had been thrown from his horse. The horse had run away and the Roman was chasing it. He had bowlegs that were probably better for riding a fat horse than for running. He was shouting at his horse in Latin.

Perhaps the horse does not understand Latin, Brecon thought. Perhaps it needs an interpreter. It might speak Greek. But not such rude words. I must be serious, like a Roman, he thought, but he wished he could have told Rhodri his joke. Rhodri and Athena always laughed when Brecon tried to amuse them.

Now the Numidian commander ordered his men to turn. Suddenly they were galloping north again, with the Romans pounding after them. They were crossing an open meadow. There was a small hill at the north end of it. They curved around it and stopped well out of sight of the Romans.

"Go to the top of the hill. Wave to me when the leader passes that white rock," the commander said to Brecon.

He could see the Romans well from the hilltop. He counted almost three hundred of them, riding heavy slow-moving horses. Sunlight flashed on their red-plumed helmets, caught the dark blue gleam of spears, showed the bronze bosses of shields. They rode in good order, keeping their lines well. Brecon saw the bowlegged man catch his horse and lumber along after the column. Far away on the southern edge of the meadow, Brecon saw men who had been wounded by javelins lying on the ground and stray horses cropping grass.

The leader passed the white rock. Brecon waved to the Numidian commander. It all began again—the fierce swift pounce of the Numidians, javelins whizzing, Numidian yells, Roman shouts, horses neighing. A few Romans fell, but they closed ranks and came on. They tried to get the Numidians within throwing distance of their spears; the Numidians were always beyond their reach.

As Brecon reached the bottom of the hill, the attack was over. The Numidians retreated again. Starlight ran with them. They went on attacking and retreating till darkness came. Then they no longer heard the feet of Roman horses following them but saw, far behind them, the glow of Roman campfires.

The Numidians did not make camp or cook. They ate dates and cheese from their saddlebags, slept on their saddlecloths, took turns on guard. Brecon lay on his leopard skin, listening to the tethered horses cropping grass, the chirp of crickets, the snores of sleeping men. He thought he would never sleep, but suddenly trumpets from the Roman camp woke him. The Numidians dashed back to the camp, buzzed javelins into it, and rode off again followed by hearty Roman curses. That day—Brecon looked at his calendar and decided he was certainly fourteen—was much like the day before. They reached Hannibal's camp in the early afternoon. A guard, which had been left behind rode off toward the Island. The Numidians ate hot stew and porridge from the kettles, groomed and fed their horses, then vanished along a wooded trail.

Brecon was not alone long. Gauls began to come to the campfire. They gobbled down what was left of the food, drank wine as fast as Brecon brought it. They were dancing around the campfire, shouting and singing when the Romans appeared.

There was no fighting. Any enemy of Hannibal's was a friend to this tribe of Gauls who had been defeated by unfair methods, their leader said. Brecon brought wine for them both and both drank it. He understood enough of their talk to learn that the Gaul said that Hannibal's men had left a little while ago—an hour? two hours? How could he say? Time had slipped by in dancing.

He meant the Numidians, Brecon knew, but the Roman commander evidently thought he meant Hannibal's main army. He sent a messenger back to tell Scipio the Consul that he could catch Hannibal if he hurried north. After that the commander and his men shoved the Gauls good-naturedly out of the camp, took care of their horses, and went to sleep.

The main body of the Roman troops appeared the next day with the Consul, Publius Cornelius Scipio himself, leading it. Brecon saw him dismount from his horse and heard him shouting for the commander of the cavalry. The Consul was a square-faced, gray-haired man with a loud voice.

Brecon heard him shout at the commander, "You found he'd just left and you didn't follow! Tell me why."

The officer gave some stammering explanation that Brecon could not hear, but the whole camp could hear when Scipio said: "Go stand on your head in the river! Find me someone who knows something."

A soldier said, "There's a young Gaul over there who knows a little Latin," and Brecon was dragged forward.

"Speak the truth now," Scipio said. "You understand me?"

"If you speak slowly, sir," Brecon said.

The Consul shouted, "When—did—the Punics leave?"

"Punics, sir?"

"Carthaginians—Hannibal—the rabble with him."

Brecon counted carefully on his fingers, bent the little one in half, raised it again, lowered it, said slowly, "Four days ago, Sir Consul."

"Four days! Take—care—now. Is that—the truth?"

"Four days. A sunny one. Two with some showers. A sunny one. And today."

The soldiers—they had been holding Brecon's shoulders—asked, "What shall we do with him, sir?"

"Give him a piece of silver. Let him go. Send the tribunes to me."

The tribunes were officers of Scipio's troops. As Brecon waited for his piece of silver he heard the Consul bellowing orders to them to see their men were fed and then march back to the sea. He also gave orders to a messenger to start at once and ride fast.

"Tell the ship captains they are going to transport troops to Spain. And have my galley ready to go swiftly to Pisa."

Pisa! Brecon could see it as if he were drawing a map of northern Italy on his sand table. It was close to the sea on a river called the Arno. Triremes brought slaves there, Gauls, Greeks, passengers seized from ships by pirates.

Athena might have been a Roman slave, he thought. Well, she's safe in Carthage. Perhaps playing knucklebones with Rhodri with the owl on her shoulder. And she'll be safe so long as we fight in Italy.

"Take this and be off," one of the soldiers said and shoved a coin into Brecon's hand.

Brecon thanked him politely. As he left, he passed a group of cavalry who were bragging to the footsoldiers about their victory over the Numidians.

"A lot of cowards—wouldn't face us. We made them run, I can tell you."

Brecon found Starlight grazing in a meadow beyond the camp where he had left her the night before. His leather sack was where he had left it, in the hollow of an old oak. Starlight came cantering across the field to him. He swung himself onto her back and rode north along the left bank of the Rhone.

Chapter 6

ONLY MOUNTAINS

IT TOOK BRECON four days of fast riding to reach the Island. It was a gloomy ride under gray skies. The path in many places was trampled into bogs by the passing of Hannibal's army. Sometimes it led through dark forests, made even darker by the rain. Sometimes he found open spaces where the army had camped. He soon used the food he had brought with him and he was glad to find scattered oats for Starlight and sometimes a crust of bread for himself.

He looked often for the Alps but all he saw in the distance was a gray wall vanishing into gray clouds. Once a ray of sun pierced the clouds and showed for a few moments the snowy shoulder of a mountain and glare of green below the snow. Once sunlight showed him a white waterfall rushing over dark rocks among black trees, but the tops of the mountains were always lost in the stormy sky.

At last he came to the Island, a rich grassy plain between two rivers, and found Hannibal's army camped there. Brecon learned from some of the first soldiers he met, Iberian horsemen from his own part of Spain, that Hannibal had found two

Gallic tribes quarreling on the Island and had made peace between them. Now he was buying supplies from them, warm cloaks and leg wrappings of wool for his shivering bare-legged Africans, leather shoes, oats for horses, wheat for men, hay for elephants. Already oxcarts were being loaded.

Many of the soldiers looked sulky and were muttering among themselves about the journey. "There are no tops to those mountains," Brecon heard one of them say. "Gods of hail and snow and thunder sit there, ready to drag us into the sky." The others grumbled their agreement.

A trumpet sounded to call the whole camp together. Brecon went with the others and found Hannibal standing on a platform higher than the heads of the crowd. Around him were men who had come to Spain with his father when Hannibal was a boy. Brecon saw Gisgo in his purple and gold and Mago Barca in his crimson cloak. He saw Sosillos, Carthalo, Synhalus, Bog, who knew the stars and kept the calendar, Hanno Bomilcar, and hawk-faced Lord Maharbal, a great leader of either footsoldiers or cavalry.

In a ring around the platform were leaders of soldiers from all the shores of the Middle Sea and the soldiers themselves, rank behind rank. Hannibal spoke in Greek, the tongue best understood by most of his troops. He sometimes repeated what he said in Spanish or Phoenician.

He began by telling them that they had all seen the chiefs of the Boii and Insubres, Gauls from Italy who had come to ask Hannibal to cross over into Italy and help them fight against Rome.

"How do you think those Gauls got into Italy? Their grandfathers went there long ago. They took women and children, horses and sheep with them. Did they fly? Did giants from the clouds snatch them and hurl them over the mountaintops? No! They walked or rode horses just as you will do. It is not an easy road but these mountains are not a wall of rock that reaches the sky as I have heard some of you say. That is not so. They are only mountains, higher than those we have crossed, it is true, but still only mountains. When we cross them we shall be in Italy."

Someone in the crowd shouted, "What about the Roman army coming behind us from the sea?"

Brecon wrote something on a waxed tablet he had in his pouch and passed it to the man next to him saying, "A message for Hannibal. Pass it along," and saw it begin to move from hand to hand toward the platform.

Hannibal was saying, "Yes—the Romans sent an army to the Rhone by sea. Where will they not send one? Will not the sea bring them to Gades, to New Carthage, to Carthage itself? Will you go home, hide your head under a blanket, wait till they come and snatch your wives and children from you? What will you say to your wives when you get home? Ask them for a good dinner because you are tired of running away from the shadow of a Roman? No!"

There were echoing shouts of "No! No!" from the crowd. Brecon's tablet had reached the platform. Someone handed it up to Sosillos, who passed it to Hannibal. He glanced at it quickly, waved it at the crowd.

"Good news, friends!" he said. "There's no army behind us. The Consul has given up and gone back to Italy. We'll meet him there—sooner than he thinks. That's how we'll keep our homes safe, fighting him in his country, not ours. We'll make Rome weary of war. Then we can live in peace where we like. March on!"

As the crowd broke up and the officers gave orders to the men, Hannibal saw Brecon and beckoned to him.

"The message came at the right moment," he said to Brecon. "Tell me more." When he had heard what Brecon had to say, he added, "You have done well. Rest yourself and your horse awhile. We shall follow the Rhone until we reach the Drome River. Chief Magal of the Boii has told me of a pass through the Alps that will bring us out among friendly Gauls. Carthalo will go ahead with gifts. Here is the pass."

He unrolled a map Carthalo had made and showed Brecon the route marked on it.

"Does Carthalo need me?" Brecon asked.

"No—but I may. Ride with the Numidians. We shall rest when we reach the Drome. You can easily catch up with us. Rest well. Go well. Farewell, cousin!"

"A good journey, cousin!" Brecon said.

The journey began at once. Hannibal rode ahead with a small party of horsemen. Behind him came the elephants. All thirty-seven had crossed the Rhone safely but some of their drivers had been drowned. These drivers were called Indos because the first ones had come from India. Brecon wondered if the new ones would be able to manage the elephants when they reached the snow. At present they were moving forward with great speed. All but one were small African elephants about eight feet tall. In the elephant stalls at Carthage, Brecon had seen the large breed of African elephants too. One was almost thirteen feet high.

Surus, the only Indian elephant in Hannibal's army, was leading the troop. Brecon noticed, as he had before, how different she was from the African breed. Her back rose in a dome shape. Theirs were almost flat, dipping slightly in the middle. Her ears were smaller than theirs, her trunk was smooth instead of ridged and it had one "finger" at the end instead of two. Surus was Brecon's favorite elephant. She was the one who had lifted him from the ground to ride with Hannibal. Her shadow had covered him and Alain when they wrestled. She was known as the bravest and wisest and swiftest of elephants. The others had a hard time to keep up with the pace she set. She was like a great thundercloud blown by the wind, Brecon thought.

After the elephants came the Numidian cavalry, moving along easily. Then came the footsoldiers, next the slingers, next wagon trains drawn by oxen, and the train of pack mules. Soldiers' wives, often with children in their arms or hanging to their skirts, trudged along behind the mules. There was a rear guard of marching Libyans and last of all the Iberian cavalry.

Alain rode by, saw Brecon, and called out, "See who's here! I thought you'd run away, toad skin, I mean leopard skin!"

Brecon answered, "Greetings, Prince! How about a little wrestling?" but Alain made no reply to such impertinence.

Brecon tried to count the troops. Gauls had joined them. There must be almost fifty thousand men now, he figured. And then, he thought that night as he went to sleep on his leopard skin, there's Alain. He ought to count extra. Why, he must weigh two hundred and fifty pounds. I'm glad I don't have to wrestle with him tonight.

The next day was sunny and he rode through a country of vineyards and golden wheat fields. The mountains were only ten miles away now. On his right they were like a herd of blue elephants, dark against a pale blue sky. Ahead they were waves of a great purple sea with a foam of white clouds where the waves were breaking.

It was a hot afternoon. When he reached the Drome, a clean,

swift, gravelly stream, he found men resting along it for miles. Many of them had swum their horses into the river and were now grooming them or drying themselves. Elephants were splashing happily in the stream. Along it were family parties, soldiers and their wives and children, eating and drinking happily in the sunshine.

Brecon found Hannibal with the elephants. He had ridden Surus into the river and was now on shore again making her show him each of her huge feet so he could be sure there were no cuts in them. She was pulling affectionately at his dark curly hair with her trunk. She was making a small noise—about like the purring of a hundred cats, Brecon thought, to show that she was pleased. There was grass growing along the stream. The elephants had eaten a great patch of ground almost bare.

Hannibal was dripping wet.

"I thought it would be only my feet, since the stream is not very deep," he said to Brecon, "but Surus squirted most of the river over me. Her Indo says it is a sign of affection. I'll dry out in the sun. Walk back with me to my tent."

As they strolled along in the warm sun, Hannibal said, "Speak to Sosillos and get him to give you a good roll of papyrus. He has some from Egypt. I want you to keep an account of our journey day by day. You have an ink bottle at your belt, I see. That bottle was blown in Carthage, but someone hammered out a case of Spanish silver for it. You did? Good. And the cork came from a Spanish tree, too. Your pen—why, it's an eagle's feather. From Spain."

"No, my lord. From Gaul. I picked it up under a great pine where the eagle had her nest, but I sharpen it with a Spanish knife."

"And your horse came from Africa, your tunic from Greece, and your sash of purple linen from Tyre."

"And from Carthage," Brecon said. "Athena spun and wove it. My cousin had it dyed. I thought, with my hair brown might go better, but my lady said purple."

Hannibal smiled and said, "It looks well and you are a real Carthaginian now, carrying things from all over the world. We must teach the Romans to let us keep doing that."

They found Sosillos. He gave Brecon a good roll of papyrus.

"Come to me for more when that is used. Write every day. Be brief. Write what you see. Remember that the biggest lies often follow the words 'they say.' I am proud you are to be our historian."

"I'm not exactly Herodotus," Brecon said.

Hannibal laughed.

"Write for Carthalo," he said. "Let the Romans worry about how it will sound in two hundred years."

This is what Brecon wrote about crossing the Alps.

First day

We started at dawn. There are more than fifty thousand men from Africa, Spain, the Balearic Islands, and Gaul. Our guides are Gauls. We followed a road at first but the valley soon narrowed and we had only a track. We had to ford the river many times, stumbling among boulders. The cliffs above us were of bare stone in shapes of strange animals and giant men. Mostly clouds cover the mountaintops but sometimes they drift apart and show a vast peak. There were Gauls hiding behind rocks on the hills watching us. They had shaggy wheat-colored hair and carried long swords.

Hannibal sent me with our Gallic guides and some officers to parley with them. Our Gauls talked with the mountain men. They say they are Allobroges, great thieves, tough fighters. They attack travelers and loot villages by day but go back to the huts in their own village at night. We camped that night on an open meadow near the river. Hannibal ordered the sentries to keep the campfires burning brightly all night. He ordered a troop of Spanish footsoldiers, heavily armed, to meet him in a dark place beyond the light of the fires. We were to climb the hill where we had talked with the Allobroges that morning.

I knew the path we had climbed, so I went ahead. It was very steep. More than once I heard men slip and fall behind me. At last we reached the rocky crest where we had met the Allobroges.

For a signal to the troops in the camp, Hannibal lighted a torch. This was to tell them to start moving through the pass below. It took a long time. The track is so narrow that only a few men can walk abreast. The elephants went first. They had to be coaxed over each foot of the way. The mules stop and peer around every rock. Our line is six miles long.

Second day

At first light, oxcarts were still being hauled up through the pass. As the sun rose, the Allobroges climbed up to their hilltop again. They started to roll rocks down on our men, but seeing us, they rushed down to rob the carts. There was thick mist below. Through it we could hear oxen bellowing, mules braying, drivers shouting. Hannibal led his Spaniards down again. The robbers fled to the meadow where we had camped. Hannibal had left African horsemen there. They made short work of the thieves. Some fled into the woods. Others were made prisoners. Hannibal found their town deserted. He seized enough food to feed the army for three days. We camped there that night.

Third day

Our guides from the Island went home saying they knew no more landmarks. Some of the officers urged Hannibal to turn back. They said we would never find the pass. We went on. He rode back along the line talking to his men. Suddenly Gauls on the cliffs above started rolling rocks down on us. Men and animals both fell into the river. Some were drowned. Hannibal made the line keep moving. He hurried forward, found Gauls killing and being killed. He hacked his way through them, made a passage for his men and held it. Blood stained the river.

The Numidians and the elephants had gone through safely. We fought our way into another valley. The track there was between a cliff above the river and much higher cliffs above. There were Gauls there too who sent boulders rolling down on us. Some of our men lost their horses. Sometimes three of them rode on one horse. Starlight carried me and a wounded Libyan the last part of the way. Hannibal rode ahead, fighting off one ambush after another, to find a safe place to camp. At last he found it, a great bare dome of rock. It rose from the valley to the height of the cliffs, where the Gauls leaped like mountain goats. We could see the whole valley. We camped and lighted fires.

Fourth day

All night I heard men reach camp, fall, and sleep where they fell. At dawn they were still staggering in as if walking in their sleep, often two with a wounded comrade between them or one with a friend on his back. Hannibal sent us back along the trail and we brought back wounded and caught horses for them to ride but there are still thousands of men missing. We rested all day. I helped Synhalus bandage wounds and give medicine to the sick. Many felt stronger after drinking hot soup in which he dissolved something. Making it is a secret of his.

Bog, the astrologer, looked at the stars last night and says we shall find our way out of these mountains. I hope he is right.

Fifth day

Stayed at our rock fortress again today. Some more men and some horses found their way to us.

Sixth day

We started at dawn. A day of sunshine. The valley widened. Pine-covered hills rose steeply above us. Above the pines were bare rocks. Higher still were what at first seemed like clouds against the blue sky. Suddenly they were mountains. No more Gauls here. Now only the mountains are our enemies.

Seventh to ninth day

We struggled on over a twisting trail. Sometimes it went downhill a little way, but there was always a higher hill again to climb. The river roars and foams below us. Above the icy wind whistles in the pines. Bog saw the Pleiades set so he says that it is now autumn and that snow will be in the high passes soon. The elephants hate the cold wind. There are no pastures for them now. So much of the packtrain was lost that there is little food for any of us—animals or men. Some of the elephants lay down and died. The men cut them up and broiled the flesh over the campfires. Neither Hannibal nor I could eat it. We had a little wheat porridge.

On the ninth day I was riding at the rear of the Numidians. The track was so narrow and twisting that I could see only three or four riders ahead of me and a few footsoldiers behind. The climb was very steep. We came to snow and the horses slipped and slid on the ice under it. I was wondering if Starlight could go farther, when I heard cheering from far ahead. At first it was faint. Then it grew louder and louder.

I could see the men ahead turn in the saddle and I heard them call, "*Hannibal's at the summit! He's at the summit!*" Then I turned and shouted to the footsoldiers and I heard the words go echoing down the trail.

Our path dipped, rose again, vanished around a great shoulder of bare rock. As we reached it, a blast of wind shrieked around it, bringing clouds of whirling snowflakes. I could hardly see the men ahead of me. Starlight slid back on the trail, almost fell, stood shivering and panting. I dismounted and led her, slipping, shivering and panting too.

The snow flurry blew on down the valley. I climbed on, dizzy, stumbling, and came at last to the top of the pass. There were the elephants dark against the snow. There was Hannibal with his officers. Gisgo's face was as purple as his cloak. Bog's teeth were chattering. His black hat with the gilt stars and half-moons on it was sprinkled with snow. His dark face was blue with cold but he was waving his wand and laughing. Suddenly the snow flurry was over. Above the mountains to the west the sun was setting. It turned the white peaks to the east a glowing pink and it shone on a wide green plain thousands of feet below us.

Our army speaks many tongues but there is one word we all know. It echoed all around us—"*Italy! Italy!*"—as the men looked down on the golden green land and the silver river below.

Ninth to fifteenth day

We camped at the summit two days, resting. It was good we had the rest because in some ways the descent was worse

than the climb. The path was narrow, slippery, and steep. Our
tired animals stumbled often. If they fell, they rolled down
and knocked down the next man and his horse. Many were
hurt in this way. Some were killed. Footsoldiers slipped on ice
under the snow. It was strange to see that elephants did better

in the snow than horses. Surus was in the lead. Her huge feet crushed the snow down into a track that the others could use.

In the afternoon we met our worst obstacle, an enormous rock, right in the path. The Indos told Hannibal when he rode down to it that we could go no farther. The ground below the rock had been broken by the avalanche that brought it down. What had been a steep slope was now a precipice a thousand feet in height. Above, a sheer cliff was almost as high. The rock was huge, as big as some of the houses in New Carthage. It towered above the heads of horses, even of elephants. Hannibal sent me to climb it. I scrambled to the top, getting foot and handholds where I could. The other side was even steeper and smoother. I reported that footsoldiers might scale it and get down the other side by cutting steps and using ropes, but that for elephants, horses, and pack animals it was impossible.

Hannibal went back along the trail to try to find a way around it. There was none. The cliffs above were everywhere as steep as those below. Soldiers gazed at the rock in despair.

I heard them mutter, "It is the end of our journey. We must go back to Spain." But Hannibal said cheerfully, "Never mind, men. We'll move it."

He ordered his woodcutters to chop down pines and make a pile of firewood against the rock. The wind blew down the pass. We lighted the fire. It burned fiercely. Even the rock itself glowed red. When the whole face of it was hot, Hannibal ordered wine that had turned to vinegar thrown on it. Soldiers brought wineskins and emptied them into buckets. Others stood ready with picks and mallets.

When Hannibal gave the word, men threw vinegar on the glowing rock, then rushed back out of the pink clouds of steam. Then the pick and mallet men took their turn, splintering off great chunks of rock. Others came with shovels and sent the pieces hurtling down over the cliff.

Hannibal took his turn with the rest of us. The men cheered him as he dashed in and out of the steam, but the work was only begun. For four days and nights we worked, taking turns chopping wood, building fires, dashing vinegar on the hot rock, splitting it and shoveling it away. The animals nearly died of hunger, for the pastures for miles were buried in snow. Some more elephants died. The smell of their flesh cooking over hot coals in the vinegar clouds made me sick and dizzy. I was cooking porridge for Hannibal's supper when Alain came through the smoke gnawing a great half-raw piece of meat.

"You ought to eat meat," he said. "You wouldn't be so skinny. I've eaten most of an elephant. The best part of course. Meat between the ribs. Gave my men the rest. You look as sick as a hungry fox," he added.

I suppose I did.

At last the rock was gone. We shoveled the track clear of the last sharp splinters of stone, spread dirt over it. Surus moved on slowly, crushing the loose dirt into a track.

In a few hours we were in Italy.

Hannibal reached Italy five months after he left New Carthage. It took him fifteen days to cross the Alps. The army rested in a green valley where there was plenty of food for the animals. Hannibal went to meet leaders of the Gallic tribes. Carthalo had arranged the meeting and had sent a messenger to show Hannibal the way. Brecon was one of the escort who rode with him.

Starlight had come through the crossing of the Alps well. Except for a mark where a piece of hot rock had struck her, scorching the hair a little, she was in good condition. Brecon had groomed her. The white star shone on her forehead. Green grass to eat and to roll on had made her so full of spirits that she reared and pranced as they rode along.

Hannibal had said, "We must not let these Gauls think we

look like beggars," so Brecon was dressed in new clothes he had bought on the Island, a loose coat and trousers the color of a frost-nipped oak leaf. He used his leopard skin for a saddlecloth. He wore his gold chain and armband and his purple sash.

He thought of Athena weaving it. Was the owl sitting on her shoulder? Could Rhodri run now? What was Sophonisba doing? When she was trying to get the armband away from him, she had told him he looked very handsome. Brecon, who had seen himself, freckles and all, in Imilce's mirror, had doubts about that. Well, at least he had combed his hair today. He had even sharpened a small twig and cleaned his fingernails with it. This made his fingers feel all new at the ends and not at all comfortable.

Even Hannibal had made himself look less shabby than usual. He had borrowed a cloak from Gisgo—not his best purple one but a crimson one, almost new. He had on a helmet instead of a headcloth and a breastplate of bronze inlaid with gold. Mago had lent him a gold clasp in the shape of a lion's head to fasten his cloak. Synhalus' new boots fitted him quite well. Even when he wore his old black cloak, he always had a well-groomed horse and splendid weapons, polished and shining with silver and gold. Today they looked especially brilliant.

Carthalo, however, looked as he always did. They met him in an open field, like a green lawn, by the river. The sheep who had nibbled it smooth were lying in the shade of a great oak tree. It was hard to believe, that warm afternoon, that a week ago they had been struggling through snow to reach this peaceful place.

The Gauls were already there on the other side of the field. Before Carthalo escorted Hannibal to them, he told him briefly what he had learned. Scipio the Consul had landed at Pisa. He had marched east along the Po River to Placentia, a fortified city. He was resting there. Probably he did not yet know that Hannibal had come. The army he had brought to the Rhone had gone to Spain. The other consul, Tiberius Sempronius, had been ordered to give up the idea of attacking Carthage from Sicily. He was marching north as fast as he could.

"I hear," Carthalo said, "that Sempronius is a very rash, energetic man and jealous of Scipio. He wants to get here and beat you first but he had a forty-day march ahead of him when he started; has plenty of it still to do."

"It would be courteous to wait for him," Hannibal said with a smile. "Still—first come, first served."

He asked Carthalo what Gallic tribes had sent men to meet him.

There were some Insubres there, Carthalo said, but the Boii were now busy fighting the Taurini, neighbors of theirs. There were no chiefs Hannibal had seen before.

The Gauls received him with shouts of welcome. He told them that he had come to free oppressed people from Roman tyranny. If the Gauls helped him, he would help them so that they might live in peace and freedom in their own fields. Rome had forced cities farther south to be her allies. They would rise against her too, he said. The Gauls shouted and beat on their long shields with their long swords but at the end of the meeting he was not sure of their aid.

He ended his speech by saying, "Your enemies are my enemies."

To prove it he attacked Turin, the fortified town of the Taurini, and took it. The Insubres and some of the Boii, who had begun the quarrel, helped a little in the attack and a great deal in looting the town afterwards. They gave Hannibal fodder for his horses and wheat for his men.

The army rested. Men and animals grew strong again. Hannibal disappeared from the camp during this time. One evening he rode off on Surus. He told Brecon to meet him a few miles down the river. When the Gauls said "the river," they meant the Po, which comes out of the Alps, runs east, empties into the Adriatic. It was still not a large stream at the place where Hannibal had told Brecon to meet him. He had given him certain landmarks—a white rock, a tall pine with a crow's nest, a waterfall.

"It's about three miles. Better walk. Bring your supper," Hannibal had said.

Brecon was sure of the place, but there was no elephant in sight. There was an old man, a Gaul, with a sweeping gray mustache and long gray hair reaching his shoulders. He was limping along the path, leaning on a heavy stick. Occasionally he put one hand to his back as if it hurt him. He had an old sack slung over one shoulder. This he put down beside the path now and then, straightened up his stooped shoulders and coughed painfully. Brecon came up with him just under the big pine with the crow's nest. He had sat down on the white rock. In a low whining voice, hard to hear over the sound of the waterfall, he begged Brecon for something to eat.

Brecon gave him some of the bread and cheese he had brought for his supper. The man took the food with a shaking, dirty hand, whined out a Gallic blessing, then straightened up and, looking Brecon straight in the the eye, said, "Have some yourself—cousin. These Gauls bake good bread, I'll say that for them."

"My Lord Hannibal!" Brecon gasped.

Hannibal looked pleased.

"You really did not know me? I told Carthalo I could fool

you. He said I couldn't. I met him here. He's taking Surus back by another road. He said riding an elephant was not an inconspicuous way to leave camp. I said that you'd be looking for a man on an elephant." Hannibal chuckled happily. "You were, weren't you?" he added. "Come, we'll go into the woods over there and make you look like my Gallic grandson."

In the old sack was a yellow wig and a small yellow mustache. There were also some ragged and dingy clothes and a smaller bag of odds and ends brought from Turin. There was a sword belt decorated with blue enamel, strings of beads, a battered drinking cup of tarnished silver, a hank of linen thread, a needle, some earrings.

"These we shall sell," Hannibal said, "or trade for food and a night's lodging." He looked Brecon over critically and added, "You look too young and your face is too clean. Rub this into it."

He gave Brecon a jar of grayish-brown stuff.

"Rub it into your neck and ears as well as into your face," he said. "And into your hands and feet too. Your toes are going to stick out of your shoes."

"It's lucky for you my grandmother can't hear you," Brecon said, but Hannibal only went on, "Here, take this gum and put on your mustache and your wig. That's good. Now stuff these rags into your shirt to make one shoulder higher than the other. Put on this coat and trousers and put your own in the bag. I'd forgotten you were so tall. Your ankles show. Rub some dirt in them."

"The Alps stretched me," Brecon said.

When Hannibal was satisfied with Brecon's appearance, they started along toward a village farther down the river. It was almost dark when they reached it, but they went from house to house offering to trade their goods for food and shelter.

Hannibal, who knew that his Gallic speech would not deceive anyone for long, would stammer and whine a few words, then say, "My g-g-grandson will s-s-speak to you," and Brecon would tell their story.

They had come with the Lord Hannibal as guides, he said. They came from an Alpine village. They would return there in the spring but now the passes were full of snow. They had goods from Turin to trade and they would spend the winter in Italy. He would also tell their hosts about the elephants and about the great rock that was heated and split with vinegar and about the fight with the Allobroges.

"They would have done better to be friends with the Lord Hannibal," Brecon would say. "Once a friend he's always a friend."

For three days they wandered from one village to the next. By the time they turned west again by a different road, Hannibal had learned a good deal about the Gauls. They were not, he thought, exactly treacherous by nature but they were easily turned from one purpose to another. They were proud, easily angered, and loved fighting for its own sake. Because of a difference of opinion a Gaul would fight the friend sitting next to him at table, perhaps wound or even kill him. The men did some farming in their green fields but they were never too busy to raid another village. Their wives took care of herds and flocks. They encouraged their men to go on the warpath against towns farther south and bring back Etruscan weaving and painted pottery.

Brecon had no difficulty in peddling the things in their sack for food and lodging, sometimes even for silver. They soon had nothing left but a few beads. One dark night they changed to their own clothes and the next morning were back in camp looking like themselves.

This was the first of several of these expeditions. Hannibal had many disguises. Sometimes he was a middle-aged Gaul from Marseilles. Sometimes an old Greek trader from Sicily or a young one from Alexandria in Egypt. It was as a Greek with a young red-haired Gaul for a servant that he visited the country near Placentia, where Scipio had his headquarters. Hannibal soon had in his mind a map of the country. He saw where the Ticino River flowed out of the Alps and into the Po near Pavia. He learned where bridges and fords were. He noticed open fields good for cavalry attacks.

Another time he explored the shores of the river Trebbia, which meets the Po near Placentia. At this time of year the Trebbia was a rushing, foaming stream, sometimes overflowing its low banks. After the Alps, the country seemed almost flat, but there were low hills here and there with sandy gullies full of straggling bushes between the hills. Although ditches were supposed to carry off some of the water, they overflowed in those rainy November days. Hannibal and Brecon squelched through acres of brown mud under dreary gray skies.

When they got back to Hannibal's camp, they found more elephants had died and had been eaten. The other animals, however, were stronger than they had been at any time since crossing the Alps. Soldiers crouched miserably in their tents. The Africans were especially unhappy in the damp cold. Hannibal found a sandy field and soon had it made into a training field like the one at New Carthage. Numidians hurled javelins, Spaniards threw lances, slingers threw stones or balls of lead. Gauls from the villages nearby watched and shouted their praise. Some of them brought their sturdy horses, their long shields and swords, and joined Hannibal's army when it marched toward Placentia.

CHAPTER 7

FIRST MEETING

THE GAULS who marched with them told Brecon about the Roman legion. There were, they said, about three thousand men in a legion, sometimes more. A legion was divided up into groups called centuries, a hundred men in each, and each commanded by a centurion. When the legion was drawn up for battle, the first line had light-armed troops in it. Besides its battle flags each legion had a standard with an eagle of gold on it. The best troops carried it at the right of the front line.

No one had ever captured one, the Gauls told Brecon. They said that there were trumpeters in the front line too, and that all the legionaries knew their calls and obeyed them. The second line was of spearmen. They were trained to make a wall with their shields and keep that wall with their spears no matter what happened. In the third line were experienced old soldiers who backed up the spearmen. All these soldiers were Romans, tough, well-trained men who never—the Gauls said—broke their lines. They might retreat, but only when the trumpets ordered them to fall back. They were afraid of nothing. The troops on the wings were Italian allies. They were not so well trained as the Romans. Sometimes they broke and ran. But not the Roman center. You might as well try to knock over the Alps!

Brecon found a Gaul who knew the messages of the trumpets. Brecon thought—he told Hannibal—that this man and some of the others had served for pay in the Roman army at some time. He could whistle the calls so that Brecon learned them. He taught them to Hannibal's trumpeters and to his officers. Mago Barca, Hannibal's brother, was especially interested in them.

On the march, the Gauls said, each Roman soldier carried his weapons, food, blankets, part of a tent, and entrenching tools. They made an entrenched camp every night. It was a walled city of tents fortified and guarded from the last trumpet call at night to the first one at dawn.

"What if something unexpected happens?" Brecon asked.

A Gaul answered gloomily, "Nothing unexpected happens to Romans."

Brecon told this to Hannibal, who laughed and said, "How dull! We must do something to interest them."

The day they reached the place where the Ticino runs into the Po, Carthalo brought the news that Scipio was encamped not far off. One of Carthalo's men was a Gaul who had joined the Roman army. He told Carthalo about a speech Scipio had made to his men about Hannibal's troops.

Scipio had said that the Punics, as he called them, were a people conquered by the Romans. They had dared to revolt. Their army was made up of slaves from many countries. They were half starved and miserable.

"Perhaps you think they were brave to cross the Alps," he said. "They were afraid not to. Many of them have died. These Punics are no match for brave hardy Romans. At the Rhone our cavalry met theirs and put it to flight a dozen times. Now they'll face our footsoldiers. They cannot escape us now."

"They all cheered," the Gaul said. "They start at first light tomorrow."

"What will you say to our troops?" Hasdrubal Gisgo asked.

Hannibal said, "I am no orator. That's a Roman specialty. Did you know, Gisgo, that no Roman ever reads anything without moving his lips? If a master sees a pupil looking at a book and not moving his lips, he beats him. I think our men will understand better if I show them something."

He summoned the troops and had them form a great ring around a field. In the fight with the Allobroges, they had taken a number of prisoners. They still had their hands and feet fettered. They had been able to cross the Alps in misery but not to escape. Hannibal had them brought into the ring. Into the ring also were thrown two richly ornamented suits of armor, helmets, and swords such as a Gallic chief might use in battle. A fine horse well saddled and bridled was also brought and a cloak lined with fur.

Hannibal said to the prisoners, "Which would you rather do—wear your fetters still or arm yourselves and fight to the death in a single combat? He who wins will receive his arms and armor, a horse and a cloak. He who is slain will be freed by death from his misery."

Every prisoner pleaded eagerly to be allowed to fight. Hannibal told them they could draw lots.

"The two upon whom the lot falls will arm themselves for the fight," he said.

The moment they heard this, the men all lifted up their chained hands and prayed to their gods to be chosen. When the result was announced, the two men chosen were overjoyed to have their fetters struck off and to arm themselves. The others sat looking on in sullen misery while the swords clashed.

At last one stood in triumph and one lay dead.

Brecon heard one of the prisoners say, "Victor and vanquished—both are happy now." His comrades muttered agreement.

Hannibal said to the troops, "Fortune has brought us all into the same pass as these prisoners. She has led us to the field of battle, has shown us the prizes. We must conquer or die. Or—what is worse—become prisoners. Our prize is not a horse or a cloak of fur. It is to be known to all men as victors over the Romans. When these prisoners fought, we thought them both lucky to be allowed to fight. It is the same for us all.

"From this moment all nations in our army are the equals of the men of Carthage. All slaves who came here with their masters are now free men. I myself will pay their masters in silver the price of their freedom. All prisoners who wish to fight the Romans shall have their fetters struck off and be given arms. After we have gained victory in Italy, all will be free to go home.

"I ask you," he added, "to go into battle as I shall do, determined to win or to die fighting. Good night. Sleep well!"

The officers of the different peoples of Hannibal's army repeated what he had said in their own tongues. Cheers rose from all parts of the camp. A strongly united army marched against Scipio in the morning.

Mist still hung over the Ticino as Brecon, riding with the Numidians, heard trumpets sounding and then caught sight of the Roman legions. The army was like a moving wall. As the mist blew away, pale sunlight gleamed on gold eagles, on flags of many colors, on shields, spears, and helmets. Horsemen on sturdy chunky horses rode on the wings at the pace of footsoldiers. Both footmen and horsemen answered the trumpet calls like one man.

Mago Barca was in command of the Numidians. As the mist vanished he waved his hand. There was a sudden thunder of horses' feet. Then came the sound of javelins finding their mark, the neighing of frightened horses, shouts, trumpet calls as the Roman cavalry scattered before the fierce swift charge.

Near a gold eagle at the right of the Roman line, Brecon saw a gray-haired man, wounded by a javelin, fall from his horse. As he fell, Brecon saw his face and recognized the Consul: Publius Cornelius Scipio. A group of Gauls tried to capture him but two Romans, one of them a very young man, rode them down with their horses, cut their way through them and put them to flight with their swords. The younger man dismounted and lifted the wounded Consul to his own horse. Both men supported Scipio between them as they rode off toward the Roman camp.

The Numidians rode on behind the legions. Brecon heard a trumpet call he recognized, saw the men of the Roman rear rank turn like one man and get their heavy spears ready. There was no target for them. The Numidians had flashed by at top speed, hurling their javelins, striking men and horses.

The legions did not break. The call to retreat sounded. They turned and tramped back to their camp in good order, carrying their wounded. Hannibal's army, at his command, went no farther.

The battle of Ticino was over.

The Consul had been rescued by his son, Publius Cornelius Scipio, Junior, seventeen years old. Brecon learned this from one of a band of Gauls who had served in the Roman army that day. They had broken out of camp as darkness fell after killing their officers. They came to Hannibal, riding horses they had stolen, and offered to join his forces. He fed them, gave them wine to drink and gifts of silver. He told them that they could help him best by returning to their own villages and telling their friends that the time had come to drive the Romans from Gallic land. He sent some of them back to camp as spies. They left after talking to Carthalo.

The Boii now saw that it was time to join the winning side. A group came to Hannibal bringing him three Roman captives, taken by them from a Roman Camp. They were army commanders. Hannibal thanked the Boii chiefs. He suggested that they should exchange the prisoners for captive Gauls.

The Numidians had also taken prisoners. These were mostly not Romans but Italian allies. Hannibal released them without asking for ransom. They could go home, he said, and tell what they had seen.

One of the prisoners was a Roman footsoldier. Hannibal asked him some questions. He told Brecon to act as interpreter.

"I will do as well as I can, cousin, but you speak Latin better than I do," Brecon said.

Hannibal smiled. "I would not like to have the Romans think I am not an ignorant barbarian," he said. "Besides, there are advantages in not asking questions directly. It gives a good chance to see the man's expression when he first hears the question and it gives you time to think up the next question. Then you sometimes learn more by looking at a man than by what he says. And it's good practice for you. How many javelins did you throw today that found their mark?"

Brecon turned red under his freckles. "None, my lord."

"None?"

"I—I didn't throw any. I can at a target but not at a man, even a Roman."

Hannibal said, "Never mind, Brecon. I have seen for a long time that you would make a better messenger and interpreter than a killer. I myself dislike killing. If today the Romans would make an honest offer of peace and give pledges I could trust to leave Carthage free to carry goods around the world, I would gladly accept it. But let's talk with our Roman. Ask him why the Romans lost the battle."

The Roman spat on the ground contemptuously.

"That was no battle," he said, "just a little skirmish. The cowardly Italians broke formation and ran. The legions did not break. Roman legions never break. We are not cowards."

Brecon repeated what the man had said.

"Ask him how he happened to be taken prisoner."

The Roman turned an angry crimson and spoke very loud.

"He says it was a dirty Punic trick," Brecon reported. "He was on the end of the rear line. The Punics must know the Roman trumpet calls. When they heard the about face, they knew he would have to turn. Four—no five—of them came up behind him and knocked him down and dragged him off. Five of them, it took. Filthy African slaves they were. 'Just give me a fair field with any two of them,' he says. He is using what sounds like some very rude words, cousin. I don't know exactly what they mean."

Hannibal said he would overlook them. He named a moderate price for the Roman's ransom and the man was dragged off still grumbling about Punic tricks. He reminded Brecon of Alain. Evidently anything that happened to a Roman was not the Roman's fault.

There were other Roman prisoners to be questioned. Their

answers were much the same. They all said that Ticino was a skirmish, not a battle, that they had been captured by Punic tricks, that when the Punic cowards met the Romans face to face, things would be different.

One said that the Romans had retired only because their consul was wounded, that it was not he but his legate who had ordered the retreat. He added that the Punics would sing another song when the consul Tiberius Sempronius came.

"Keep him talking," Hannibal said to Brecon, "I want to learn about this consul."

"Sempronius," the Roman said, "is a great fighter. Acts fast, wastes no time waiting for an enemy to attack. Comes in like a hungry wolf, seizes his foe, hangs on till there's nothing left of him."

"So in the battle at Ticino, he would not have gone back to camp?"

"Battle! That was no battle!"

"Just a skirmish," Brecon said.

"Right!" the Roman exclaimed approvingly. "And the dirty Punics did not dare attack our camp. Have no siege machinery, I hear. You're not a Punic. You're a Gaul. I can tell by your hair—I notice things like that. Not much gets by me, I can tell you. Now you ought to join Rome, my boy. Sempronius will be here tomorrow or next day. We'll have forty thousand troops against you. Get on the winning side, boy."

"I'll think it over," Brecon said.

"And if you can get me out of the fetters and back to camp without ransom, I'll pay you well. Understand?"

"Yes," Brecon said, "I understand."

Hannibal gave the sign to have the prisoner removed. When they were alone, he said to Brecon, "You know of course that these men are right. It was only a skirmish. They did stand their ground. They retreated in good order with most of their forces. It's true that we lost our siege machinery in the Alps and can't attack their camp. I'd like Sempronius to know how weak we are. I think you had better take that man's bribe and set him free. I'm glad Sempronius is coming soon—I am anxious to meet him."

Hannibal met Sempronius near the river Trebbia.

When he and Brecon had tramped over that country, he had noticed a place suitable for an ambush. Between two low hills was a gully with a small stream in it, more like a ditch with steep banks than a river. The banks were covered with brambles and other prickly plants and dry brown bracken. Reeds grew at the edge of the water.

When he learned that Sempronius had arrived, Hannibal called his officers, including Mago Barca, together. Hannibal told them about the gully. He said that a watercourse like this one could hide not only footsoldiers but dismounted horsemen. They must lay their shields face down to hide the markings and hide their helmets under their shields.

He said to Mago, "Choose ten of your best and bravest men. Let each of them choose ten and let each of this second ten choose ten more. That is for the horsemen. Do the same thing with footsoldiers. Brecon will lead you to the place. Take your best ten horsemen and your best ten footsoldiers and study it carefully today. Be ready to steal out to it quietly an hour before dawn. I will bring the Romans to you."

Then he added to his officers, "Since Scipio is still suffering from his wound, Sempronius will command. He plans, Carthalo says, to ride in triumph through the streets of Rome and be chosen consul again. We must give him a real battle, not just a skirmish."

Roman elections were held in January. It was now December, a wet dreary day. During the afternoon some Numidians came close to the Roman camp. Roman scouts reported their presence and Sempronius eagerly led two legions out of the camp gate. He would have fought then and there but the Numidians hurried off and were soon on the other side of the flooded Trebbia. Sempronius felt sure that the Punics would never stand against his men.

One of Hannibal's sayings was, "Make the ground fight for you." Half a mile from the hidden river gully was a slope of hard earth. Hannibal had a trench dug behind it. The trench made that slope into an invisible fortress.

Mago, who had been out to inspect his gully, said, "Your ditch is good. Mine is even better," and Hannibal said, "Yes, they are both good hiding places—no one will be looking for us in either of them."

To his officers he said, "Tomorrow the roads to many Latin cities will be open. Do you really think they hold great wealth—or is that only talk?"

Gisgo and some of the other commanders were sure it was true.

"Don't keep it a secret from your men that there are rewards from battles won," said Hannibal.

There were no trumpet calls to summon Hannibal's army to battle. The men were quietly wakened long before dawn of that icy day. They were well fed and were given olive oil to rub themselves with. Hannibal said it would help protect them from the cold. They had plenty of time to arm themselves and to feed and groom their horses.

An hour before dawn Mago's chosen men left the dark camp

and hid themselves in the gully. They hid their shields and helmets as Hannibal had ordered. Their well-trained horses lay down quietly among the bracken.

Still in darkness, before the hour for Roman trumpet calls, there was wild shouting and cheering from Hannibal's camp. Several thousand Numidian horsemen splashed across the flooded Trebbia, through a muddy ford to the Roman camp. There they leaped over the outer defenses of the camp, flinging javelins at the astonished Romans, who rushed out of their tents, and then were gone as suddenly as they came.

Trumpets sounded, sentries shouted, centurions barked orders. Half asleep, the Romans stumbled into formation and, without food, marched out into the mist of that cold dawn.

The Numidians came back saying that the Romans were moving.

Brecon, who had ridden with them, told Hannibal, "In the torchlight I saw Scipio, looking ill, leaning on his crutch. He was at the door of his tent speaking to Sempronius. He tried to hold Sempronius back but Sempronius shouted, 'No! No! The hour has come!' and called to his officers. Then we jumped back over the camp wall and I saw no more, but they will ford the Trebbia soon, I think."

Hannibal said, "Ride fast to Mago and tell him that. He must stay hidden and let them pass. Lord Maharbal, Gisgo, and I will drive them back toward Mago again. He must wait till we outflank them, then attack. Go!"

Brecon dashed off on Starlight. Liquid mud splashed around him. Freezing rain fell steadily. The north wind brought a flurry of snow as he entered the gully. He was hiding there near Mago when they saw the Roman footsoldiers at the ford. They waded through it with muddy freezing water breast-high around them. Sometimes they fell but they struggled to their feet again, climbed the slippery bank, and took their own places in the Roman lines.

They had to wait, shivering in the icy wind, until the cavalry had crossed too. Mago said, "They have about two thousand cavalry on each wing, I think."

"Yes," said Brecon, "and four Roman legions at least. I can see four eagles. The footsoldiers on the wings are Italian allies. See, they are moving."

The Romans moved forward slowly, steadily, solidly. They passed the gully without looking toward it and only pushed on straight ahead through the swirling snow. Facing them were the Balearic slingers. Behind the slingers were heavily armed Spaniards, Gauls, and Africans. There were five thousand cavalry on each wing with groups of elephants in front of the horsemen. Lord Maharbal and Gisgo were in command there. The Romans passed not only the gully but Hannibal's ditch, which faced it, and saw neither.

Snow hid the battle from the men in the gully. The Roman charge and the men who met it were only shadows in the snow. Brecon heard trumpet calls, shouts, shrill threatening cries from the charging Numidians, the whizz of javelins, trumpeting of elephants, the wild scream of dying horses. Then the snow blew away and he saw the elephants, great gray shadows, trampling down the Roman cavalry. They fell back, leaving the flanks of infantry exposed.

In the center the legions fought stubbornly, slipping on ground where frozen blood mixed with snow, holding their own in spite of slingers and javelin throwers, but they fell back nearer and nearer the gully and Hannibal's ditch. Then came Hannibal's charge from the trench, outflanking the legions.

Brecon could see him leading his men, always helping when help was most needed. The Roman lines were still unbroken, the eagles still held their places, but now, under the charge of the elephants, the thrust of Iberian and Numidian cavalry, they began to fall back more quickly. Soon they were facing their attackers on three sides.

Now Mago waved to his men. Footsoldiers leaped to their feet, seized their shields, jammed on their helmets. The horsemen threw themselves on the backs of their horses. With javelins, spears, and swords ready, they dashed toward the retreating Romans. First they rode in a column. Then, spreading out into a great crescent, they completed the circle around the Roman legions.

This blow was too much. The legions broke and ran back toward the Trebbia. Thousands were cut down and died where they fell. Some were trampled to death by elephants.

Many were drowned. Yet the Roman center bravely held its formation. Several thousand men even broke through the Carthaginian lines and reached the Roman camp. Among them was young Scipio. He found a litter and had his father carried to Placentia, but more than thirty thousand Romans were dead, dying in the freezing rain, or prisoners.

These prisoners, when questioned by Hannibal, did not say that Trebbia was only a skirmish. They blamed the weather and the Punic trick of hiding in ditches for their defeat. In a fair fight, they all agreed, Rome would have won.

Sempronius was of the same opinion. His message to Rome said, "Our army has met Hannibal. Unfavorable weather prevented a victory."

Sempronius did not have a Roman triumph. He was not re-elected consul that January.

CHAPTER 8

ARMY IN THE CLOUDS

THEY SPENT the winter in the country of the Gauls near the river Po. It was strange to Brecon to live under a roof again and be sure where his next meal was coming from. Chiefs of many Gallic tribes came to visit Hannibal and promised to join him against Rome. Ligurians came from the west of Italy, Veneti from the east. Boii and Insubres pledged their loyalty again.

Hannibal dressed himself in purple and gold to receive the ambassadors. A lion's skin was at his feet. On it lay something a soldier of Sempronius had dropped on the battlefield at Trebbia. It was one of the fasces of a consul, a bundle of bronze rods with the blade of an axe sticking out of the middle of it. This sign of authority was always carried before a consul wherever he went.

Other spoils of the battle—Roman shields, swords, spears, trumpets—were leaning against the wall or had been piled on the floor. On a table were Roman belts ornamented with gold, the golden seal rings of Roman knights, gold chains. The ambassadors received these things as gifts. Hannibal's footsoldiers wore such ornaments too, for things found on the battlefield had been fairly divided. The Gauls might see a dark-skinned Libyan, formerly a slave, armed with the shield of a Roman officer.

However, most of the time Hannibal wore his old cloak and drilled new soldiers in the training ground. Ten thousand Gauls joined him that winter. He still wanted to learn for himself about the Gauls and the Romans and the country, so he continued to slip away at times, dressed in one of his disguises. Brecon sometimes went with him, but more often with Carthalo. Once Carthalo took him so far south that they saw the walls and hills of Rome with the red sun sinking behind them, and the curves of the yellow Tiber. On the way back they went to Firenze on the Arno. There were peddlers there who kept him supplied with news. He gave them Egyptian perfumes and beads of carved ivory to carry in their packs. You might find almost anything in the packs—wooden flutes, bells, shoestraps, beeswax, lamps, linen cloth. The peddlers bought or traded as well as sold and picked up information as they did so.

One of them told Carthalo that Scipio had recovered from his wound and had gone to Spain to fight the Punics there. He added with a sneer that he supposed the Consul would rather fight someone else than Hannibal.

After he had left them, Brecon said to Carthalo, "Scipio's no coward. I saw him quite close. He looked brave even when he was so badly wounded. I think he knows he can hurt Carthage most in Spain. I liked his son. He paid no attention to javelins buzzing around him. Just saved his father's life as if he did it every day."

"How does he look?"

"Like a Roman. Handsome. Square-faced. Carved out of

marble. He's not much bigger than I am but I doubt if I could beat him wrestling."

"Oh, you might—think of Alain!"

Brecon was glad he could not hear Alain's voice. Alain loved to tell about the men he had killed at the Trebbia. The number was growing larger every day. Alain had put the Roman cavalry to flight. He had captured Romans and had been paid their ransom in silver. He would have captured a gold eagle if the Romans had not run away. If you listened to Alain, you wondered if Hannibal had been at Trebbia.

"One or two more such battles and we'll seize Rome," Alain boasted.

In Firenze they learned that the Romans were training new legions. New consuls had been elected—Servilius, a patrician, and Flaminius, a man of the people. He had held the consulship and other offices before. The great well-paved road that ran northeast from Rome for two hundred miles had been named after him—the Flaminian Way. He had planned it to make it easy for the legions to march against the Gauls.

"We followed it for a while last week," Carthalo said.

"Hard walking on those stones," said Brecon, "but it's well built. Might last a hundred years. Or a thousand, for all I know."

They went next into a land of peaceful villages and pleasant valleys. White oxen were plowing the fields. It was a country of olive groves and vineyards and dark cypress trees. Long ago the Romans had taken the land away from the Etruscans. Everyone spoke Latin there now.

"It was from the Etruscans," Carthalo said, "that the Romans learned to build aqueducts and bridges and great sewers. Romans invented none of these things. Whatever people had that was good they turned to their own use. They even copied Etruscan armor."

"What will they take from Carthage?" Brecon asked.

"Whatever they can get," Carthalo said.

One evening they missed their road. They had planned to spend the night in Cortona at the house of one of Carthalo's agents, but they took a wrong turn. The sky clouded up suddenly. It began to rain. They were soon tramping through mud. There were no houses in sight but they came to a wall of light-colored smooth rock. There were dark holes in it like the mouths of caves. From one of them shone a faint light.

As they went toward it, Carthalo called, "Is anyone there?"

A boy about Brecon's age came to the doorway. He was dark and slender with dark wavy hair and large dark eyes.

"Come in," he said. "It's only a tomb but it will keep you dry."

They stooped and went through the low entrance. The place smelled of burning olive oil. The lamp was a small one. It had smoked enough so that what light it gave was dimmed by the smoke. At first Brecon could see nothing. Then, as his eyes grew used to the half darkness, he began to see figures on the wall. The chief color was a glowing red. Dancers wore cloaks of red. Their bare feet and arms were drawn in the same color. Lines of it at the top of the wall enclosed a border of grape leaves and fruit. Just when he began to see nothing but red, Brecon noticed a shadowy blue horse beside a red one, dark blue fruit on a red tree, blue and red dolphins leaping over an almost black sea, red and blue birds flying above them. It was all strange but he felt at home as he had not done since he left his own cave with the bison on the wall and a thin ghostly horse something like the blue one here.

There was a bench with some food on it—olives, some wheat porridge, a little cheese.

"Help yourselves," the boy said. "You must be hungry."

"Not hungry enough to take your supper," Carthalo said.

The boy drew his heavy dark eyebrows together.

"I am Lucius Tarchon," he said. "This tomb and the others here belonged to my ancestors. They were Tarquins, not the rulers of Rome but cousins of theirs. This place is mine. I am the last of my family, but I am not so poor I cannot give a stranger a little porridge. Please eat."

"I would like to," Brecon said. "I am as hungry as a— as a Gallic wolf."

Lucius smiled for the first time.

"Are they hungrier than other wolves?" he asked. "Are you a Gaul? You do not speak quite like a Roman."

"I'm not a Roman," Brecon said. "And you don't sound quite like one either."

"Good," said Lucius.

"You don't like Romans?" asked Carthalo, helping himself to an olive.

"Why should I like them? They conquered our people and took our land. They still let us work on it, like peasants. I am lucky. I have an ox and a plow, my own wheat field, my own grapes and olives. They let us build roads and bridges for them too. For a while they left us our tombs. Then they broke into them and took what they found."

"What did they find?" Brecon asked.

"Treasures belonging to our ancestors—drinking cups, shields, swords. Collars of gold. Warm cloaks for their journey into the underworld, jars for wine and oil."

He stood up and poured them some wine out of a jar with twisting snakes and leaping dolphins on it. Brecon thought he looked like the pictures on the wall. He had the same arched nose, large eyes, firm chin.

When they had eaten, Lucius said, "No one will disturb you if you choose to sleep in the next tomb. There are mattresses of straw there. There's nothing left to steal. The Romans haven't thought of a way of getting the paintings off the wall—yet."

They thanked him and picked up their packs. Brecon's contained the leopard skin. It was beginning to get bald now in spots.

Before they left, Carthalo asked, "If someone tried to throw off the power of Rome, would you and your people help? Don't answer now. Tell me in the morning."

The next day was sunny and warm. Lucius guided them to a place from which they could see the towers of Cortona against the soft blue sky. As they parted, Lucius said, "You know where to find me now if you need me. My neighbors will not rise against the Romans—they have been conquered too long—but I will help you—who is coming?"

Carthalo told him about the peddlers who carried the news for him, the names of those who might come to him from both north and south, the signs that would be given and received.

"Yes, yes. I understand. But who is coming? I will not speak his name except to you."

"Hannibal", Carthalo said.

When Brecon turned and waved to Lucius, he was still standing staring after them.

They explored the country around Lake Trasimeno as Hannibal had asked them to do. On the northern side, hills came down close to the lake. They saw it first one evening. It was like a blue-green inland sea. The next morning they hunted for a road they had seen twisting along the edge of the lake. The morning mist was so heavy that it was a long time before they could find either the road or the lake. They moved along in a narrow valley with steep hills at both sides and another hill rising sharply at its eastern end. The road ran toward this hill and vanished around it. It led to the lake. This morning it was gray like the sea in a thick fog.

"My lord will need a map," Carthalo said. So when the mist burned away, Brecon drew one. It showed how rocky hills, not very high and covered with bushes and olive trees, pushed down into the lake and how a narrow road ran from west to east along the lakeshore.

When they got back to Hannibal's headquarters, it was spring and the army was ready to march. Surus was the only elephant left now. The others had all died during the winter. Their flesh had been eaten and their hide used in many ways. Shields were covered with it. Horsemen used the tails for whips.

Alain had one of them. It was well tanned and had a handle of ivory and gold. Alain stood snapping it against his leg while he greeted Brecon.

"You look as skinny as a weasel," he said.

"Last time it was a fox," Brecon replied.

Alain must have had plenty to eat. His little blue eyes were almost lost in cushions of pink fat. He asked many questions but got no answers that satisfied him.

At last he said, "This journey seems to be a big secret between you and Hannibal. Come on—we're old friends. It must be wonderful to know so much and be so mysterious. Tell me where we're going."

"You know more than I do, I'm sure," Brecon said. "But why don't you ask my Lord Hannibal? He'd be glad to tell you, doubtless." Alain gave a growl that ended in a squeak. His voice was changing. But not enough, Brecon thought, as he hurried toward Hannibal's house. He found him alone and gave him the map of the road along Lake Trasimeno.

It was a long time before he saw that road again. Carthalo brought the news that the Romans expected Hannibal to go south and were guarding the best route. Hannibal chose another. It took them through the flooded marshes of the Arno. For four days and nights they waded through mud up to their waists. Horses and pack animals had to be coaxed along. If a man fell, it took two friends to get him up again. Sometimes they stumbled into whirlpools of liquid mud yet they would stumble out again and follow where Hannibal led.

He himself was ill. His head and eyes gave him such pain that he could hardly see. He shook with cold and burned with fever. Synhalus made him ride Surus so that he would at least be out of the mud and above the thickest of the cold mist. Surus made her way carefully through the swamps as if she knew the path. The men struggled after her. At night she stood patiently in the mud while Hannibal slept on her back. For beds the soldiers threw their baggage in heaps on the squelching ground, threw themselves on the heaps of packs, and fell into exhausted sleep.

When at last they reached dry ground, many dead men, horses, and oxen were left behind in the swamp. Hannibal recovered from his illness but he lost the sight of one eye.

To anyone who expressed sympathy for him, he said quietly, "I am lucky to have one left."

He could still, Brecon thought, see more with one eye than anyone else could with two.

Carthalo had not been with them on the journey. He had been on a journey of his own, gathering information for Hannibal. He met them in a smoky, dark little inn near Clusium.

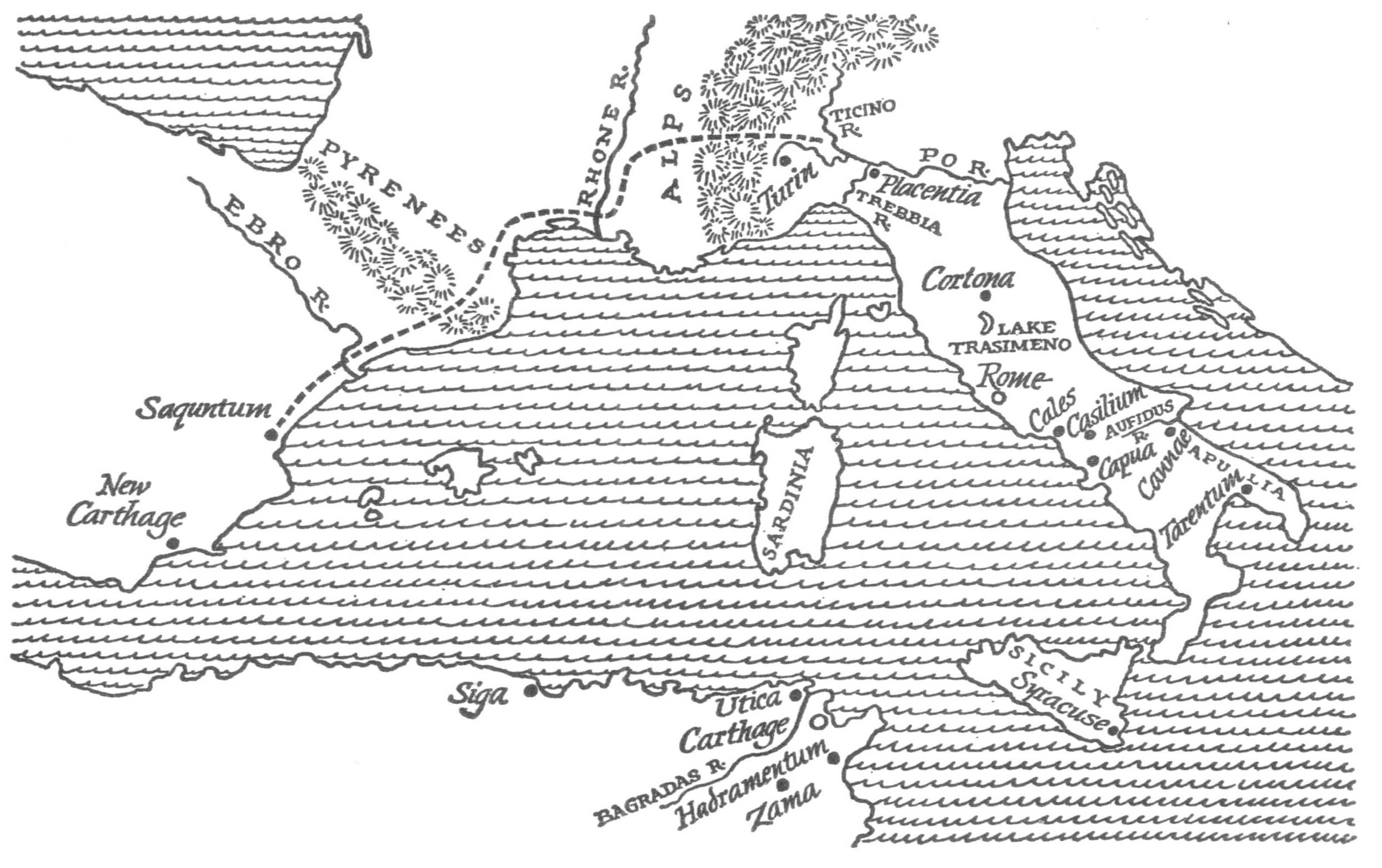
PYRENEES
EBRO R.
RHONE R.
ALPS
TICINO R.
Turin
PO R.
Placentia
TREBBIA R.
Cortona
LAKE TRASIMENO
Rome
Cales
Casilium
AUFIDUS R.
Capua
Cannae
APULIA
Tarentum
Saguntum
New Carthage
SARDINIA
SICILY
Syracuse
Siga
Utica
Carthage
BAGRADAS R.
Hadramentum
Zama

There he found Hannibal sitting with his hand over his eyes and Brecon reading to him.

Carthalo had learned that the consul Servilius was at Rimini near the eastern end of the Flaminian Way. The other consul, Flaminius, was west of the Apennines near Cortona. Carthalo told the numbers of their troops and how they were armed.

Hannibal thanked him. Then added, "It is good to know numbers, but what I need is a look into the mind of Flaminius."

"I have brought someone," Carthalo said, "who will show it to you."

Brecon had seen that someone was standing behind Carthalo, but the light from the one lamp was too dim for him to see who it was. Now Carthalo waved to him and he came forward. It was Lucius Tarchon. He smiled at Brecon and bowed before Hannibal.

He said that Flaminius owned land not far from his own small field. Lucius had seen him many times. The Consul, he said, was a proud man, easily angered. When angry he would do the first thing that came into his head.

"What makes him angry?" Hannibal asked.

"To cross him in any way. To doubt his judgment. If he decides on a course, he is sure it is the right one. Just now he is angry with the Senate because they say he should have marched north and attacked you near the Po instead of here in the hill country. He says the right thing is to fight you in the hills where your cavalry will be no use. He expects you to attack him, my lord. He is ready for you. He says he and Servilius will catch you in a trap. He says so to everyone he sees. He has carts ready, driven by slaves and peddlers, to follow the army. They will collect the spoils of battle after he has defeated you."

Hannibal smiled for the first time in many days.

"I suppose those same peddlers could help clear up the battlefield in case of a Carthaginian victory," he said.

"Yes, my lord. Some of them are Carthalo's men. But Flaminius is very sure of victory," Lucius said.

"Thank you for what you have told me. It will help me," Hannibal said. "I must think of a way to annoy Flaminius."

He did not go into the hills to find Flaminius. He crossed the fertile plains, driving off the ivory-colored oxen, taking grain and wine, burning villages. He hoped the smoke might tempt the Consul out of the hills to fight on open ground but Flaminius had made up his mind to meet Hannibal in hilly country.

He watched from an old Etruscan tower in Cortona until Hannibal had passed, and then came down and began to follow the Carthaginians. Both armies were going east now toward Lake Trasimeno. If they kept on in that direction, they would reach the Flaminian Way, down which Servilius was marching. Hannibal would soon be caught in a trap between the two armies in hilly country. Flaminius need only follow.

He did this so closely that the Numidian scouts, who were at the end of the long lines of Hannibal's army, were sometimes in sight of the Roman advance guard. In this way they reached the road through the hills that leads to Lake Trasimeno.

It was a June day, one of the longest days of the year. They had been marching all day. They heard the trumpet calls that meant the Romans were making camp. Before they themselves made camp, Hannibal looked at Brecon's map.

"Are we now in what you call the defile?"

"Yes, my lord. Here are the hills north and south of us. Here is the steep one at the east end of the defile. The road curves around the hill and comes out soon on the lake. About two days' march away is the place where Flaminius has set his trap for you, where he plans to catch you between his army and that of Servilius."

"You say the mist is heavy here in the mornings?"

"Yes, my lord."

Hannibal rolled up the map.

"The trap," he said, "will be here."

While his troops were encamping, he rode on and saw the lake. Across it fishermen in long, flat boats were hauling in their nets and bringing their catch ashore. The lake was greenish blue offshore, the color of pale violets where the rocky hills met it, brown near some reed-grown mud flats. Mist was already rising from the lake. They could now barely see the opposite shore. On their own side cliffs towered above the narrow road between them and the lake.

They turned and rode back to the defile. During the short night, Hannibal led his Spaniards and Africans to the hill at the eastern end. On the hills south of the defile, he placed slingers and javelin throwers. Just below the brow of the northern hills, he placed his cavalry and his Gallic troops. They were in a line that reached from the entrance of the defile almost to the lake. By dawn, when the Roman trumpets sounded, the trap was set.

Brecon was on one of the northern hills. It was bright and clear there as the sun rose, but the defile below was a narrow white river of mist. He could hear the Roman legions moving through it—the thud of horses' feet, the creak of saddles, the clink of bridles. Then came the regular tramp of footsoldiers and at last the squeaking of cart wheels.

The peddlers, he thought, ready to collect the spoils.

The carts carried chains to put on captives, he remembered.

It was a long column. By the time it reached the end of the

defile the Romans saw what they thought was Hannibal's rear guard just ahead of them. They fought it bravely, hand to hand, and it retreated before them, vanishing into the mist. They knew that victory would soon be won. Yet they began to hear a strange sound. It seemed to come from an army floating in the air above them.

Javelins whirred out of the mist. Lead balls crashed into Roman shields. The legion could not form regular ranks and face the enemy. It was all around them and invisible. Though they could not see, they could hear the groaning of their own wounded and the voices of the floating army. They heard Libyan yells, Gallic roars, Numidian howls.

The Romans looked in all directions but the mist still hid the enemy. They began to throw aside their packs, their shields, even their swords. Some ran back toward their camp of the night before, others ran toward the lake, others uphill through brush and rocks.

Wherever they turned, armed men came leaping down from above. Companies were surrounded and cut to pieces. Huge, half-naked Gauls rushed out of the mist swinging their great swords. Spaniards in their white tunics striped with the color of blood came at them with spears. Numidians made one of their headlong swift charges.

Flaminius fought bravely. Wherever he saw men retreating, he rallied them to face the enemy. He was a handsome figure in his splendid armor. He was ready to fight Hannibal single-handed, but he never found him.

One of the Gauls saw him. "See, friends! This is the consul who laid waste our lands along the Po and murdered our brothers!"

Putting spurs to his horse, he dashed through a dense group

of Roman soldiers, killed the Consul's bodyguard, and ran Flaminius through with his lance.

It was now three hours after sunrise. The Romans, who had thought they were chasing Hannibal's army into the arms of Servilius, had reached a hilltop from which they could see both the defile and Lake Trasimeno. The last of the mist burned off and the lake was calm and peaceful in the hot sunshine. Along the road lay the corpses of fifteen thousand Romans. Carts moved slowly along the road. The drivers stopped and stripped the dead men of their arms and armor.

Some footsoldiers had tried to escape by wading into the lake. Iberian horsemen rode into the lake and killed them where they stood. Some, heavy with their armor, stumbled and were drowned. Others staggered to shore again. The Numidians were waiting for them. Many surrendered and were fettered by the chains in the peddlers' carts.

The Italian allies were released and sent home. The fettered Romans were held for ransom. Hannibal sent one of his officers to find the body of Flaminius so that it could be given honorable burial. It was never found. To the vultures of Lake Trasimeno, one corpse was like another. The Consul's fasces and gold eagles of the legions were either surrendered or found on the battlefield.

Hannibal now marched his army toward the Flaminian Way. Servilius had not heard of the disaster at Trasimeno. He had sent four thousand horsemen ahead to catch Hannibal in the trap. Hannibal sent Lord Maharbal with a force of Spanish spearmen and Iberian cavalry to meet them. Half of the Romans died in that meeting. The rest surrendered themselves and the eagles of the legions to Maharbal.

Carthalo and Brecon went almost to Rome to learn how the city was taking its defeat. This time the truth was told.

A praetor stepped to the rostrum and told the anxious crowd, "We have lost a great battle. A consul is dead."

For days great numbers of women stood at the northern gates of the city, waiting for their husbands or sons or news of them. One woman, hearing her son had been killed, was mourning his death at home when he appeared, alive and well. Her joy was too great. She fell dead at his feet.

Another strange piece of news that Carthalo brought to Hannibal was that during the battle of Lake Trasimeno, all the country around the lake had been shaken by a great earthquake. The shock was so severe that towers and houses had fallen in many towns. No one on the battlefield had noticed it.

The news of the disaster to the forces of Servilius seemed to upset the Romans even more than the greater defeat at Trasimeno.

"But," Carthalo told Hannibal, "Romans are never so brave as in times of real danger. They have elected a dictator. He is Quintus Fabius. When he was a boy they called him the Lambkin because of his light woolly hair. Now he is fifty years old and is called Verrucosus because of the warts on his face and hands. He is the man who told the Senate that war was different on the battlefield and in the Senate chamber."

"It seems that I am now to face a sensible man," said Hannibal.

GALLOPING TORCHES

HANNIBAL WAS RIGHT. Quintus Fabius was a sensible man. He realized that the Romans had met a new kind of enemy, one who did not fight the kind of battles Romans liked. Hannibal used Punic tricks. Fabius thought of a Roman trick to use against him.

He felt sure that Hannibal could not conquer Rome unless the Italian allies deserted Rome and helped him. Fabius did not think they would. Hannibal's army was small compared to the legions Rome could raise. Time, Fabius said, would work for Rome and against Hannibal. Fabius said that the Romans must never engage the Punic in an open battle. They must follow him, not too closely, and cut off parties he sent out to forage for food. They must keep to the hills, where his cavalry could not make their encircling attacks. They must delay him, always delay. Not speed but slowness would defeat him.

While Fabius was making these plans, Hannibal was capturing Romans in Umbria and selling them for slaves. This news terrified the Romans.

Fabius said to them, "Why speak the name of Hannibal in

fear? He is only one man. No more than a third of the army he brought across the Alps is left to him. He is far from home. He must get food for his army every day. Each day he is weaker. Each day we are stronger."

The Romans had made Fabius their dictator. They had to obey his commands. Of course it was true Hannibal was only one man, but somehow his shadow kept many Romans awake at night.

He had crossed over the Apennines, the mountains that are the backbone of Italy, and was in Apulia on the Adriatic. There he rested his men and horses. In the past fifteen months they had—besides fighting the Romans—marched eighteen hundred miles. Hannibal liked this country of green plains and gentle hills. He liked to ride through it learning how its hills rose, how its rivers ran to the sea. Brecon was with him on many of these journeys. Hannibal would often say, "Draw me a map, cousin," and Brecon would trace for him the course of a river and note the shape of hills and their heights. He did not always understand why one place was more interesting to Hannibal than another.

Why, he wondered, did Hannibal want a map of a little town of old stone houses called Cannae? And of the twists and turns of the river Aufidus. The land there was flat and sandy. On the hot afternoon when they rode along the Aufidus the wind blew so strongly from the southwest that the air was full of gritty dust. A peasant with whom they talked said that this wind was called the Volturno. It came from the direction of the Volturnus River. Through the dust clouds the sun looked like an enormous red orange. Even the papyrus on which Brecon drew his map felt gritty.

There were no real hills here, but he drew the gentle folds

in the plain as well as he could, sneezing and coughing and with his eyes full of dust. He was glad when they rode back into greener, cooler country. Their days of peace did not last long. Fabius followed Hannibal into Apulia and carried out his plan against him.

He did not face Hannibal in battle but stayed in the hills. His army was large. It had plenty of food and weapons. If a small party of Hannibal's men went out to collect food, a large, heavily armed troop of Romans would attack them. The Carthaginians were usually quick enough to escape, but some men were lost and food was scarce. Hannibal set traps for the Romans. Fabius did not fall into them. Sometimes Hannibal's men, in plain sight of the Romans, would snatch a crop of ripe grain, set the field on fire, and disappear in the smoke. Then they would wait around a turn in the road for the Roman army. Numidians would hide in some bushy hollow ready to pounce on it and Hannibal's whole force would be ready to join the battle.

No battle followed. Cautious Fabius sent scouts ahead and ordered them back into the hills as soon as they saw the enemy. In Rome, Fabius was no longer the Lambkin or the Warty. Now they called him Cunctator, the Delayer. Which was more annoyed by his policy—Hannibal or the Romans—it is hard to say.

One thing that helped Hannibal in Apulia was that sometimes a galley from Carthage managed to slip past the Roman fleets between Africa and Italy. There was no large port nearby so there was little shipping to avoid. There was a sandy cove where a galley could come on a night without a moon and stay hidden among rushes and scrubby trees at the mouth of a little stream the next day. On dark nights that summer Brecon often put his leopard skin on the beach and lay there till dawn. He was awake much of the time watching the stars. They seemed very close to the land on those warm nights. Even if he dozed, the signal, a cry like the screech of an owl, would wake him. He would be at the water's edge by the time the prow of the galley touched the shore.

Sometimes the galley would not stay the next day but would leave at once. On those nights Brecon would help her crew dig a hole in the sand and hide the chests they had brought in it. Carthalo or Hannibal himself would come with an oxcart the next day, dig up the chests, and take them to camp. The chests often held coined silver from Spain and also things for Carthalo's peddlers to use in trade—beads, perfumes, fine linen, belts with gold clasps. There would also be a sack with letters in it. This the captain would deliver to Brecon. Before dawn he would be at Hannibal's camp with news from Carthage.

Once that autumn, besides news of Spain and Carthage, there was a letter from Imilce for Hannibal, one from Rhodri for Brecon, and one for him too from Athena. Rhodri's letter was about his horse and a very large fish he had caught. The sentence in it that Brecon liked best was, "I am hardly lame at all now. I have thrown my cane away." Athena's letter was mostly about her owl.

Brecon [she wrote], the owl is very well. I have named him Socrates because he is so wise. I leave the door of his cage open at night and he flies out the window. At dawn I hear the soft flutter of his wings when he comes back. He goes right into his cage and goes to sleep. In the daytime he often sits on my wrist or my shoulder.

Sophonisba does not like him because he brought a mouse and dropped it on her bed. It was alive. I picked him up and put him out in the garden. He was quite soft and his tail was cool. Sophie is more beautiful than ever. She has a new dress of white linen. A prince is in love with her. His name is Masinissa. At present he is disinherited but Sophie says she will marry him just the same as soon as her father comes home and brings enough gold for a dowry. Then the prince can get his kingdom back and they will live happy ever after. His Numidian horsemen will be a help to Carthage, she says. She loves Carthage and talks often about how she will save it from the Romans. Rhodri often takes little Hamilcar to ride on his horse. He says, "When will my father come?" We would all like to know.

Your friend—
Athena

Rhodri's letter, when he had finished telling about his fish, also mentioned Sophonisba's prince.

This prince is quite old, almost twenty, much too old for Sophie, who is only twelve though she says she is fourteen. My lady Imilce laughs at her and says she will soon be taking years away instead of adding them. Sophie does not really know this Masinissa. She just saw him riding past one day. He waved to her so now she says he is in love with her. I shall never understand women.

How is Alain? Are you and he killing lots of Romans? How is Surus? Come soon.

Rhodri

Brecon thought of the cool green garden in Carthage. Water would be dancing from the fountain and making rainbows above the pool. They would be playing some game—knucklebones, perhaps. Did they still play knucklebones? Or would they be eating ripe peaches, dripping cool golden juice? Or would Sophonisba be playing her lute and singing?

Whatever they were doing this hot, hazy day, here the Volturno was beginning to blow. It was hard to breathe the dusty air. Still, whatever the weather, snow in the Alps, sleet at the Trebbia, mist at Trasimeno, mud in Tuscany, hot wind in Apulia, Brecon would rather be with Hannibal than in the freshest, greenest garden in the world. In that he was like all Hannibal's men.

He wrote to Rhodri and Athena.

Thank you for your letters. This one is for you both. It was late—almost dawn—when the galley came last night so it could not get away in the darkness. It is hidden today in a little river where the bushes grow over it. They will be starting as soon as the sun sets so I have not much time to write.

Rhodri, I was glad to hear about your new horse and that you are not lame and about the fish. Are you sure it was not a whale? It sounds big enough to swallow you whole. I am glad your horse is chestnut-colored like Starlight. She looks beautiful now that she is rested and well fed. All our horses had the mange after our journey across the Alps. Synhalus told us to wash their coats with wine. We did and now they are all right again.

Athena, I am glad the owl is well and that his name is Socrates. I have a book Plato wrote about Socrates. I read it aloud often to my lord. It is one of his favorite books and one of mine too. Have you read it? Yes, I know you are only ten years old, but who taught me to speak Greek when she was only seven?

When Hasdrubal Gisgo read Sophonisba's letter, he roared like an angry bull. I do not think he will give her to any prince just yet. As to killing Romans, Alain says he has slain hundreds and perhaps he has. Lord Maharbal, a fine commander who leads the Iberian cavalry, speaks well of Alain. I have not killed anyone. I am just a messenger for my Lord Hannibal and sometimes I help Synhalus set broken bones and bind up wounds. Surus is well. I ride her into the river, the Aufidus, and she gives herself and me a showerbath. I am writing this in her shadow. It is the coolest place this hot afternoon. It is time now for her bath. She is tickling my neck with her trunk. That means she wants me to stop writing. Write again soon.

Brecon

It was a long time before they heard again from Carthage. Hannibal grew tired of trying to draw Fabius into a trap and failing. He set out suddenly and crossed the Apennines again. This time he went into the country near the Bay of Naples. Fabius followed, still keeping to high ground, never giving Hannibal a chance to fight him. Hannibal came to Campania, some of the richest land in Italy, and tried to stir Fabius to anger and to battle by laying waste its fields. Villages and farms burned, but Fabius watched the smoke and did not attack. He was still on the hilltops when Hannibal entered a fertile valley between Casilinum and Cales.

Minucius, one of the Roman commanders, was becoming very impatient. One of Carthalo's peddlers reported that Minucius had tried to rouse his soldiers to demand that they fight the Punics.

Minucius had said to the troops, "Are we supposed to enjoy seeing our allies sold as slaves and their houses burned? Should we not be ashamed not to protect them from a man from the end of the world who is here because we are too lazy to stop him?"

"I asked the peddler," Carthalo said, "what the soldiers answered. He said that some called Fabius a coward. Still, he was the dictator and they would obey him. Others complained to Fabius. He answered that he had you trapped in this valley. That you will never escape."

Hannibal said, "Show me the trap, Brecon, on the sand table. Help him, Carthalo. I will sleep a little."

Night and day were much the same to Hannibal so far as sleep was concerned. He could fall asleep anywhere, anytime, and wake full of energy in an hour. When he came back from his rest this time, the map on the sand table was ready. At the entrance to the valley at Casilinum there was a strong fortress with Roman troops now guarding the entrance behind them. Fabius was on the hills nearby. The exit was a narrow pass near Cales. Here Fabius had placed another strong force to keep Hannibal from leaving. The tops of the ring of high hills around the valley were all guarded by Roman troops.

Hannibal looked carefully at the model and said, "Yes, a very neat trap. We can't spend the winter here—there's not enough pastureland for our cattle. How can we drive thousands of cattle out of the valley? How shall we carry our oil and wine? How shall we keep our prisoners? We can't get out by Casilinum or Cales. If we move up any hill, the Romans will jump down our necks. Fabius has thought of everything—almost."

"What will you do, my lord?" Carthalo asked.

Hannibal said, "We'll rest tomorrow and give Fabius a chance to attack us. Perhaps we can set a trap of our own. I might think of something." Then he added to Brecon, "How old are you, cousin?"

"I saw Orion, belt, stars, feet and all last night," Brecon said. "I think I'll be seventeen tomorrow or the next day."

"We must celebrate your birthday," Hannibal said. He was silent a moment and then added cheerfully, "Of course if I set a trap for Fabius, he would know it was just a Punic trick, wouldn't he? Or a Spanish trick? He would be much too cautious to come down out of the hills, wouldn't he?"

He began to whistle softly an old Spanish song. He did this, Brecon knew, when he was pleased about something. He felt sure that Hannibal had already thought of his trap.

They rested the next day. The day after, they traveled slowly toward the exit of the valley, the high pass at Cales. The thousands of oxen were driven along ahead of the army. They grazed as they went. Women, children, pack animals, and carts with loads of plunder were with this part of the army too. It was a tempting bait, but Fabius was too cautious to take it.

The army was not far from the pass when they camped that night. The soldiers were fed well and sent early to sleep. The drivers of the oxen were busy. They were doing a strange thing, something Hannibal had once seen done in Spain. Brecon knew what it was. They were binding the horns of the oxen with branches of pine and wisps of hay. At midnight the troops were quietly set on the march. Hannibal himself and a troop of Iberian soldiers drove the oxen up a gently sloping hill south of the valley. They carried fire pots full of live coals with them.

When they were halfway up the slope, Hannibal said to Brecon, "Happy Birthday, cousin. Now we must light our torches so Fabius can see them and join our celebration—if he likes."

They began lighting the hay and pine boughs and driving the oxen uphill. At first there were only a few flashes of light, then hundreds. They dipped, swayed, circled but moved always toward the heights. The roar of the frightened oxen echoed through the valley.

Sentries on the hills woke their officers shouting, "Hannibal is escaping over the hills! Catch the Punics! Kill them, kill them!"

There was a rush of Roman soldiers toward the lights. The guards in the pass all left their posts and hurried where the torches blazed. They stumbled in the dark as they ran. Lord Maharbal led the army into the unguarded pass. Soon it was guarded again, this time by Hannibal's Africans.

On the hillside, the Roman guards had almost reached the glaring, smoking torches. Above them they heard shouts and trumpet calls as the hilltop troops chased the imaginary enemy. Suddenly one of the Romans reached a torch. He had his sword ready but the torch carrier bellowed, plunged at him, and knocked him down, goring him with his burning horns. This happened many times and at last the guards realized they had been fooled by another Punic trick. The torches were burning out now. Their angry wearers pursued the Romans as they hurried down what they thought was an empty hillside toward the pass.

Dark shadows moved below them. More oxen, they thought. Then, one after another, they were speared, cut down with swords or pierced with javelins. There were Iberians wherever they turned. The Romans fought on bravely, trying to reach the pass, stumbling over rocks behind which armed men rose up in the darkness. Many were killed. Others were captured and dragged off toward the pass.

When they reached it, Hannibal's army was marching safely through it. There were torches—real torches—blazing on both sides of the pass. While their fetters were being put on, the captives saw, in the smoky reddish-light, yellow-haired Gauls with their great helmets, bronze-skinned Numidian horsemen, gigantic Libyans wearing captured Roman shields and swords. There were Balearians with their coiled slings. There were shepherds and peasants from Tuscany and Apulia who had joined Hannibal.

All these men, as they reached the top of the pass and started down the other side, shouted, "Hannibal! Hannibal!" and held up their hands.

Few Romans had ever seen Hannibal. The captives had heard he was a fierce-looking magician seven feet tall. Not a soldier you could meet in a fair fight. He won battles by casting spells and by trickery. They had been under one of his spells tonight or they would not have been caught. He rode an elephant with wings, they had heard, and he had a magic wand that turned men to stone.

It was hard to believe that the Punics were shouting "Hannibal!" to the man in the black cloak. This man was neither tall nor fierce-looking. He had a battered helmet in the fold of his arm. His brown curly hair was tousled and tumbled. Behind him rose a great gray rock. Suddenly it was alive. It moved slowly out of the shadows. There was a noise like a dozen trumpets. Part of the rock turned into a gray snake and began to tickle the man's neck.

He spoke to the snake quietly, patted it and said, "Yes, I know, Surus, it's time to go."

A redheaded boy, a Gaul probably, brought the man something in a leather cup and the man drank part of it. The gray snake drank the rest. A magic drink, probably.

The man said in Latin, "Thank you, Brecon. That's good milk."

"Milk indeed! Lion's milk, serpent's milk, crocodile's milk!" the captives muttered to each other.

At last followed peddlers with their carts. Fabius had carts like these, the Romans knew, to carry off the spoils of the battle-fields after he had trapped Hannibal's army in the valley and destroyed it. These carts contained Roman shields and swords.

One of the captives said to the man next to him, "Why, I saw that peddler at Fabius's camp yesterday. He's a spy, I tell you!"

The other Roman said gloomily, "Don't tell me! Go and tell old Lambkin Warty Fabius the Delayer."

The soldier never told Fabius anything. He was sold as a slave in a Greek market and spent the rest of his life in Crete. He was, however, quite right about the peddler. It was Carthalo.

Carthalo told Hannibal that at Fabius' camp he had heard Minucius shout when he saw the lighted torches twinkling on the hill.

Minucius had called to his officers, "The fool thinks he can get away over the hills. Go quickly to Fabius. Ask him to order us down to the pass now. Only a few have started. We can catch the rest if we hurry."

"I went along ahead of the messenger," Carthalo said. "You know the best way to follow anyone in the darkness is to go ahead of him. I was hidden near Fabius's tent when they woke him.

"He said loudly and angrily, 'Tell him No! This is just another Punic trick to get us down into the valley. Our guards in the pass will stop the Punics. We will stay here till dawn. We have them in a trap. I will snap it shut when I can see what I'm doing.'

"Then Minucius came to the tent. He pleaded to be allowed to cross the valley and capture the torchbearers. Fabius said, 'Don't move. I forbid it.'

"All this time there were more and more lights dancing up the hills across the valley. They went flashing and glittering up to the crest like fireflies on a June night. Then I heard the oxen bellowing. I thought I had better get back to my cart. I got down to the valley. Our carts were all there. My men collected a few Roman arms on the hill. The last thing I heard Fabius say was, 'It's another trick. Sempronius and Flaminius fell into traps through rashness. I will be cautious. I will not move till dawn.'"

Hannibal smiled and said, "I thought he'd be cautious. If he'd been rash he could have destroyed us." Then he added, "Surus is right. It's time we were moving."

Brecon saw the light begin to change. Brightness began to fall into the dark valley. When Hannibal and the last of his troops left the pass, the Roman trumpets were beginning to sound. Fabius would soon see that the valley was empty.

CHAPTER 10

WIND, SAND, AND SUN

HANNIBAL DID NOT HURRY back to Apulia. There were many rich Romans in this part of the country. Some were tax collectors, others had seized many small Italian farms and had joined them to make great cattle ranches. Some had simply settled down to live in pleasant villas stolen from them long ago, the Italian owners said.

Hannibal did not trouble the poor peasants. In fact, he often shared the grain and cattle he took from the rich land-owners with their poorer neighbors. Many of these peasants knew they might soon find themselves in the Roman army. They joined Hannibal's instead.

The rich men protested to the Senate that they had no protection against the invaders. They called Fabius names, of which "the Delayer" was the most polite. Once Hannibal devastated a number of big cattle ranches but left an estate belonging to Fabius untouched.

One of the few times Brecon ever heard Hannibal laugh until he could hardly breathe was when Carthalo brought the news that Roman senators were saying that since Fabius' estate had not been damaged he must be in league with Hannibal.

"What could possibly make them think that?" Hannibal gasped, wiping his eyes. "I do love the Roman senators. If I had a house of my own, I would like to have one stuffed for an ornament."

"They've summoned Fabius back to Rome to explain," Carthalo said. "Now you have Minucius against you." Hannibal looked pleased.

"A splendid rash young man," he said.

"Yes, but left with orders never to meet you in battle," Carthalo said. "He's just allowed to cut off your foraging parties."

Hannibal began to whistle that Spanish tune again.

"Minucius deserves a little sport, a little taste of victory," he said. "Perhaps someday, if he knew my camp were almost undefended, he would attack it. Could you arrange that—let's say day after tomorrow—Minucius will hear that news?"

Carthalo said he could.

So Minucius attacked Hannibal's camp. He sent an enthusiastic account of his victory to Rome. He had done much damage to the camp, he wrote; would have destroyed it completely, but some large Punic foraging parties returned unexpectedly so he had retired. He would have engaged them only Fabius had ordered him not to fight a battle on open ground. The next day Hannibal had moved his camp and his whole army eight miles away.

"We could soon have him on the run," Minucius said. "I hope the policy of not facing the Punics will be changed," he added. "Dash and courage will defeat them."

This message caused great excitement in Rome. The victory grew as it was talked about. Fabius was more unpopular than ever. His Master of Horse, Minucius, had not been afraid to face the Punic. Why was Fabius such a coward? Minucius would not have let Hannibal escape at Cales. He would have ended the war right there.

Terentius Varro brought forward a bill to make Minucius co-dictator with Fabius with equal powers of command. The bill was passed. Before long Carthalo brought news to Hannibal that Minucius now had an army of his own and a camp six miles from the camp of Fabius.

Hannibal said, "And Minucius is waiting impatiently for a chance to use his army, I feel sure. Can you show me the shape of the hills near his camp on the sand table, Brecon?"

As at the Trebbia, there was a hollow between two hills where cavalry could be hidden. The next day a troop of Punic horsemen appeared near the camp of Minucius. They retreated hastily when the Romans hurried out to meet them, and escaped being encircled. Minucius and his men dashed after them and were soon drawn up on a wide plain in line of battle, facing Hannibal's troops. They moved forward to crush the Punics, but suddenly five thousand Numidians and Iberians swooped out of a gully between the hills and crashed into the rear of the Roman army. It broke and fled. It would have been utterly destroyed if Fabius, who had been watching from his hilltop, had not come to the rescue of the fleeing troops. Already many had been killed or captured.

Minucius learned his lesson that day. He gave up his separate army and went back to the hilltops with Fabius.

"They hang there like a dark storm cloud," Hannibal said to Carthalo, "but sometimes a storm cloud breaks and rains down into the valley. Perhaps this one will."

He spent the winter and the early spring improving his army. He trained new troops and taught them to use the Roman arms he had seized after Ticino, Trebbia, and Trasimeno. His Spanish troops preferred their own short curved swords. The Gauls liked the Roman long swords, the Roman spears and shields. The clothes of many of his soldiers had been worn almost to rags. Now they had clothes of good strong cloth. They were well fed, too, and their horses looked very different from the mangy half-starved animals that had crossed the Alps.

It was two years now since Hannibal and his army had crossed the Ebro and had begun their long journey. For two years he had kept the Romans too busy to attack Carthage. People there—his wife and his son among them—could sleep safely at night. In Rome it was different. In the Forum citizens complained that the Punic might charge into the city any day with his wild elephants. They still feared the elephants, though he had none left. Even Surus had died now. One spring evening, just before Brecon came to take her for her swim, she lay down quietly on her side and never got up again. Her heart had stopped beating.

Everyone in camp grieved for her and told stories about how wise and brave she always was, how she used to pull Hannibal's hair, how well she carried him through the swamps.

"We shall miss her when the Romans come down from the hills," Brecon heard one Gaul say to another.

No one doubted now that the Romans would come down and fight. Fabius was no longer the dictator. There were two new consuls. Aemilius Paulus and Terentius Varro. Aemilius was a patrician, Varro was the son of a rich meatpacker, but both believed that Hannibal and his army must be destroyed.

Men shouted approval when Varo said, "Fabius and his

friends in the Senate say they are preserving the Republic. I say they are only keeping us from conquering Hannibal."

The people in the Forum were sure that Varro would stop the war in the only way it could be stopped—by fighting the Punics and winning.

No one believed Fabius when he said, "In battles the Romans will find Terentius Varro a more dangerous enemy than Hannibal."

Eight new legions were organized. More than a hundred senators volunteered and joined these legions. All the Roman knights joined the cavalry. Poorer citizens were told by Varro that they would loot the Punic camp and capture slaves themselves. Many of them volunteered. There were eighty-five thousand men, the largest army Rome had ever put in the field. Hannibal, as everyone knew, had not half so many troops. Besides, the Romans had learned his tricks now.

Varro shouted from the rostrum, which was trimmed with bronze beaks taken from captured Punic galleys, that the Roman legions would stand firm on open ground in clear Italian sunlight. "What Punic trick could make them vanish?" he asked.

Among the young patricians who joined the army was Publius Cornelius Scipio, Junior. He had not been in a battle since the skirmish at Ticino, where he had saved his father's life. His father and his uncle were still fighting in Spain. They reported victories over the Punic forces, but Hasdrubal Barca had not been conquered yet. However, if Hannibal were once defeated, dealing with his brother would be easy.

Young Scipio preferred studying and politics to battles, but now that Rome was in danger he put away his books and became tribune of one of the new regiments. It was his habit to do well what he undertook. He studied war as he had studied oratory. He knew Minucius and with him studied Hannibal's battles and figured out the tricks by which he had won. This new Roman army, they felt sure, would not be fooled by men hiding in a gully or traveling on hills in the morning mist or at night by oxen made into torchbearers.

The troops that had watched Hannibal so long were still keeping an eye on him. Two proconsuls, Servilius and Atilius, were in command in Apulia now. Their orders were not to risk a general engagement. They might, however, give their troops practice by cutting off foraging parties. The new army was well drilled when they arrived. They already, the Proconsuls said, kept their lines like veterans when they were attacked in practice battles. They formed in maniples of one hundred and twenty men as if they had been doing it all their lives. They wheeled out of a marching column into long lines bristling with spears. They obeyed trumpet calls briskly. They pushed against the enemy from behind a wall of shields. They learned to take the shock of a charge and never yield an inch but move forward, always forward.

They had left Rome sooner than Varro and Aemilius had planned. News had reached Rome that Hannibal had appeared suddenly at Cannae, a little town near the river Aufidus. Cannae was important for only one thing, Varro told the Senate. Most of its old stone houses were in bad repair, but there was one large building in which grain and other supplies for the Roman army were stored. Hannibal had broken into the building almost under the noses of the Roman troops and had carried off all the supplies.

The Senate agreed with Varro and Aemilius that this sort of thing must be stopped. It not only injured the Romans; it also helped the Punics. They must be destroyed. There were open plains around Cannae. There the eight Roman legions would surround Hannibal's small army and the war would be over.

It was blazing-hot summer weather when Varro's troops at last saw the Punics. They were in a golden wheat field reaping the grain. Even after their long march, the Romans would have dashed at once into battle but the consuls and proconsuls decided that it was too soon. They must do nothing rash.

Varro and Aemilius had agreed to take turns commanding the army. Aemilius' turn came first. He thought the country too favorable to Hannibal's cavalry. He kept to the hills. What Hannibal called the Roman storm cloud had not yet broken.

"It will, I think, tomorrow," Carthalo told Hannibal, who at once sent Brecon for Bog, the astrologer.

Hannibal asked him what he thought the weather would be like the next day.

Bog said, "Sunny but the sun will be seen only by eagles."

"What does he mean? I wish magicians did not always talk in riddles," said Hasdrubal Gisgo, who looked hot in his purple tunic.

Hannibal looked cool and comfortable. He was dressed in linen the color of dust.

"It means it's time to put out a little bait," he said.

Some of Varro's troops found the bait that evening. It was a deserted Punic camp. There were tents, cooking fires still burning, half-empty kettles of food. In some of the tents were silver cups. In one was a gold chain with a jeweled clasp. It was almost as if these things were waiting to be picked up. Perhaps if anyone had seen Hannibal's deserted camp on the Rhone, this one might have reminded him of it, but no one had been at the Rhone. The Romans snatched the bait and then pursued what they felt sure must be the rearguard of the Punic army.

They were horsemen moving along rather slowly on thin horses.

"A Roman horse would make two of them," Varro said to Aemilius. "Let's put on a little speed and catch them."

They did not catch them that day. The Punic horsemen increased their speed too. They seemed to drift off into the hot, hazy air. The last Varro saw of them, they were crossing the Aufidus and joining what must be Hannibal's main force. The Punics were making a new camp not far from Cannae. The Romans saw the tents and the cooking fires.

"We have brought him to bay," Varro said.

It was his turn to command the next day. This time, he vowed, Hannibal would not escape.

The plain of Cannae looked level from where Varro had first seen it. Actually, as Brecon remembered, because he had modeled a map of it once for Hannibal, it sloped gently up from the river. Hannibal was on the upperpart of the slope at dawn the next morning. The Volturno was already blowing from the southwest. The sun was only a blurred spot a little brighter than the haze around it. First a coppery spot, then a brassy one, then only a faint yellowish gleam in the yellowish clouds that shut the sky away from the earth. The wind brought dust and heat that felt as if it came from some vast underground oven. The dusty haze held the heat close to the burning ground.

With Hannibal were messengers from all the different peoples of his army. He and Brecon between them spoke all their languages, so they could give orders to each one.

A dark-skinned African smiled happily at Brecon and said, "Fine day for a battle. Fine and hot!"

Brecon thought, Why, he means it! and said, "Better than the Alps!"

The man pretended to shiver and make his white teeth chatter.

"Much better, Sir Leopard," he said. "No leopard skin today?"

Brecon was messenger to the Spanish troops that day. He and the African set out together to carry orders to Spanish and African cavalry. Hanno Bomilcar was commanding them. They were at the left of the Carthaginian lines. Hannibal ordered them to move slowly down the slope and toward the cavalry at the right of the Roman lines.

As he rode toward Bomilcar, Brecon could see Roman horsemen already crowding into the space between the Aufidus and the line of Roman footsoldiers. That line must be a mile long, he thought. He gave Hannibal's message to Bomilcar and to the Spanish commander serving under him. They were not to attack until they saw smoke from the hill top. Then, Hannibal said, they were to carry out the plan they had talked about the night before.

Other messengers had ordered the slingers and the Gauls into Hannibal's front line. Blocks of Spanish and African veterans were posted at the ends of the line of footsoldiers but slightly higher on the slope. The front line, much shorter than the Roman line, was a long shallow crescent with its center curving out toward the Roman line. Far to the right Lord Maharbal was in command of the Numidians. Carthalo was near him with a special group of five hundred men. No one had to tell him what to do—it was his own idea—but Brecon would tell him when to do it.

Everyone was in place now except Hannibal, his brother Mago, the messengers, and a few officers. They stayed at the top of the slope as the Roman lines began to move toward them. Through the clouds of dust came the dull gleam of thousands and thousands of bronze helmets. Dimly, as the wind dropped for a moment, they saw the gold eagles of the legions high above the marching men, the flags of the different regiments, the bright wall of shields, the threatening line of spears.

Hasdrubal Gisgo, shaking his head and panting a little, said to Hannibal, "It's really extraordinary, most extraordinary to see such a number of men."

Hannibal smiled at him.

"Yes, Gisgo," he said, "you are right. But do you know something even more extraordinary?"

"No, my lord—what is that?"

"Why in all those tens of thousands of men there's not a single one called Gisgo!"

Then, above the bray of the Roman trumpets, rang out Gisgo's laugh like the roar of a bull. Men saw him slapping Hannibal on the back, saw them both laughing. Others around them joined in. The messengers, who had been tensely darting their eyes along the Roman lines, began to laugh too. When they carried messages, men asked them, "What did he say? What did Hannibal say?" Then, hearing the joke, they would laugh too and pass it along.

"Do you know the most amazing thing about the Roman army?... There isn't a single man in it called Gisgo!... That's what he said—that's what Hannibal said." The laughter ran along the line. They were still laughing when Hannibal took his place near the curved center of the front line, the point closest to the Romans.

The Romans were close enough now so that some of them could see that the Punics were laughing. Some of them wondered if one of Hannibal's magic spells were being repeated along the lines. They marched forward, keeping their solid wall of shields and spears, until they could see the slingers uncoil their ropes and whirl their slings. Then stones crashed against Roman shields. A great roar from the Romans was echoed by yells and cries in many tongues from Hannibal's men. Some Romans fell but the soldiers closed ranks and came on steadily. Now javelins were flying like a flock of pouncing hawks through the dusty air. One struck the consul Aemilius and he fell bleeding from his horse. The horse, terrified, wheeled and fled toward the river, trampling wounded men.

Hannibal said to Brecon, "Light the fire."

Brecon made his way up to the place where dry brush and hay were heaped up in a tall pile. He poured oil on it, dumped coals from a fire pot onto the heap, knelt with his back to the dusty Volturno, and blew on the coals. Soon thick black smoke was blowing toward the Roman lines. Brecon saw Bomilcar raise his purple banner to show that he had seen the signal. The Spanish cavalry plunged forward as if it had been hurled in one mass from a giant sling. In a moment Bomilcar was driving the Roman cavalry along the river, cutting them down as he went.

Now to the commanders all along Hannibal's front line the messengers carried the one word, "Retreat." It was Hannibal's plan, Brecon knew, to draw the Romans into a hollow in the slope and surround them. Gallic troops had been trained for hours in this very spot to make the retreat at exactly the right pace. They must move back slowly, so slowly that the Romans would follow up the slope in the face of the dusty wind, fast enough so that the Romans, trying to get them—the cowardly Punics—within reach of their spears, would not see that they were marching into a hollow with Hannibal's strongest troops above them on their flanks.

It was one thing to make this retreat in practice with your fellow soldiers pursuing you and pretending to be Romans. It was quite another thing to move step by step up the slope with real Romans stabbing and slashing at you. Soon many Spanish red-bordered tunics were reddened with blood. Both Spaniards and Gauls lost men, but they kept their ranks around Hannibal and moved slowly out of reach of swords and spears.

The Romans began to move faster. Now they had flattened the curve of the Punic crescent. Now it was curving the other way.

"The cowards are retreating," shouted Terentius Varro.

He was with the cavalry on the Roman left wing. The dust had dropped for a moment and he had seen quite clearly across the plain. Then the dust swirled between them again and he saw no more.

Suddenly a change took place in the Roman lines. They found themselves surrounded by Punics. Africans and Spaniards on both sides of the hollow had plunged down against the Roman flanks. Soon these veterans spread out behind the Romans as well as beside them. The Gauls and Spaniards of Hannibal's front lines retreated no longer but came forward through the dust.

There was a wild Gallic yell. Some of the Romans had heard it before at the Trebbia. When they tried to answer it, they found themselves choked with dust. They could not see their standards now. The maniples could not keep their position. They would have broken and run but there was nowhere to go, nothing to do except face the keen curved swords, the short sharp pikes.

Varro could not see through the dust what was happening. Besides, he had his own troubles. The Numidians had been retreating in front of him and he was hurrying after them. Now Lord Maharbal and Carthalo got the message, brought by Brecon, to charge. Lord Maharbal was to charge, retreat swiftly, and charge again. On the second charge Carthalo's men were to go forward too.

Swiftly the Numidians came out of the dust cloud, riding with both hands free, buzzing javelins at the Roman cavalry. Varro's men held their ranks and took the crash head on. The Numidians retreated and wheeled back to higher ground.

Then Carthalo said to his lieutenants, "Sheathe all swords; keep them under your cloaks."

The sharp curved swords disappeared under the men's long linen cloaks the color of sand. The Numidians charged again. Carthalo's men went forward more slowly. Brecon could see their red and yellow flag through the dust clouds. After some time he saw it dip. This was the signal that Carthalo had found Varro and had offered to join him against Hannibal. Would Varro see through this Punic trick? No! The Roman cavalry charged the Numidians and the red and yellow flag moved with the Romans.

This was the signal for Brecon to carry a message to Bomilcar. He galloped Starlight all around the battle until he came to what had been the Roman right wing of cavalry. It was broken up into little groups of fugitives who were riding desperately toward the river to try to cross it. Riderless horses raced for the river and plunged into it. Men without horses tried vainly to catch them.

Brecon saw a wounded man sitting on a stone. A young officer, one of the few who had succeeded in catching a horse, led it up to him.

"Take this horse, Lucius Aemilius," he said "Ride to safety."

"Thank you, Lentulus. No. I will... die here... with my men... You go to... Rome... Say Fabius was... right... Tell him to... guard... Rome."

He fell over into a pool of his own blood. Lentulus bent over him, tried to raise him, let the dead body fall. A group of fleeing horsemen came up to him. He joined them and escaped across the river.

Brecon found Bomilcar and told him that the time had come to ride along the rear of the battle line and attack Varro's cavalry from behind.

"Carthalo's five hundred are with Varro," Brecon told Bomilcar.

Soon Varro's men had Punic horsemen all around them. They tried to turn and escape. Many were killed by Carthalo's men. Varro got away. The Numidians pursued him and killed many of his men. About fifty were left with him when at last he crossed the river.

Maharbal and the Numidians then returned to the main battle. With Bonilcar and his Spanish horsemen they surrounded the whole struggling mass of Romans and Carthaginians. Now the Roman footsoldiers were twice surrounded, first by Hannibal's footsoldiers, again by his cavalry. There was no chance to break through and escape across the river now. Those who tried it were killed or captured. A few climbed to the hilltop and made their way to Cannae. Maharbal captured them there.

Varro was the only commander who left his troops. The others—Servilius, Atilius, Minucius, Aemilius—all died with their men. Eighty Roman senators, most of the young tribunes of the new legions, and almost all the Roman knights were killed. Yet though they were crushed together around their eagles with no hope of escape, the Roman soldiers fought on. When their weapons were seized, they fought with their nails and teeth. At the end of the day more than seventy thousand Romans had died. Hannibal had lost six thousand men.

In all her history Rome had never suffered such a defeat.

Toward sunset Hannibal rode out over the battlefield. He ordered his wounded men to be carried to the tents where Synhalus, helped by Brecon and other messengers, was binding and anointing wounds. Hannibal ordered his men to find the

bodies of Aemilius and of the other commanders and give them honorable burial. He gave orders also for his men to rest and told the cooks to give them the best meal they could prepare.

"Hannibal," Lord Maharbal said, "are these men to waste their time feasting when Rome lies helpless? In five days we can all feast in Rome. I will start now with my horsemen. We will be at the gates of Rome before they know of the battle. Start your men marching."

Hannibal said quietly, "Yes, we could get there quickly but to think of it will take a long time."

"Truly," Maharbal said, "the Gods do not give all gifts to one man. You know how to win a victory, Hannibal, but not how to use one."

Hannibal only repeated patiently, "I must think of it, Maharbal." Then he added to the head cook, "Give the men the best food you have, the best wine."

He went next to the tent where Synhalus was treating the wounded and spoke to the injured men, praising them for their courage that day. Brecon saw that even some of the most seriously wounded men were better after he had spoken to them.

It was late at night before Synhalus told Brecon to go to bed. He rode Starlight to the place where they had stood at dawn. The Volturno had stopped blowing now. What breeze there was came from the north. Stars were beginning to show faintly. Some of the sentries were throwing dice in the light of a small fire. Beyond them Hannibal slept on his black cloak Brecon fed Starlight. He took the leopard skin off her back and lay down on it. Soon he was asleep too.

CHAPTER 11

SHIPS SAIL THE LAND

BRECON WAS RIDING beside Carthalo on the road to Rome. They were escorting ten Roman prisoners. They were among seven thousand men who had surrendered the day before. Hannibal's men had surrounded the Roman camp and had told the Romans that if they surrendered, they would not be killed but would be held for ransom. Out of the thousands who surrendered ten young men of noble birth had been chosen to go to Rome and arrange for the ransom of themselves and all the others. The prices asked by Hannibal were five hundred denarii for a horseman, three hundred for a footsoldier, one hundred for a slave. The prisoners were not guarded or fettered. They had sworn on their honor to raise the ransom or to return to Hannibal's camp. If they did not come back, all the other prisoners would be sold as slaves.

To Brecon, Hannibal had said, "Will you go with Carthalo, cousin? Or will you stay and collect spoils on the battlefield? There is great wealth there."

"Forgive me, my lord," Brecon said, "but—I would like never to see a battlefield again. I will gladly go with Carthalo—if I can help him. Or stay and work with Synhalus." Hannibal said, "If this is the last battle I ever fight, I shall be glad. There has been enough killing. I hope that when Carthalo meets the senators, they will accept the terms of peace I am offering. Perhaps we shall return soon to Carthage across a peaceful sea. Go with Carthalo. Keep a journal for me as you have done before."

Brecon wrote:

First day

We stopped at an inn not far outside the city walls. The innkeeper is one of Carthalo's men. I waited there, feeding the horses while Carthalo and the prisoners went to the gate. The Romans went into the city but Carthalo was turned back. No Carthaginian is allowed to set foot in Rome. The guard gave him till sunset to leave Roman territory.

He started at once back to Cannae, so you will know, my lord, long before you read this, that there is no chance Rome will make peace. I am staying. I hope to get into Rome tomorrow or the next day. Great trains of mules and oxen carry food into the city every morning. The innkeeper says that one of Carthalo's men is a miller. He comes often with sacks of flour for the bakeries in the city. The innkeeper says he will get the miller to take me as a driver.

Second day

The miller did not come today but I am ready to go. The innkeeper has given me some dusty clothes proper for a miller. He has dyed my hair dark brown with walnut juice. He says my red hair would be sure death. It looks Gallic and Gauls are always much hated but more than ever since they joined Hannibal. The augurs say the gods are angry with Rome. Yesterday, to turn aside this anger, the priests had a Gallic man and woman and a Greek man and woman buried alive.

The innkeeper said, "These are the people who call Hannibal cruel!"

Third day

The miller came at dawn. I drove one of his carts into the city. The streets are dark and narrow and the noise of wheels on the stone paving is awful. It smells awful too. It's as hot as if the Volturno were blowing. The brick walls of the houses hold the heat all night. Carthalo gave me money before he left and told me how to find Lucius Tarchon. Lucius had been in Rome several months. He works in the shop of one of Carthalo's men, a jeweler. Lucius has taken me to live with him. He lives in a very large house called an insula. Many families live in an insula, sometimes seven people or more in a room. Lucius and I are lucky. There are only three others in our room. Two of them work in the cookshop where we buy our food. The other is a barber. If I had a beard, he would shave me for nothing, he says. All the time he is talking, which is most of the time, he sharpens his razors on a leather strap. He loves his work.

Fourth day

The barber is a Greek. His name is Philip. He was a slave in the Scipio family. He bought his freedom and now he has his own shop near the Forum. I am working for him now. The boy he had before had a fever and died. Philip gave me his clothes, which are cleaner than what the innkeeper gave me.

I open the door for customers. I take down and put up shutters and carry water. I hand Philip towels to put around the customers' necks. I sharpen scissors for hair cutting and sweep hair off the floor. Sometimes I brush a customer's hair and once in a while, if Philip is very busy, I am allowed to trim someone's hair and beard but not to shave anyone. I told Philip I used to shave my master sometimes, but he doubts if I have the skill to shave an important customer. I wonder what he would think if he knew my master's name.

Fifth day

Lucius came in today and Philip let me shave him.

"If Lucius is brave enough, I will be," he said.

The jeweler's shop where Lucius works is near Philip's. They sell pearls and the owner is a goldsmith and makes seal rings. He told Lucius that after Cannae more than a bushel of seal rings belonging to Roman knights were picked up on the battlefield besides armbands and clasps and chains of gold.

Philip says I did quite well shaving. Only I don't talk enough. He says it is necessary to keep a patron entertained because then they do not notice so much if you cut them a little or tweak too hard when you pull hairs out of their eyebrows with tweezers. He says, too, that I must learn the right way of taking hold of a patron's nose when I want him to turn his head. You should be firm yet gentle. He says it is like riding a horse. Never let a patron know you are afraid of him.

"Suppose he bites me," I said.

"Patrons growl sometimes. They never bite," Philip told me.

He has something he rubs into a patron's face before he shaves him. It is called "Cream of Roses." I am supposed to tell the customers that this stuff is an old Egyptian secret and is scented with the essence of a thousand roses. (To me it smells rather like a flock of goats!) Philip is willing, as a special favor, to sell his patrons some of this secret cream. Part of the secret is that Philip makes it himself, a gallon at a time, in the back room. I don't know what he puts in it besides olive oil, goat's tallow, and ashes of beechwood, but if I would promise to stay with him he would teach me to make it. Somehow I would rather not be a barber all my life. Besides, Lucius says we must leave soon or we'll find ourselves in the Roman army.

Eighth day

We have been so busy at the shop I have not had time to write lately. We have been here a week now. Things are very bad in the city. They are giving slaves their freedom and putting them in a new legion. The walls are guarded night and day. There is a new dictator but Fabius seems to give most of the orders. They don't call him the Delayer any longer. Now he's Fabius Maximus.

Ninth day

Philip is very proud today because of news about young Publius Cornelius Scipio. He was one of the few not killed or captured at Cannae. The other officers with him said Rome was finished and they would escape to Sicily.

Scipio drew his sword and said, "You may go after you have fought and killed me. If I kill the first man, I will fight the second on the same terms. And so on until you are all dead—or I am."

The men said they would not kill him but follow wherever he led. He made them swear this oath: "I swear I will not desert the Roman Republic. If I break my oath, O Jupiter, supremely good and great, may you visit my house, my family and my fortune with destruction!"

The men all took the oath. They went with him and joined Varro, who is supposed to have ten thousand men now.

Tenth day

The Senate has been debating about paying ransom for the prisoners who surrendered at Cannae. Some were in favor of paying but a man named Torquatus spoke against it. This is what he said to the prisoners: "If you were fighting for Rome again, what would you do if you had to die for your country? At Cannae thousands lay dead around you. If this did not stir you to fight, nothing will. You did not follow the brave men who fought their way out of the camp. You chose not to fight for Rome but to betray her. Why should we pay gold and silver for such men?"

The senators voted to send the prisoners back to you, my lord, with the message that you may do as you like with them. No ransom will be paid. All went but one, who broke his word. They found him and are sending him to you under guard.

Eleventh day

The shop was very busy today. Philip allowed me to do some shaving, not of course of what he calls important customers. There is no use pretending that we have many of these. Really rich patricians have barbers among their slaves. So have rich contractors who have made fortunes out of the war. They are not likely to come to a little shop like this. Most of our customers are other shopkeepers or farmers in from the country for a day's trading. A few rich men come in to hear the news from Philip. Also, if they have something they want everyone to know they tell it to him, I notice.

Twelfth day

This day we really had an important customer. It was P. C. Scipio, Junior, himself! I knew him at once from having seen him at Ticino. Philip almost stood on his head, he was so pleased. A crowd followed him to the door cheering him and waited all the time he was in the shop to see him come out.

Most Romans, even senators, look dirty. Their togas are a dingy yellowish color. Scipio looked as if everything he had on had just been washed and dried in clean air and clean sunshine. (Philip says he always looks that way.) He is of medium height and very strong looking. Philip washed his hair and trimmed it and shaved him. He would not have any Cream of Roses. We have another cream that has a little spice in it and something else, one of Philip's secrets of course, that makes it smell like pine needles. It's called "Roman Pine." Philip used some on Scipio's hair.

He enjoyed his shave and said it would be his last good one for a long time. Philip asked him why and he said he doubted if there were good barbers in his father's army. He said he was going to Spain to join his father and uncle who were still fighting Hasdrubal Barca there.

"I hope to learn something," he said.

"You are a fine soldier already," said Philip. "Everyone says so."

"Then everyone's wrong," Scipio said. "But at least I know how little I know. That's a start."

Philip said that conditions at Cannae were unfair to the Romans. He'd heard all about it. There was the Volturno blowing sand in their faces, the great heat, a hill to climb that didn't look like a hill. It was all a Punic trick to get the Romans into a place where they could be surrounded and cut down. They were stabbed in the back, he said, and the tendons of their knees cut from behind. Besides, for most of them it was their first battle.

"And their last," Scipio said quietly. "Philip, you must never make those excuses again. Hannibal planned it that way. Tell people so. He chose a day when the Volturno was blowing. If it had not been blowing the battle would have been fought another day. He left a camp with fires burning so it would look as if he were running away from us. He sent his horsemen to come near us and then retreat till they led us to the place he had chosen.

"I learned from a peasant near Cannae that for weeks his troops had drilled on that very spot, where we had to climb that hill in the face of wind and dust. We couldn't see what we were doing. We were surrounded twice, first by footsoldiers, then by a ring of cavalry. We were like cattle in a slaughterhouse. Some of us were lucky enough to fight our way out. Most were not so fortunate. Our only excuse is that we were fighting the great-est soldier since Alexander—and were too stupid to know it."

I never knew Philip just to hang his jaw open and not say anything before. I brushed the hair off Scipio's toga and he gave me a piece of silver. He paid Philip generously and said, "I'll see you when I come back from Spain. Perhaps by then I'll know something."

Then he went out into the crowd. They cheered him but fell back, leaving him space to move.

Thirteenth day

We have your message, my lord, and I send this by the mes-senger. Lucius and I will leave the city tonight and go back to the miller and work for him until we can start for Capua. We will be there as soon as we can.

Capua was a city almost as large as Rome. It welcomed Hannibal and it became the capital of his part of Italy. He marched there with the carts and pack animals of Varro's army carrying the spoils of Cannae. Among them were eagles and standards of the legions and fasces of the consuls. Cities of southern Italy now began to open their gates to him in Apulia, Samnium, Calabria, and Bruttium.

He needed a port. Naples, the great port city, did not join him. He used a much smaller port at Locri. From there he sent his brother Mago to Carthage to ask the Council to send him horses, elephants, and money. Hannibal used his own money and the spoils of battle to pay his army. The great merchants of Carthage felt that he ought to get along without help, but the Council finally sent him forty elephants and four thousand Numidian horsemen. They also sent help to Hasdrubal Barca, who was fighting in Spain. Hannibal hoped Hasdrubal would defeat the Scipios, cross the Alps, and join him in Italy.

Hasdrubal resembled Hannibal in many ways, especially in his appearance and in his military skill. He was only a little younger than Hannibal. When they were boys people used to think they were twins. Hannibal felt sure that if Hasdrubal came they could conquer Rome.

The Gauls would certainly help Hasdrubal. They had already risen against Rome and defeated one of the newly trained legions. Far to the south in Sicily, Syracuse was ready to turn against Rome.

If he only had a port! Tarentum would be a good one, Hannibal thought. By the time Brecon and Lucius Tarchon reached Capua, Hannibal was encamped on a mountain above the town—Mount Tifata.

"The rich men of Capua wanted him to stay in the city," Carthalo told Brecon. "He had one dinner with them and it was all he could stand. They lay on couches for hours and ate food that they said was fit for the gods. Hannibal sat on a stool. He ate some bread and olives and drank a little of their Falernian wine. The soil in the plain below us is fertilized by ashes from Mount Vesuvius. See it smoking over there? The ashes are supposed to grow especially fine grapes. I wish you could have seen the expression on the noble Capuans' faces when Hannibal praised their wine and said they must come up to the camp and have some date wine from Carthage sometime."

"He told them," Carthalo added, "that it came in the same fleet that brought his elephants. I expect they think it is about right for elephants to drink."

Brecon asked, "Does he like it here?"

"Yes. He likes to meet men who have copies of books by Plato and Aristotle and who talk sensibly about the art of healing. Synhalus says they do not rely on powdered bats' livers and ground-up pearls to make people well. He says they seem to understand that a man's mind and body are one thing and must always be studied together. They have great respect for learning. One of them has been to Syracuse lately to talk with Archimedes."

"Archimedes!" Brecon exclaimed. "Is he still alive?"

"More alive in his mind than most of us ever are," Carthalo said. "He still invents extraordinary machines, works at it all day and half the night. If Roman ships attack Syracuse, they'll learn something about mathematics."

"I'd like to go to Syracuse," Brecon said.

"It's one of the most beautiful cities in the world," Carthalo said, "but it's cut off from us by the Roman fleets. We can't get through the Strait of Messina."

He unrolled a map and showed Brecon a map of southern Italy and of Sicily with Syracuse on the east coast, the narrow

Strait of Messina, the toe and heel of the Italian boot with the Gulf of Tarentum between them.

Brecon said, "If we held Tarentum, we could reach Syracuse easily. We could get to Tarentum through Apulia."

"Hannibal is thinking about it," Carthalo said, "but it may be some time before the right moment comes."

It did not come for two years.

There was news from Rome. When the Romans had seized Tarentum many years before, they had demanded hostages as a pledge that the city would be loyal to Rome. Ever since then sons of the noble Tarentine families had been sent to Rome every year.

About the time Brecon was eighteen years old, Carthalo sent him to Rome on an errand. When he came back to Capua, he told Hannibal that some of the Tarentine hostages had tried to escape but had been caught. In punishment all the young Tarentines had been thrown from the Tarpeian rock and killed.

Tarentum now had no loyalty to Rome left, only hatred. Two messengers managed to slip out of Tarentum and reach Hannibal. At that time there were three Roman armies in the field against him. One was commanded by Fabius, one by Gracchus, one by Marcellus. These were all able commanders. They did not defeat Hannibal in battle but they kept him from seizing Nola near Naples. So long as Nola resisted, he could never make the port of Naples his.

He besieged Nola but he did not have proper siege engines. He could not use cavalry against stone walls. Neither he nor his troops could bear the monotony of a siege. Rapid motion, surprise attacks, setting traps for the enemy were what both he and his men enjoyed. When the envoys from Tarentum appeared, he suddenly left Nola and led his troops back to Mount Tifata.

In Capua they heard that he was ill of a fever. Perhaps he was. A great many soldiers burned with fever one day and shivered the next. If he was ill the Tarentines did not notice it. There were two of them, both of whom had brothers among the hostages killed at Rome. One was named Philemenus, the other Nico. With Carthalo, they went over maps of Tarentum and made some corrections. On the whole the maps were good, they said. Brecon, who had visited Tarentum secretly several times in the past two years and who had made the maps, was pleased.

Nico and Philemenus had a scheme for seizing the city. There was no use in besieging it, they said. The citadel above it was strongly garrisoned with Roman guards.

"But," Philemenus said, "the Governor is too fond of a sociable evening of food and drink to be in command of a city threatened by Lord Hannibal Barca."

"What is your plan?" Hannibal asked.

"Before I tell you, I must ask you to promise that you will leave all Tarentines free and that your men will plunder only Roman houses," Philemenus said.

"I promise," said Hannibal.

"Tell him, Nico, what you will do."

Nico showed them on Brecon's map how Tarentum was a triangle. One side faced the sea, another was protected by a small lagoon which had a narrow inlet running into the land. The third faced the land. On all three sides were walls of stone and tall towers, with the citadel higher than any of them on a rocky hill near the inlet.

"There are many Romans there," Nico said, "but if we take

the city we might starve them out. If two gates can be opened at exactly the same moment, we can do it."

"Which gates?" Hannibal asked.

"This one," Nico said, "is close to the place where we bury our dead. Between midnight, when the gates are shut, and dawn an army can march through it unseen and unheard. Be outside the gate at midnight. There is a little hill here." He put his finger on a spot on the map. "If you light a torch there when you are ready, I shall see it and light one in return. Then you light a second and I will open the gate. Now, Philemenus, tell your part."

Philemenus smiled at Brecon and asked, "Do you like hunting?"

"Yes, when I used to go with my father in Spain, I did. I have not done much lately."

"Did you ever hunt a wild boar?"

"No," Brecon said.

"The Governor loves game, especially a boar's head, roasted. I have his permission to go hunting. I give the guard at the gate part of the game I kill—a pheasant or a rabbit perhaps—for his trouble in opening the gate for me if I come in late from hunting. He listens for my whistle and opens the gate for me when he hears it. He's fond of a nice piece of venison, but if I have no game for him he kindly accepts silver. He has been helping me in this way since he first came, several months now. He happens," Philemenus added, "to be one of the men who threw my brother from the Tarpeian rock."

He had spoken quietly and now he was silent for a moment. Then he added to Hannibal, "That is two gates, my lord. You will know better than I what to do when they are open."

Hannibal said to Brecon, "When will there be a night without a moon?"

Brecon pulled out his parchment calendar and studied its dingy surface.

"Next week, my lord, there will be several moonless nights," he said.

Hannibal turned to Philemenus, "And you said the Governor has invited you to a feast?"

"Yes, seven days from now, but I shall be late for it. I shall be out hunting."

"Perhaps I can be present," Hannibal said. He pointed to a spot on the map and said to Philemenus, "I shall camp here west of the forest. Meet me there. Brecon will go back with you now and learn more about the city. Thank you for your courtesy. Until we meet again..."

They left early the morning of the party: Brecon, Philemenus, and a dozen friends of his armed with javelins and spears. Philemenus knew where the boar slept. They made a wide circle around it, sounding their hunting horns, moving slowly toward the den. At last they saw him. He was making fierce rushes, first in one direction then in another.

Philemenus blew his horn in a rhythm that brought the hunters closer to him and to the boar too. At last the tawny, bristly plunging mass came near enough so that Brecon threw a javelin. It was close, almost touched his great snout, but whizzed past it. The boar came ahead, angrily, ready to tear his enemies to pieces with his yellow tusks.

Brecon hurled another javelin. This one pierced the boar's shoulder. He grunted furiously but came on. Philemenus was ready for him. He met the charge with his spear, thrusting it deep into the boar's throat. The thrust was so strong, so well aimed that it brought the boar to his knees. He died where he fell.

The other hunters stayed behind the carcass. Philemenus and Brecon walked to the forest until they saw the green fields north of it. The sun had sunk into a great mass of purple cloud. Now the clouds drifted away and in a golden light Numidian horsemen moved swiftly. Spanish cavalry followed. Elephants towered above them. Gallic and African troops, Italians from Bruttium and Apulia marched sturdily along. Behind them white oxen dragged carts with squeaking wheels. Brecon saw familiar figures:—Lord Maharbal, dark and slender; Hanno Bomilcar; Alain, enormous on a dappled-gray war horse; Gisgo laughing at something Mago Barca was saying.

"But where is Hannibal?" Philemenus asked.

"Wherever the greatest danger is," Brecon said. "Today with the rear guard, I think. In case one of the Roman armies has followed him. Yes—see our Iberian troops in white and red? There he is on the brown horse, dressed like them. Come!"

They ran toward him. Behind them the field was suddenly becoming a camp. When they turned and walked back toward the field with Hannibal, they found tents, smoking fires, and tethered horses grazing. Brecon wished Starlight were there instead of in a stable in Tarentum—perhaps with tarantulas in the straw.

They walked on toward the low hill on which they could see the cemetery of Tarentum. Philemenus showed him the place where Nico would wait with his men and watch for the light from Hannibal's torch. The sun had just set. The gate tower was already dark against a sky of gold and bronze and purple, with the new moon slipping down through the clouds.

Hannibal went back to the camp. Philemenus and Brecon made their way through the forest. After what seemed like endless wanderings in the darkness, they came at last to the carcass of the wild boar, where their friends were waiting. They took turns, two of them at a time, in carrying the boar toward the edge of the woods. Here the land sloped toward the city. They could see the dimly lighted watchtower and hear the trumpets that marked the changes of the guard. It was a warm night, with only a faint breeze stirring. They could see the torches that lighted the Governor's guests toward the Temple of the Muses. As the night wore on, they heard singing and laughter from the temple. Still there were lights there, but the rest of the city was dark.

At last more torches were lighted near the temple. They could see its columns looking pink in the glow and dark figures against them. The torches began to weave through the dark streets. The guests were going home, still singing.

"Nico and many of our friends are with them," Philemenus told Brecon. "They are pretending they have drunk too much wine and they are staggering along the streets singing. Really they are as sober as we are. They will escort the Governor to his house and be sure he and all the other Romans are safely in bed. Then they'll go to the cemetery."

It was a long time before all the houses of the city were dark again. Philemenus and his party moved closer to the gate. From there they could see the hill on which Hannibal was waiting. At last they saw a spurt of flame from a torch on the hill, an answering flare from the cemetery, and the second light from the hill. Finally, in the starlight they could make out a dark mass of moving men. At the foot of the hill it divided into two groups. One group came toward them. The other went to the cemetery gate farther along the wall.

Philemenus said to Brecon, "It's time. Tell Hannibal's men to follow close behind us to the gate and to rush in behind you and me when the door is opened. When you are sure they understand, come back and help me with the boar."

Brecon spoke to the leader of Hannibal's men and told them what to do. They were Africans, veterans of Cannae and other battles. Then Brecon went back to Philemenus and helped him carry the heavy carcass of the boar to the gate, where his friends were waiting.

Philemenus whistled three times, a whistle like that of a hawk flying. They heard Titus stumbling toward the door, heard the heavy bar lifted and the creak of the door on its hinges.

A crack of light showed as Titus called hoarsely, "How about that boar? Where's my roast pig?"

"Plenty for you, Titus," said Philemenus. "Open the door wider so we can get it in." Then, as the door swung open, he flung the boar at the guard's feet and said, "For you, Titus, for all the guards at the Tarpeian rock. And this is for you too."

As he spoke he ran Titus through with his spear, saying, "For you and for all tyrants."

Hannibal's Africans now followed Philemenus's men into the gatehouse and overpowered the guards in the tower before they could throw aside their dice and wine cups. Farther along the wall Nico's men had made the guards prisoner and opened the gate. Hannibal's Iberians were already quietly moving through the cemetery. The city still slept.

Two thousand Africans now started to pass through the gatehouse where Philemenus still stood with the boar's carcass and the dead Roman beside him. He stayed with his friends to guard the gatehouse against possible Roman attack and sent Brecon to lead the Africans to the marketplace. Brecon set off in the starlight with the dark men following.

Hannibal was already in the marketplace when they reached

it. He had posted groups of Gauls and Iberians along the different streets leading to the square. With each group were some of Nico's Tarentines. They were to warn any of their fellow citizens to go home and stay there in safety.

Just before dawn the trap was ready. Now it was time to spring it. Philemenus and Nico, leaving the gatehouses well guarded, had come bringing Roman trumpets with them. Piercing blasts from the trumpets summoned the legions from their quarters. Soldiers, half asleep, stumbled into the streets. The Gauls cut them down before they knew who the enemy was. More trumpets sounded, more Romans fell. The Governor was still half overcome by wine but he was prudent. He hurried not toward the fighting but away from it, found a boat, and escaped to the citadel. Some of the soldiers managed to follow him there. Others surrendered and became prisoners.

When the Tarentines came out on the streets in the morning light, they found the Roman soldiers lying where they had fallen.

Criers were going through the streets shouting, "Liberty! Liberty! Hannibal is here! No more Roman tyranny! Hannibal is here—meet him in the marketplace!"

Roman citizens fled to the citadel. Tarentines flocked into the marketplace. There Hannibal's Spanish, African, and Gallic troops were drawn up in good order, the sun shining on their weapons. On the rostrum stood Hannibal. There was a great shout of "Liberty! Liberty!" from the Tarentines, then silence as Hannibal began to speak.

He said in Greek, "I have come to free you from the tyranny of Rome. You have nothing to fear. Go home. Each of you must write 'Tarentine' on his door. A house so marked will be safe. Do not set marks falsely. Any Roman who does so will be slain. All Roman property is the prize of my soldiers. Go in peace and freedom!"

Hannibal now had possession of another rich Italian city and of a port, but while the Romans were in the citadel he could not use the port. The Romans had machines by which they could drop great stones on ships as they entered or left the harbor. The citadel was well stocked with food and wine. Their own ships could enter and bring them more. Indeed, there were ships in the harbor that had not been unloaded yet. They could hold the city indefinitely, the Governor said. He gave another supper party, at which all the loyal Romans ate and drank heavily with him.

When they woke up late the next morning, all the ships were gone. The guards of the harbor entrance were severely punished for not knowing how it had happened. They swore that no ships had passed by their tower. They spoke the truth.

While the Governor and his party were shouting defiance of Hannibal and gobbling tunafish and singing, Tarentines and Africans had seized the ships and overpowered their watchmen. Then they had rowed the ships into the lagoon and up the inlet and dragged them ashore. There, other troops were waiting with rollers made of tree trunks. These were put under the ships. Hannibal's oxen were hitched to the galleys. They had dragged them to the marketplace with soldiers pushing and moving the rollers to the front of the galleys as they were needed.

Every man in Tarentum helped shove, lift, tug, drive oxen, move rollers. By the time Marcus Livius and the Romans had wakened after the party, the ships had crossed the city and were anchored off a beach on the ocean side of Tarentum.

It was not exactly a port. The ships were not sheltered from storms. There was no quay at which they could land. The sailors had to leave the ships offshore and land from small boats. Still, Hannibal was in touch with the sea again.

"A Carthaginian," he said, "is content with that."

GIANT CLAWS

ONE SPRING AFTERNOON in the marketplace at Tarentum, a ragged old beggar spoke to Brecon. He was a short, stooping man with a black patch over one eye and long gray hair straggling over his shoulders. Like many Tarentines, he spoke a mixture of bad Latin and worse Greek as he whined a request for a small piece of silver to buy a bit of bread.

Brecon was starting to take a coin from his pouch when a tarantula suddenly flashed out of a pile of fresh asparagus stalks. The beggar hopped quickly aside. Brecon dropped the coin back into his pouch.

He said to the beggar, "Follow me. I will see that you get a good meal." The man muttered, "To the beach." A short street led down to the sea. The beggar limped along until they came out on the beach, below the sea wall. Two galleys were anchored some distance offshore. Two small boats were drawn up on the pebbles. Except for them the beach was empty.

Brecon sat down on a rock and said, smiling happily at the beggar, "Are you hungry, my Lord Carthalo?"

Carthalo smiled too.

"As a matter of fact I am. I could eat a big slice of blue fin, broiled, a pound of fresh asparagus, and a dozen almond cakes. But that's not why I spoke to you."

"Practicing speaking like a Tarentine, I suppose," Brecon said. "You do very well."

"Thank you. How did you know me?"

"A Tarentine does not drop his jaw when he sees a tarantula and skip out of its way. They are the pride of our fair city. Named for it. We have the biggest ones anywhere. A Tarentine either speaks a polite word of blessing to it or steps on it, according to how he is feeling that day."

Carthalo chuckled and Brecon went on, "I had a good master who taught me to notice things like that. What can I do for you, my lord?"

"You can come with me to Syracuse," Carthalo said. "I have just been with my Lord Hannibal to show him something. He says you and I must go to see Archimedes."

"When do we start?" Brecon asked.

"As soon as you are ready. Row me out to the nearer galley. Then go ashore, get what you need. We may be gone a long time. The captain and crew of the galley are ashore. If they come back before you do, I'll send the boat back for you. I'll be watching. Tell your friends you are going on an errand for my lord to Croton. That will be our first stop. Say nothing of having seen me. No one must know where I have been or where I am going. Bring some papyrus. I want you to make some drawings for Archimedes."

Then as Brecon stared at him, only half believing what he heard, Carthalo added, "Yes, you've taught me about tarantulas today. Next week you'll be teaching Archimedes! Start along now. Don't show you are in a hurry but get back as soon as you can. The wind is just right."

To avoid being seen by Roman ships, they traveled chiefly at night. In the daytime Brecon worked at making drawings from Carthalo's notes and rough sketches. They were for a new kind of Roman war vessel, invented especially to attack Syracuse. The Romans had been besieging Syracuse for months because her people were friendly to Hannibal. They had not been able to break through the walls anywhere. At present they had withdrawn their troops. The new ships were quinqueremes, lashed together in pairs with only the outside oars able to move. Each could be separated from the other and be rowed as usual. While fastened together they made a broad, steady foundation. At the bows were high ladders that were raised and lowered by ropes and pulleys. Landing platforms projected from the tops of the ladders.

In an attack these ladders would reach the top of the wall and be held firmly to it by the platforms. Carthalo had seen the Roman soldiers training for the attack on Syracuse. They filled the decks of the lashed galleys. They were armed with shields of iron and heavy swords. At the signal to attack, they raced up the ladders, dashed across the platforms, and moved along the walls, cutting down the defenders and seizing watchtowers. No soldiers of Syracuse, a place where people loved books and beautiful statues and painted bowls, where they studied the stars and music and mathematics, would ever be brave enough to beat off such an attack, the Romans boasted.

The quinqueremes with the ladders would not be the only ships. Between each pair would be a large galley carrying slingers and javelin throwers. There would be men armed with scorpions, a kind of whip made of knotted cords with steel spikes at the end. This was an old-fashioned weapon, Carthalo said, but a painful one. It was used chiefly for beating prisoners.

The name scorpion was also given to a more modern weapon, a machine for hurling heavy stones against the walls. This could be done at one spot to draw the attention of the defenders while the soldiers used the ladders in another place.

Brecon said, "You say it's more than ten miles around it and that some of the walls are great cliffs. And that the Romans have been besieging it for two years."

"It is true that Syracuse has never been taken by direct assault," Carthalo said, "but if the Romans make a real breach in the harbor wall, their whole army might pour through it like—like—"

"Like troops going through a gap made by heating a rock and dashing vinegar on it?" Brecon asked.

"Yes," Carthalo said, "but I believe Archimedes will think of something when he knows the problem."

They found the mathematician at his sand table. He was working on a quick way of adding large numbers, his secretary said. His master was expecting Carthalo's visit but no one must speak to him at present, he said. It annoyed him to be interrupted. He showed them a bench at the other end of the big room. They might speak softly to each other. Or perhaps they would prefer to read. They chose books. He brought them each one, both by Archimedes. Carthalo's was about the measurement of the circle. Brecon's was called *On Floating Bodies*.

The palace where Archimedes lived had been given to him by the King of Syracuse. There were many beautiful things in the rooms through which they had walked. The one in which they were sitting was bare except for cases that held rolls of papyrus, the sand table, and some benches. A door led to a sunny terrace. Through it Brecon could see the sea wall and its towers, the dark blue harbor and its ships.

He tried hard to understand what he was reading. He kept saying over to himself, "A body wholly or partly immersed in water loses weight equal to the weight of the body's volume of water."

That's why ships float, he told himself. That's why a ship can carry an elephant from Carthage to Locri. But he knew he did not really understand it.

He looked at Archimedes. The mathematician was a small man, bald, with a fringe of silvery hair, pink-faced, with clear blue eyes. It was hard to believe he was almost seventy-five years old.

Suddenly Archimedes wrote something—only a few figures, a few words—on a piece of papyrus, then brushed the sand evenly over the table, stood up, and smiled at his guests. He was much interested in Brecon's drawings of the Roman ships with their ladders and platforms.

"We must welcome them," he said. "It will take some thinking."

Though the two men were so different, Archimedes reminded Brecon of Hannibal. Neither thought defeating the Romans was easy.

"Who will command this attack?" Archimedes asked. "Marcellus," Carthalo said.

"Why was he chosen?"

"Because he has not been defeated by Hannibal yet," Carthalo said. "The Romans call him victorious because Hannibal stopped the siege of Nola while Marcellus was defending it and took Tarentum instead. The Romans call him the Sword of Rome. I think he is an able commander," Carthalo added.

Archimedes said, "Whoever planned these twin ships with the ladders was not stupid. How much time have we?"

"Three months, not longer. Perhaps only two."

"I must leave my sand table and talk with the King and his engineers," Archimedes said regretfully. "You write and draw well," he added to Brecon. "I shall need help from you."

During those next weeks Brecon spent much time copying drawings made by Archimedes for the King's engineers. When at last the drawings were finished, Archimedes said, "I would like to give you a present—something by which you will remember your visit. You admired those bowls the other day. Would you like one?"

The bowls were made of bronze, embossed outside with a pattern of gold, gilded inside. There was a border of grape leaves around the edge and a band of dancing figures in gold that made Brecon think of the walls of Lucius Tarchon's tomb.

"Take one," Archimedes said.

Brecon said, "They are the most beautiful I have ever seen. But there is something I would like even better."

"What is that?"

"To make copies of your books—about the circle and the cylinder and the floating bodies and the others—and for you to help me understand them. Then I can learn them and carry them in my head. That way I'll always have them. I have no house to put the bowl in but I will carry a picture of it in my head too."

Archimedes smiled.

"Of course you may copy the books, and we'll talk about them. And if you change your mind you may have the bowl too. Surely you will have a house someday. In the meantime my house is yours."

Carthalo came and vanished many times in those weeks. He would trust what he learned of the plans of Marcellus to no messenger. At last he came with the news that the Roman fleet—ladders, twin ships, platforms, iron shields, scorpions, and all—had started. Marcellus was commanding it in person.

"They'll come," Archimedes said, "some windless night without a moon. Any night now."

Brecon wrote in his journal for Hannibal:

First night

I am in one of the harbor watchtowers. It is hard to stay awake because we must not speak to each other but listen always for the sound of oars. Carthalo is here too, and Archimedes. The tower is the one nearest the new engines. Archimedes wants to work one of them himself. He's like a small boy who is going to ride his new pony.

Second night

Another dark night in the tower watching the empty harbor. All the ships have been moved to the inner harbor where goods are unloaded. There was a brisk wind tonight and we did not really expect the attack but we kept watch anyway.

Third night (or, rather, morning)

Last night they came. The sea was calm. I could see stars sparkle in the harbor almost as brightly as in the sky. At last I heard the first faint creaking of oars. I touched Archimedes on the shoulder and whispered, "They are here."

We had boys ready to slip quietly along the wall from tower to tower and warn the engineers and the guards. Archimedes was at his engine as soon as anyone. I stayed in the tower to send a message to him and the others as soon as the ships passed it. Now the noise of the oars grew louder. I could hear water lapping against the sides of the galley. Suddenly the stars in the water below me broke into faint sparks of light. The ships began to pass my tower. They were great dark shadows. The ladders made dark stripes against the sky. I sent my runner to Archimedes. Now the ships were in the darkest place in the harbor, next to the wall. I could not see them but I could hear men moving, hear the clink of metal on metal as one shield touched another and low voices muttering commands.

They must feel safe now, I thought. They had passed the place now where giant engines, designed by Archimedes, had been dropping great stones on Roman ships for years. He felt sure they would avoid that place and attack farther along the wall. He was right. Now I knew my runner had reached Archimedes, because dim openings suddenly appeared along the wall on a level with the decks of the ships. Spears as sharp as porcupine's quills bristled out from the wall and flew against the lines of soldiers waiting to climb the ladders.

There was no longer silence on the ships but shouts, trumpet calls, moans of wounded men. Still the ships moved in. From above them chains rattled, long arms swung out, giant claws bit into the bows of the ships. I heard the wood crashing and crunching. The bows began rising higher and higher. There were choked shouts and the splashing of shields as the heavily armed soldiers slid helplessly into the water. And water must be pouring into the sterns of the ships now, I knew.

Then I heard great splashes as the claws of Archimedes dropped the ships suddenly. Many sank. Ladders and platforms crashed. Now I could see the ships. Balls of flaming pitch were whizzing into them. Woodwork caught on fire. The ladders of those still above water were like torches of flame. Through the smoke and flames I saw great balls of lead fall onto the single galleys between the quinqueremes, crash through the hulls, and sink them.

Once in that smoky red-orange light I saw Archimedes standing on the wall watching his giant claws at work. Then, from a ship that had not yet reached the wall, I heard the trumpets sounding notes that you and I, my lord, first heard at Ticino. It was the call to retreat, sounded from the ship of Marcellus.

Those ships still able to move hurried out of the harbor after the Sword of Rome. I think they will not return soon.

So the genius of one man, Archimedes, defeated thousands.

CHAPTER 13

A SLAVE IS SOLD

MARCELLUS NOW TRIED to take Syracuse from the land all, but Archimedes had engines to fight off the Romans here, too. They settled down to starve out the city.

It was still possible to enter Syracuse and get out again without being captured by the Romans if you chose the right place at the right time. Not long after the harbor attack by Marcellus had failed, Carthalo and Brecon left the city. They went first to Tarentum by sea and then to Capua by land. Hannibal was at Mount Tifata. The Capuans needed his help because their crops were ripe and they were afraid to harvest them without Hannibal's soldiers to protect them. So few Capuans came into the fields that it ended by the soldiers doing most of the work.

Bomilcar, whose soldiers had reaped most of the grain, was in Hannibal's tent. He said disgustedly to Carthalo, "Hunger makes even dogs work—but not Capuans," and went off still grumbling.

Hannibal said that he had enjoyed Brecon's journal but that he wanted to hear about Archimedes again, so he and Carthalo told the story all over again both talking at once.

When they were both too tired to speak, Hannibal said to Brecon, "I am going to ask you to do something for me. I need Carthalo here and in Italy but also I must have someone I can trust near Rome. Now this means great danger for you. Carthalo and you have always been in greater danger than soldiers on the battlefield. We all know this, though we do not usually speak of it. I want you to be my head spy for the country north of Capua.

"Carthalo would rather I would say 'head of my information service' or 'news gatherer' or 'news messenger,' but we might as well speak as the Romans will if they catch you. If they do they will kill you—after torturing you, of course. Now if this seems too bad to you, say no. I will never blame you. If you say yes I will be grateful and I will give you the same secret weapon that I carry against the Romans."

Brecon said, "I say yes, cousin. What is the weapon?"

Hannibal took a small wooden box out of his pouch. In it, wrapped in several thicknesses of linen, was a tiny glass flask.

"A few drops will put you quickly beyond the reach of Roman cruelty," Hannibal said. "Mine, which I always carry, will keep me from ever being a Roman prisoner. I shall never be dragged through the streets of Rome in triumph like a crocodile in a cage. If they ever catch me, I shall have my last victory over them. And if they seize you, cousin, you can defeat them too."

Brecon held out his hand for the flask.

"Don't uncork it," Hannibal said. "Even to breathe a little or to let it touch your skin might poison you, Synhalus says. It smells of bitter almonds," he added. "I always liked the smell. I remember the almond trees in Carthage and in Spain. The white flowering trees have bitter nuts and the pink ones sweet.

Imilce liked them too. Remember the honey cakes she used to make out of the sweet ones?"

"Yes, I remember," Brecon said.

He wrapped the flask up carefully again, put it into the box and the box into his pouch.

"Now I will tell you Carthalo's plan," Hannibal said. "You may still change your mind if you do not like it."

They left Capua next day and went back to Syracuse to carry out Carthalo's plan.

There were the usual peddlers around the camp of Marcellus. Many of them were Greeks. Among them was a Greek with yellowish-brown hair and beard. He was a small man, a little lame. He carried a scorpion, one of those whips of cord and steel spikes. This was to beat his slaves with. He was a slave trader.

This bright morning he was riding a thin chestnut mare with a star on her forehead. His slaves were in a line behind him. Their ankles were chained together. Two men, one of them a blacksmith, were guarding the slaves. At the end of the line was a young man, nineteen or twenty years old, perhaps. He was better and more cleanly dressed than the other slaves and he was carrying a leather sack with some rolls of papyrus sticking out of it. He was freshly shaved. His hair was the color of his masters horse, only darker. He stood very straight and in spite of his fetters he moved as if he knew where he was going. The other slaves stumbled along, groaning and mumbling except when a crack from their master's whip silenced them for a few minutes.

The slave driver spoke to one of the soldiers who were guarding the entrance to the camp. He spoke in Latin with a strong Greek accent.

"The consul Marcellus wishes to see me," he said. "He wishes to buy some slaves. I have just what he wants."

The soldier said, "What makes you think Marcus Claudius Marcellus would even look at such trash? Take them away!"

The slave dealer pressed something that clinked into the soldier's hand and the man said less roughly, "Oh, you say he sent for you? Well, I'll find out if he'll see you. Guard the gate," he said to another soldier and marched off toward the largest tent in the camp.

It seemed a long time as they waited in the hot sun for him to come back. When he came, he said loudly to the slave dealer, "Get off that horse! You don't think you're going to ride a horse into a Roman camp, do you? Leave her at the gate with one of your men to hold her."

The slave dealer said meekly, "Yes, sir, of course, sir—but could I lead her in? I hope to sell her too." He gave the soldier another piece of silver and added, "She's a real Numidian horse, sir. Crossed the Alps with Hannibal."

"That's a great story!" the Roman said. "Every horse anyone has for sale crossed the Alps too. But I'll say this for yours—if anyone wants a horse you've got the framework to start with." He laughed heartily at his own wit, adding, "Well, take her in. Too bad you didn't bring an elephant! Ho! Ho! Ho!"

The slaves clanked along toward the tent of the Consul. Marcellus, a big handsome man, splendid in bronze armor inlaid with gold, came to the door of the tent and looked down at the slave dealer and the line of chained slaves.

"I asked for a well-trained tutor and secretary, and you bring me this riffraff, Carthalodes," he said, scowling.

The slave dealer whined, "Forgive me, my lord, but sometimes different kinds of slaves are needed. I have a carpenter here. Some good workers in the field, a goatherd, a metalworker, a cook..."

Marcellus said impatiently, "The tutor, man—the tutor! I haven't got all day to talk. I have a war to fight."

"The young man at the end of the line, sir. From a Greek family living at Taormina. Speaks Latin well. Captured at sea by pirates on his way to visit Greece. Fine mathematician, sir. Studied with Archimedes, sir. Writes a good hand, Greek or Latin. Those rolls in his sack, he calls his treasure. I don't know about such things but he says they are copies of works by Archimedes. Valuable, he says."

"M'm—what's his name?"

"Breconides, Sir Consul. He's in good shape, good teeth, muscles, eyes. Ought to last a long time, sir. Only twenty years old, he says."

"Unchain him. Bring him over here."

The blacksmith struck off the fetters. Brecon walked over to Marcellus and bowed before him. The Consul went over him carefully as if he were buying a horse or an ox, examining his eyes and teeth, feeling his muscles.

"Let me see those books," he said. "Oh, Greek—I can make nothing of them. Here, read me some in Latin. What does it say there?"

Brecon began, speaking rather slowly: "This one is *On Floating Bodies*, sir. It explains that a body wholly or partly immersed in water loses weight equal to the weight of the body's volume of water."

Marcellus laughed and said, "It does, does it? Very interesting, I'm sure. I suppose you know how to make these machines they use against us, do you?"

"No, Sir Consul, only the principles."

"If you could make them you'd be worth something but you just teach—is that it?—typically Greek." He turned and said to the trader, 'Well, Carthalodes, what do you want for him? Seems strong, as you say. Speaks Latin without much accent. If he were a practical engineer I could use him right here, but—as I said in my message—I want to send him to my sister for a present. She has a son—poor boy. He's lost the use of his legs. He'll never make a fighter. All he'll be able to do is study."

"Hard for a noble Roman, sir," the trader said sympathetically.

"Yes, he was a fine boy. Jumped higher, ran faster than all his friends. Only eight years old but already practicing with a sword and shield I gave him. One night he had a little fever, my sister writes. Next morning he couldn't stand. Every medicine no matter how costly, even pounded pearls, has been tried. He has to be carried everywhere. Will never walk again. Now—how much for the tutor?"

"Three hundred denarii."

"You're joking! Why that's the ransom for a Roman knight and his horse! I'll give you a hundred."

"Not many knights know the Odyssey by heart and have studied with Archimedes," the trader said. "But—I'm sorry for your nephew. I'll take two hundred and throw in this mare. Real Numidian. Crossed the Alps with Hannibal."

"Got pretty worn out on the way and hasn't recovered in six years," Marcellus said. "Still, perhaps it might cheer the boy up to have a horse, and he might ride some day. Look, I'll give you a hundred and fifty. That's my last word. Take it or leave it."

With a good deal of grumbling the trader accepted the offer, signed a paper describing the tutor and saying he was sound in wind and limb. He put the money in his pouch and, while Marcellus was not looking, slipped the pouch into Brecon's sack.

"Sure you wouldn't like a good carpenter, Sir Consul? No? Well, goodbye, Breconides, work well. Sometimes a tutor gives extra lessons to other pupils. Earns a little money. Gets a chance to buy his freedom. Maybe you can do it. And here's this old leopard skin. It was thrown in with Starlight in trade. That's the mare's name. Starlight. Take it along. Nights will be getting cool now. Keep the chill off."

For a moment Brecon could not speak. He always had known when he and Carthalo parted even for a day, that they never might meet again. This time the feeling was as if someone were clutching his throat.

At last he managed to speak. All he could say was, "Thank you. Thank you for—everything."

He stood with Starlight's muzzle against his cheek and watched Carthalo and his chain of slaves out of sight. All the men were really soldiers of Hannibal's, he knew. Two of the dirtiest and raggedest, those called goatherds by Carthalo, were Greek soldiers who would lead the fight against Marcellus. They would enter Syracuse that night by a door in the sea wall.

Marcellus said, not unkindly, "We shall take the city soon and when we do, the great prize will be—what do you think?"

"I don't know, Sir Consul," Brecon said. "There are many fine things in it, much gold, statues from Greece, bowls that cost more than a man—"

"It's a man I'm thinking of," Marcellus broke in, "Archimedes, of course. He's wasted on these cowardly Greeks. I'll take him to Rome. He'll be one of my best weapons against Hannibal. Those giant claws! I know a good thing when I see it. Backed up by Roman courage, such ideas will amount to something." He gave a loud confident laugh and added, "Come into my tent and write a letter for me to my sister. Your ship sails soon for Ostia. I will write to her about you. You can carry it to her."

His sister's name, Marcellus told Brecon, was Claudia Scipio.

She was the widow of a cousin of Scipio, the former Consul, who was now fighting in Spain. She had a house on the Palatine Hill in Rome but spent most of her time in a villa outside the city.

The letter was quite long. By the time Marcellus had scrawled a few words and his name at the bottom of it, the galley that took Brecon to Ostia was ready.

He was not fettered for the journey.

"You seem like an honest fellow," Marcellus said. "I never make a mistake in people. Just give me your word not to escape, that you'll go to my sister and do your best for the boy."

"I give you my word to go to your sister's house and to do the best I can in every way for her son," Brecon said. "Perhaps I can even help with his lameness. I know an Egyptian physician who taught me something of his craft."

"He's had the best medicines," Marcellus said, "but if you know others, no matter what they cost—"

"This would not be a matter of drugs," Brecon said. "Sometimes by rubbing the muscles in a certain way, by baths, swimming, later by rowing a light boat, by using braces and crutches, it is possible to help such a patient to walk again. Did this happen long ago?"

"No, about two weeks."

"There may be a chance, then," Brecon said. "I promise nothing except to do my best."

This was all written in the letter he carried in his bag to introduce him to Claudia Scipio. The bag held the few things he really cared about—the leopard skin, his calendar, the works of Archimedes, the purple belt Athena had woven, the box containing Hannibal's flask.

Would he ever see Hannibal again? Or Carthalo?

Perhaps not, he thought as the galley started its journey. But

I would not turn back if I could. Some news I send might help Hannibal make peace with Rome. Then we can all go back to Carthage. It might be a day when all the almond trees are in bloom.

He tried hard to believe it might be so.

He wondered about Rhodri, whether his lameness was all gone, and about Sophonisba. Was she in love with a new prince now? Did Athena still trot after her like a good little pony?

I should have written from Sicily to her and Rhodri, he thought. Too late now.

It would be dangerous to send letters through Roman territory, Hannibal and Carthalo had both said. All messages must go by word of mouth along the twisting chain of Carthalo's men. Brecon's men now, Carthalo had said.

"It's like a grapevine," Hannibal had said, "twisting, turning, reaching everywhere. It moves but you never see or hear it move."

Brecon liked the idea of the grapevine.

"Since Bacchus is the god of grapes and wine, I shall begin each message with 'Bacchus says' or with some word about grapes or wine. Then our messengers will know the message is a true one," he said, and Hannibal had approved.

It was a long time before he sent or received any messages. The galley, heavily loaded with grain from Sicily, moved slowly. Rome was short of food, the captain told him. The Punic Fox, as he called Hannibal, either destroyed crops or stole them for his own troops. And besides, so many young men were in the legions, so many had been killed in battle that the few farmers left could not grow enough grain.

"They're beginning to buy it from Egypt now," the captain said.

This news, Brecon decided, would be one of the first messages he would send to Hannibal. Would he really be able to teach his pupil and manage the grapevine too? Well, he could only do his best. He thought a great deal about his pupil. Marcus Cornelius Scipio was nine years old, Marcellus had said. That was a little younger than Rhodri was when Synhalus taught him to walk again, when Brecon used to swim and row with him in the inner harbor at Carthage. He was only a little lame now. Perhaps someday, Brecon thought, I can say the same of Marcus Cornelius.

CHAPTER 14

GRAPEVINE

THEY REACHED the villa of the Scipios one afternoon when cold mist was rising from a pond where cattle were drinking. Crickets were chirping slowly. Their voices would soon be quiet until next summer. The captain of the galley turned Brecon over to the steward and went back to Rome. The steward was a sensible-looking elderly man. He gave orders for Brecon and Starlight both to be well fed. The captain had told him that the horse had come over the Alps with Hannibal.

Piccus—that was the steward's name—was much interested in the horse, more of course than he was in the tutor. After all, you could ride a horse. The voyage had done Starlight good. She had been well fed and rested, looked almost fat. After a stall had been found for her and a groom started rubbing her down, Piccus led Brecon into the main house of the villa. There would be food for him in the kitchen later, he had ordered it. Good porridge made of their own wheat.

They crossed a courtyard with low pinkish-yellow buildings on three sides of it. It was paved with stones like a Roman road.

Claudia Scipio was sitting at her loom in the atrium of the

villa with her maids around her. They were spinning wool for her weaving, the yellowish-white wool of which Roman togas were made. The maids sat on benches or stools. The only chair in the room was occupied by a small bright-eyed boy. He was leaning his dark curly head on his left hand, resting his elbow on the arm of the chair. His eyes looked large in his thin face. He was dressed in a toga edged with purple. His sandaled feet were propped up on a small stool. His right hand rested on the head of a reddish-brown, bristly-haired dog.

The dog whined and then barked as Brecon came into the room. The boy said, "Quiet, Rufus," stroked the dog's head, and added to Brecon, "Don't be afraid. He won't bite."

The steward went over to Claudia and said, "I have brought a young slave, mistress. Here is the bill of sale and a letter from your brother. It is sealed with his seal."

Claudia got up from her loom. She was a large woman, somewhat like her brother, except that her expression was sad rather than cheerful. She held out her hand for the letter, unrolled it, and read it herself. Not all Roman women could read, Brecon knew.

After she had finished reading, she said to her son, "Marcus Cornelius, this is your new tutor, Breconides. He is a present to you from your uncle. Bid him welcome."

"You are welcome, Breconides," the boy said. "Rufus says so too, don't you, Rufus? Speak to him Rufus."

The dog gave a sharp bark, then crossed the room, wagging his stumpy, bristly tail, and put his cold nose against Brecon's bare knee.

"He knows you already," Marcus said smiling. "Here, Rufus! Good dog. Do your tricks—some bread, Piccus, please—lie down, Rufus. Good boy! Roll over! Sit up! Please put a piece of bread on his nose, Breconides. Wait, Rufus—not yet, not yet!'"

The dog sat up, whining a little, balancing himself and the bread with difficulty. Then Marcus snapped his fingers and the bread vanished. Rufus was so pleased with himself that he barked happily, chased his tail, and rolled over. Then, panting hard, he sat down again by his master's chair.

Brecon saw that Claudia had tears in her eyes.

He said hastily, "Why, Marcus Cornelius, if I am half as good a teacher as you are, you will soon know Aesop and Euclid."

"Why are we waiting?" asked the boy.

His mother smiled for the first time.

"Because your tutor has had a long journey and needs food and rest," she said. "And because daylight is almost over and we shall all soon be going to bed. Breconides's room will be the one next to yours. You will see him as soon as you are ready for the day. You will be called at first light," she added to Brecon.

His room was small, dark, cold. It contained a mattress of straw with a thin blanket on it and a wooden chest. The top of the chest could be either a chair or a table, according to whether he sat on it or put his writing materials on it. There were two pegs on the wall. Brecon hung his cloak on one and his best tunic on the other. He put his leopard skin over the blanket, his books and other clothes into the chest. While he was on the ship, he had sewn the silver Carthalo gave him into his belt. Hannibal's flask he put into the pouch attached to the belt. He laid his extra sheets of papyrus on top of the chest beside his pen and his ink bottle. He was settled.

For months, he thought. For years perhaps. How many years?

Perhaps it was fortunate he did not know.

Two slaves soon picked up Marcus' chair and carried him off to bed, Rufus trotting behind them. His nurse followed to undress Marcus and get him into bed. The maids went off to their own quarters.

Claudia said, "Please stay a few moments, Breconides. I did not like to speak of my brother's letter while Marcus was here. It has given me hope and it might have made him too hopeful. I would not like him to be disappointed. Is it true he can be cured?"

"I can only tell you about one case that seems like his," Brecon said. "The boy—an orphan about your son's age—lived in our house. He had a sudden fever and seemed to have lost all use of his legs. An Egyptian physician treated him. He was only a little lame when I last heard from him. I used to help the doctor by rubbing the boy's muscles and exercising his legs in various ways. I see you have a pool in the garden beyond the atrium and I noticed a pond as we rode in. Both might be useful, the pool for swimming, the pond for rowing a boat later. The swimming helps very much. He can float and use his legs without putting weight on them. You probably have a good carpenter."

"Yes," Claudia said.

"I could show him how to make braces and crutches. We can at least get Marcus Cornelius out of that chair. How well he recovers will depend much on his own determination. I think he has plenty. And patience—see how he taught the dog."

"Yes," Claudia said. Her voice trembled and Brecon saw that she was crying.

He looked away and said, speaking rather quickly, "The boy I knew walked first with crutches and braces, then with crutches and one brace, next just with crutches. Then he threw his crutches away and used a cane. Now not even a cane."

Claudia said, "The day Marcus Cornelius walks again, you shall have your freedom."

"I thank you, my lady," Brecon said. "I wish I could promise that he will. All I can promise is to do my best."

"Will you begin in the morning? Never mind about Greek and geometry."

Brecon smiled and said he thought there would be time to study too.

"I can see he has a good mind—it's worth having some good furniture in it," he added.

"Yes, yes, of course," Claudia said. "His guardian, his cousin Publius Cornelius Scipio, Junior, would agree with you, I know. So would his father too. But in these times... My husband was killed fighting the Gauls when Marcus was a baby. This estate will be his as soon as he is of age. He must be trained to manage it, even from his chair. But if he could only walk—and fight against the invader!"

Brecon was silent. It would be a strange thing if he were to spend his time training a man to fight against Hannibal.

But I've promised, he thought, then said aloud, "By the time he is a man I hope there will be peace in Italy."

Claudia got up from the bench on which she had been sitting.

"Never," she said fiercely. "Rome will never make peace while there is one Punic soldier on the soil of our country."

Then she added more quietly, "You cannot help thinking like a Greek, I know. Anymore than I can help speaking like a Roman. Perhaps you will learn here—as well as teach."

"I hope so," Brecon said.

He learned many things during the next months. Almost every week peddlers came to the villa. Some of them he had known in Rome as Carthalo's men. Before long, messages beginning "In the words of Bacchus" or "The vintage is good this year" began to reach the villa and leave it again. In this way Brecon learned before anyone else at the villa that Marcellus had seized Syracuse. He never broke through the walls. The city was taken by treachery during a feast.

Brecon thought of Tarentum. Were the Romans learning that a headlong attack was not always best? He remembered Hannibal saying "The Romans are a hardy and courageous people quite innocent of the arts of war." Perhaps they are not innocent any longer, he thought. Worse to Brecon than the loss of Syracuse was the death of Archimedes. Marcellus had given orders that the old mathematician should be taken alive and brought to him, but soldiers, who had not received his orders, were already looting the palace. When they reached the library, the room Brecon knew so well, Archimedes was sitting at his table working out an equation. A soldier shouted at him. Archimedes was annoyed.

"You are disturbing me," he said. "Go away."

The soldier ran him through with his spear and hurried on, looking for gold.

The peddler who was telling Brecon this news said suddenly, "Pull yourself together. Don't let anyone see you look like that."

Some slaves were carrying Marcus in his chair toward the peddler's cart. The peddler began to recite in his singsong cry a list of the things he had for sale. The whole household gathered around him. Brecon had a chance to get control of himself. When, later in the week, he heard the news again, this time from Claudia, he was able to express his regret for his old teacher calmly.

"My brother feels badly about this accident," Claudia said. "He had given special orders that Archimedes should be brought to him alive. He greatly admired his genius."

"Yes," Brecon said, "he said so to me."

"However," Claudia went on, "he has ordered a splendid tomb for him. Archimedes will not be forgotten."

"No," Brecon said, "not so long as ships float and lead sinks."

Perhaps Claudia noticed a certain non-Roman feeling in this remark. She changed the subject.

"What of Marcus Cornelius this week? Do you see improve-

ment? It is a long time now that you have been working with the rubbing and exercises."

"I was about to tell you," Brecon said. "This morning when I had him in the pool, he really kicked out with his feet. I think the time has come to have his braces made. I have talked with the carpenter. He has some beechwood that is well seasoned. He says it will be just the thing."

The day Marcus first stood up, using his braces and crutches, was a day of rejoicing at the villa. There were special treats for everyone, great kettles of stew with meat in it for the field workers, roast fowls for the family table, walnuts to crack, honey in the comb, a cask of last year's wine opened, chestnuts roasted among the hot coals of a big fire. The days were short now. There was a dusting of snow on top of the mountains that ringed the valley where the villa was.

After supper was over, Marcus sat in his chair with his hand on Rufus's head. Some of the maids were shelling chestnuts and cracking walnuts. Two of them played knucklebones. Two others played with a cord, each taking it from the other's fingers in a different pattern.

"Almost bedtime," Claudia said.

"Oh, please, Mother," said Marcus, "Let Breconides tell one story, just one. Then the day will be perfect."

"Well just one—what shall it be?"

"Something about Ulysses, a story I haven't heard. Something frightening, Breconides."

Brecon laughed.

"I'll tell you about Polyphemus," he said. "First I'll say it in Greek, then in Latin."

When Ulysses had outwitted the terrible one-eyed giant both in Greek and in Latin, Marcus was carried off to bed.

Claudia said to Brecon, "This is the happiest day I have known for many long weeks. He walked! Only two steps and with the crutches, but he walked. Freedom is yours if you ask for it, Breconides."

Brecon said, "He will walk freely by himself before I ask for it, my lady. It will be many months before that day comes, but I feel sure now that it will come."

"That will be a happy day for you as well as for me, I know." Claudia said kindly.

"Yes," Brecon said, "but I am content now with the day we have just had."

During the next months the news that Brecon sent over the grapevine was mostly bad. A Carthaginian fleet tried to seize the island of Sardinia and was destroyed, partly by a storm, partly by Roman ships. Carthage sent troops to try to take Syracuse from Marcellus. Some died of a plague. Others were defeated. Once Bomilcar attacked Syracuse with a fleet of many galleys from Carthage. He hoped to free the city but he was driven off by a Roman fleet. In Spain the Scipio brothers defeated Hasdrubal Barca. Carthage sent troops to his aid, twenty thousand of them, with Mago Barca in command.

Not long after this news came, Claudia Scipio and her family moved into Rome for the winter. The winter before, because of Marcus's illness, they had stayed at the villa. Because it was easier to meet his peddlers at the villa, Brecon would in some ways have preferred to stay there. Still, Rome had advantages too. There was always news—true or false—in the Forum. Also, more visitors came to the pleasant house on the Palatine.

A very distinguished one came soon after they were settled. It was young Publius Cornelius Scipio. His father had sent him to Rome. He did not say why. Brecon thought it might be to urge the Senate to send more troops to Spain to face Mago's new army. Young Scipio was twenty-four years old now, still spotlessly dressed and well shaved. He must visit Philip often, Brecon thought. There was a pleasant scent of Roman Pine about him. Brecon himself did not need to visit a barber's shop. He had grown a beard on his voyage from Sicily to Rome. One of Claudia's slaves cut his hair for him. It was quite dark now but his beard was reddish and curly like his hair. He looked, he felt sure, very different from the boy who had waited on Publius Cornelius in Philip's shop.

Yet Publius Cornelius fixed his keen gray eyes on Brecon and asked, "Haven't I seen you before somewhere?"

"I've been here only a few weeks," Brecon said.

Marcus said to his cousin, "The last time you were here, Breconides was being captured by pirates. And it's lucky for me he was because he is making my legs well. Soon I shall try standing with no braces—just my crutches."

Brecon said that Marcus was making his own legs well.

"The doctor who taught me the small amount I know used to say that a wound's cured from inside not from outside. Marcus Cornelius is growing better because he has a mind full of patience and courage."

"Yes," Publius Cornelius said, "but I still agree with Marcus that he is lucky you are here."

He and Claudia had business about the estate to talk over. Brecon and Marcus went out to a sunny terrace. Marcus moved slowly with his crutches and braces but he managed the distance, the longest he had walked without stopping to rest. Brecon set up the sand table in the sunshine, and they did problems in geometry until the warmth of the sun began to fade and shadows began to fill the city below them.

The next time Publius Cornelius came, he brought Marcus a book of Aesop's fables, written in Greek.

"You will soon read Greek better than I do," he told Marcus.

The next morning Marcus began to read the story of the Fox and the Crow. By the time Publius made his next visit, Marcus had made some verses that told the story.

"They are rather bad," he told his cousin, "but you will have to hear them because you brought me the book. First—as Breconides would say—I will say them in Greek, then in Latin.

Young Master Crow sat up in a tree,
Eating a chunk of cheese, was he.
Clever old Fox, he came along
And asked the Crow to sing him a song.
"Your feathers are splendid," he said, "they glisten.
If your voice is as fine, I'd love to listen!"
The Crow, much flattered by words like these,
Opened his beak and dropped the cheese.
Fox quickly snapped it up and said:
"Now get this lesson into your head—
If you swallow flattery without sense,
The flatterers live at your expense.
This is wisdom for earth and trees.
Worth silver and gold—as well as cheese."
A little too late the Crow now said
"I won't be caught again unfed.
Whether you meet them in trees or on rocks I
See that with foxes you have to be foxy."

Publius Cornelius clapped his hands together and said, "I must have a copy of that, Marcus. There's a lesson for me in it. People in Rome who don't know the Pyrenees from the Pillars of Hercules say, 'You know all about Spain, Publius Cornelius.' All I know about Spain is that a big army can starve there and a small one can be surrounded and destroyed by one of the Barca brothers."

"Did you like Spain?" Brecon asked, and then thought, What a stupid question!

He had asked it because he had felt suddenly homesick for his old stone house, for the strange paintings on the walls of the cave, even for his grandmother's voice telling him to comb his hair. He would have liked to ask a hundred more questions, but he knew he must not show his interest.

Publius Cornelius said, "Oh, it would be a useful bridge to Africa, if the Barcas were somewhere else. But—perhaps we shall learn that with foxes you have to be foxy," he added and patted Marcus on the shoulder.

Scipio's father and uncle did not learn about Punic foxes in time. Their armies were caught separately by the Barcas. Masinissa, the Numidian prince Sophonisba had admired so much, brought his horsemen to help them. Gisgo led another army against them. Both Scipio brothers, with most of their troops, were killed.

This news did not come secretly to Brecon. He heard it in the Forum when he went into the city to do errands for Claudia. The crowds were frightened. "More Punics will cross the Alps," they said.

He heard it a dozen times as he walked to the shop where he bought parchment for Marcus to write on.

"And Gracchus!" another groaned. "I never thought Hannibal would catch Gracchus in a trap."

Gracchus, a dashing leader of cavalry, had been caught in a river, where he was bathing, and killed. Poemula, who commanded two legions, vowed to find Hannibal and kill him. He found him but came back without his legions.

"But Marcellus is still the Sword of Rome," men said. "The Punic can't hold out against Marcellus."

They sounded, Brecon thought, rather as if they were whistling to keep their courage up.

"Young Scipio will save us," others said, but they were told, "He spoke foolishly in the Forum. Fabius Maximus said so."

What Scipio had said in the Forum was, "You talk only of Hannibal, but Carthage is your enemy. Attack Carthage."

A senator had replied, "Hannibal is a week's march away. Carthage is across the sea, Publius Cornelius."

Then Scipio had said, "Yes, but if we attack Carthage, who but Hannibal will come to defend it. For eight years he had defended Carthage by attacking Rome. We ought to learn a lesson from him."

Rome was not ready to learn the lesson, but they did elect Scipio Proconsul and send him to Spain. He could at least, the senators thought, keep the Barcas from crossing the Alps.

CHAPTER 15

AT THE GATES

NEWS CAME over the grapevine that a Roman army was besieging Capua, that Numidians had dashed out of the city and had almost broken the siege, that Hannibal and his elephants had done much damage to the Romans but had not driven them from their trenches.

Claudia and her family were back at the villa when this news came. The peddler who brought it was Lucius Tarchon. He and Brecon did not greet each other. Lucius said to Piccus, the steward, that he had been to Capua but had left because of the siege. After that all Brecon had to do was to listen to the steward's questions and Lucius's answers.

"What else is the Punic doing?" Piccus asked.

"Well," Lucius said, "he sends messages by fire from one hill to the next. You never can tell what they say till the next disaster. Strange things happen. A Roman commander received a letter written in good Latin and sealed with a Roman seal. The letter warned him not to go to a certain place on a certain day, or he would meet destruction. He scorned fear, went, and was slain."

Piccus shifted his feet uneasily and asked, "Is that all?"

Lucius said that another commander was warned that the Punics would cross the river near his camp. He laughed because the river was in flood. But the Punics crossed it—on a bridge of boats. Their men brought the boats on oxcarts. The oxcarts crossed on the bridge. Then the carts carried off the boats. The boats were full of spoils, some of them from the commander's camp. They say too, Lucius added, that when he has broken the siege of Capua he will march on Rome.

After the peddler had left the courtyard of the villa, Brecon said to the steward, "Will you see that Marcus Cornelius gets back to his room. I forgot that I need new straps for my shoes. I must catch the peddler before he goes too far. Smooth out the sand on the table, Marcus Cornelius. I will be back soon for our geometry lesson."

He hurried after Lucius. They had not seen each other alone for months.

"We could talk all day," Brecon said, picking up some shoe straps. "Tell me quickly—he is really coming? When?"

"Soon," Lucius said. "He's across the Volturnus already, elephants and all. He wants it known he's planning to attack Rome so the besiegers of Capua will come and fight him in the open. Or that the legions in Rome will."

"They won't," Brecon said. "Fabius Maximus is in command in the city. Tell him that."

"Anything else?"

"Yes. Ask him if I may leave here and join him again."

"He knew you'd ask that," Lucius said. "The answer is no. He needs you here. He also sent you a warning. Alain—he says you will know whom he means—has gone over to the Romans. He helped betray Syracuse to Marcellus. He may be in Rome. Be sure he does not find out who you are—and—there is someone coming—watch out for elephants on this road, soon, soon—oh, the shoe straps are too short, sir? Sorry sir! I'll bring longer ones next time I come."

Piccus hurried up to them, out of breath.

"Marcus Cornelius sent me for shoe straps for him too, Breconides," he panted. "Says he will walk soon. Needs new straps."

"Take these," Brecon said. "They are all he has left and they are too short for me."

Piccus paid for them and said to Lucius, "Do you believe he will come?"

"Hannibal? This young man just asked me that. I'll say again what I told him. Watch out for elephants!"

"How soon?"

"Within a week he'll be at the gates," Lucius said, and started his donkey toward the road.

Brecon said, "I can't believe it."

"I believe it," Piccus said.

They were not thinking of the same thing. What Brecon could not believe was that anyone, even Alain, could be disloyal to Hannibal.

The news that Hannibal would march on Rome traveled fast, as he meant it to do. From all the countryside men hurried to the city to be safe behind its walls. Claudia received a message from Marcellus urging her to go to the city. They set off immediately. Marcus rode Starlight, with Piccus beside him on an old gray horse. Even the slaves who were gathering in the grain went. They took grain with them. Mules carried it and skins of wine and of newly pressed olive oil. As they came near the city, the road was crowded with people from other villas. The women, like Claudia, rode in oxcarts with furniture around them—lamps, figures of the household gods from the shrine, blankets, earthenware. Claudia even had her loom on a separate wagon.

Brecon walked, carrying his old leather sack with his clothes and books in it. When they were within a mile of the city, the crowd filled the road and they could only move forward a foot at a time. It was dark long before they passed through the city gate where blazing torches dazzled their eyes.

The next day Brecon went to the Forum. The name Hannibal seemed to blow through it with the smoke of burning villages. The speakers had seen the red glow last night in the south. This morning the south wind brought the smoke. You could smell it even in the Forum.

"Hannibal did not dare to do this even after Cannae," men said. "He must have had a great victory at Capua. Our armies must have been destroyed."

Brecon saw an old man standing just outside the Senate house. He heard someone say, "There's Fabius—Fabius Maximus. Let's listen to him."

In all Brecon's visits to the Forum, he had never seen Fabius. Now he could see him and hear his voice—a voice surprisingly loud and clear to come from such a frail-looking, stooped old man. Brecon could see the warts on his face and the woolly hair, white now, that had given him the nickname of Lambkin when he was a schoolboy.

Fabius was saying to the men around him, "You ask me why I do not send to the armies at Capua to come and save Rome. With Jupiter's help we shall save it—never fear. We have ten thousand soldiers to man our walls. Has Hannibal ever taken a large city by siege? What makes you think he will storm the walls of Rome? He has not come for that but to make us think so and call our troops from Capua. We will not call them."

The people around Fabius were calmed by his words but women with their hair unbound still sobbed and prayed in the temples, and the words "Hannibal at the gates" were still a terrifying sound along the dark crowded dirty streets. No one, Brecon noticed, ever said "gate." It was always "gates," as if he could be everywhere at once.

After several days the watchers on the walls saw villages burning along the Tiber, northeast of the city. This brought new terror. It meant that Hannibal was not in the south, where everyone had thought he was. He had in fact swung widely around the city and was now encamped not far from the walls.

This day, so terrible for the whole city, was for Claudia Scipio one of the happiest of her life.

Marcus Cornelius walked across the terrace of the house on the Palatine without his crutches.

He carried a cane in his hand but he never once touched it to the ground. Hannibal and danger to Rome were forgotten. Slaves gathered around clapping their hands and laughing. Two of them, sturdy reapers of grain, snatched Brecon up and carried him in triumph in a chair made by their hard arms, shouting, "Breconides, the good physician, great magician!"

He struggled to get down but they were too strong for him. They carried him all along the terrace while the other slaves joined in clapping and chanting, "Good physician—great magician!"

At last they set him down before Claudia and, at Piccus's orders, went back to their work.

Claudia said, "There is no use my trying to thank you, Breconides. I am sorry I do not have the record of your freedom to give you today. It is at the villa. I was so sure it would be needed that Publius Cornelius wrote it on parchment before he left and we both signed it. You are free from this moment. I hope you will not leave us but stay on as tutor to Marcus Cornelius. At a salary, of course," she added, and named a generous one.

Brecon thanked her and said he would gladly stay for a time.

"Sometime before long I would like to visit my friends again. And today I ask your permission to go to the villa and get it— the parchment with the words of my freedom written on it."

"A dangerous journey at this time," Claudia said.

"But I would make it in freedom."

She asked him if his days of slavery had been so unhappy.

"No," Brecon said, "they have been some of the happiest of my life."

"I will not try to stop you," Claudia said. "Piccus shall go with you to the gate and tell the guards you are going on an errand for me. But go into the Forum first and learn the latest news about Hannibal. If the danger seems too great, I trust you not to go out to the villa."

"Take me with you, good physician, great magician," said Marcus, getting up from the bench where he had been resting.

"Not today, Marcus Cornelius, not today!" his mother said, and Brecon added, "You must stay and take care of things while I am gone."

He found men laughing in the Forum. Even Quintus Fabius Maximus was laughing. A dealer in land had just put up the site of Hannibal's camp at auction. It had been sold at a good price.

"I will send a messenger to Hannibal to tell him so," the purchaser shouted. "He must either get off my land or pay rent."

"What rent are you going to charge?" called a high-pitched voice from someone behind Brecon.

There was a burst of laughter. Brecon stood as if he had been turned to bronze. He did not need to look to see whose voice it was. No one but Alain had that peevish twang. Yes, it was certainly Alain, now calling again, "What rent? What rent?"

"An elephant a year!" shouted the purchaser and the crowd roared with laughter again.

Alain took up more space than ever. He smelled of musk and roses. He was wearing Roman armor, including a helmet with bristling red plumes rising from it. It made him look seven feet high.

And I threw that giant! Brecon thought. He smells like a goat with a wreath of roses around his neck. Oh—I know! He gets shaved by Philip. An important customer. Uses Cream of Roses.

"If I am to be back before dark, I must go," he said to Piccus.

The road to the villa was almost empty now. Brecon moved fast along it until he could see the villa. No smoke rose from the fields or buildings around it, he was glad to see, though he had passed scorched fields and charred houses. He cut across the golden stubble of wheat fields, made his way under the twisted branches of olive trees and across the vineyard, where young elm trees carried the weight of the vines and their purple fruit. Then he went over fields of cabbages, turnips, and beets. Beyond them cattle and sheep were grazing in the hillside pastures as peacefully as if Hannibal were no nearer than Capua.

Brecon thought, He might have burned the villa and destroyed the crops. He spared it all on purpose.

There were two old Greeks, brothers, freed slaves, who had refused to go to the city. They were in the garden picking broccoli.

"It's just right," they told Brecon.

They had a habit of saying the same thing. Sometimes they

both spoke at once. Sometimes one repeated what the other had just said. It was rather like listening to two crows talking, Brecon thought.

"Broccoli must be picked before the yellow flowers come," they told him. "Marcus Cornelius likes it—likes it, he does. You must take back a basket for young master—for young master. How is he?"

"He walked," Brecon said, "all alone, without a stick, even."

"A miracle—magic—magic—Hermes. Breconides should carry a winged staff, brother. Yes, brother—a caduceus with wings and a twisted snake. We should make one for him. The wings of a cock would do—where is the old rooster we killed for supper? Here is a snake!"

The old man plunged his hand into a grassy place between two rocks and came up with about a foot and a half of twisting brown snake.

"Let him go," Brecon said, laughing. "I'd rather have broccoli."

"Yes—yes—broccoli—basket. Something else? You are right, brother—The bag, the letter—From Marcellus—from Marcus Claudius Marcellus—Yesterday—came yesterday..."

Brecon said, "I must find something in the house, a casket for the mistress. "It's in the atrium. Is the bag with the letter there too?"

"Yes—yes—in the atrium—unlock the door, brother. The key—you have it—no, I have it."

When Brecon started back to the city he was carrying the leather sack from Marcellus, a basket of broccoli, and a small bag with the casket in it.

And in the casket, he thought, freedom, freedom! I never knew I had it till I lost it. It's like water, you don't miss it till the spring runs dry."

This time he kept to the road. It dipped into a valley, rose, dipped, and rose again. Then below him were tents, a stream with men bathing in it, Numidian horses grazing, elephants squirting water over each other. Beyond them the stream met the yellow Tiber, which looped away toward the walls of Rome.

He started running, ran until two Africans with sharp spears barred his way at the gate of the camp. He knew them and called them by name, but they did not know him.

"How do you know our names?" one asked scowling.

"Because we crossed the Alps together. I'm Brecon of the Leopard Skin. Why, we poured vinegar on the hot rock together. And you were there when we brought the wild boar to the gate at Tarentum. Take me to my Lord Hannibal—he'll know me."

At last they were convinced. They called other guards to the gate and took him to Hannibal's tent, talking all the way about old times in a mixture of Greek, Libyan, Latin, and Phoenician.

"Why, you are just a boy when we pour that vinegar. No wonder we don't know you, Leopard Spot. You have such a beard. How old now?"

"Almost twenty-two," Brecon said proudly.

"Great age, great age! Like to be back in Africa and twenty-two."

"What would you do?"

"Just nothing at all, Leopard Spot, nothing at all. Find little oasis. Lie around. Eat dates. You come see us."

When they reached Hannibal's tent, there was a guard, another African, walking up and down in front of it.

"Lord Hannibal, he's asleep," he told them. "No sleep for three nights. I must not disturb him unless it's important. Is this man important?"

"He's *mighty* important," they told him.

"No, I'm not," Brecon said. "I'll wait." But he did not have to.

"I know that voice," he heard Hannibal say, and in a moment there he was, with his old cloak over his shoulders, bright-eyed as if he had never needed sleep.

"The disguise is good," he said, "but I see through it. The beard pulls off, I suppose"—he gave it a tweak—"why it's real! And an extra foot of height, shoulders inches wider, hair's new color, voice deeper, but there's still a good Iberian twang in it."

As it always was with Hannibal, Brecon thought, they might have seen each other yesterday. With one look he seemed to understand Brecon's life—everything he had done, seen, cared about.

"So young Marcus can walk and you have your freedom! Yes, you see, I keep an eye on you. I heard it before noon today... Yes, you may come to me, but not until I send for you. I hope Hasdrubal, my brother, will cross the Alps soon. When he does you must join him. You know, I think, how it would help me to have Hasdrubal in Italy. All three of us were always good friends, but I always felt more than twice as strong with Hasdrubal beside me."

They talked about Marcellus.

"He and Fabius," Hannibal said, "are the Romans who have given me the most trouble. Fabius is my schoolmaster, always setting me some unpleasant task. Marcellus is a wrestler who changes his hold on me. Fabius keeps me from getting into mischief. Marcellus does me damage. When he is defeated he doesn't know it but goes on fighting. When he is victorious he gives his enemy no rest, takes none himself. He is well called the Sword of Rome. I have not met him yet on an open field," he added thoughtfully.

"Will you attack Rome?" Brecon asked.

"You know the answer to that as well as Fabius does," Hannibal said. "I have no siege engines. Archimedes is dead. And perhaps not even he would have thought how to break these walls."

They talked for a long time. Hannibal told Brecon that the night before he and a dozen of his men had crossed the Tiber and ridden all around the city. There was a pale hazy moon with drifting clouds over it, he said. They had ridden elephants and far enough from the walls so that if the guards had seen them, they would have been only gray shadows among other shadows. No one challenged them.

"I hear that in the city the women are all sobbing, 'Hannibal at the gates!' Last night that was true. I was within a javelin's cast of every gate. At one of them—the Collina Gate, they call it—I could hear the guards snoring. I did something foolish. I took a javelin and cast it over the wall. Then I rode away. That is my attack on Rome!"

He was silent for a moment and then asked, "Is it true that in the Forum today they sold this campsite for a good price?"

"Yes," Brecon said. "I was there." Hannibal smiled.

"I like that," he said. "Roman bravado—well, they shall have some from Carthage before I go."

"Let me go with you, cousin," Brecon pleaded.

"Not yet. I need you here. You have done well. Carthalo greets you and says he is proud of you. After Hasdrubal comes, things will be different. And I promise to send for you before if I need you. The message will say 'Come' and the name of the place. I warned you about Alain," Hannibal said. "You got the message?"

"Yes," Brecon said, "and I saw him today. And knew him partly by his Spanish twang," he added smiling. "I must be careful of my own. I must speak more like a Capuan, a Capuan who is discussing Plato's Republic after eating turbot cooked in cream with fresh asparagus and lifting a cup of Falernian wine."

He imitated the voice of a well-fed Capuan and made Hannibal smile, but only for a moment.

He said seriously, "This means that we have lost Capua. I hoped the Romans would break the siege and follow me. There would have been another Cannae if they had."

"Fabius warned them that you wanted them to attack you."

"Ah, my Roman schoolmaster, I might have known," said Hannibal.

"Why did Alain turn traitor?" Brecon asked.

"Because he has decided Rome will win," Hannibal said quietly. "I once heard my father say this: 'Win a victory—even your enemies will join you. Lose a battle—even your friends will leave you.'"

"Not all friends, I think," Brecon said.

"No, there are always a few a man can trust. But there is some truth in the saying. Alain is more Roman than the Romans now, I expect."

"Yes," Brecon said. "You should see his helmet! And he's smeared with scent from a Roman barber shop. It was only a little shop once. Now it's moved and is one of the most fashionable and expensive in the Forum."

Hannibal said, "When Hasdrubal comes, we may find Alain crawling back saying it was all a mistake—that the Romans dragged him off as a prisoner. I'm glad he's gone, and others like him. But look out for him. He must not recognize you. Speak like a Capuan."

"Better like a Roman, perhaps. I'll get Marcus to teach me. I must go back to him," Brecon said, but he did not go. He sat there in silence a moment and then said, "It must seem strange to you that I am doing all I can to train up a healthy, intelligent Roman soldier."

Hannibal said, "I prefer honorable Romans to traitors of any race. Before Marcus grows up I hope Rome and Carthage will be at peace."

"There is something else I feel strange about," Brecon said. "I have a letter here in this bag from Marcellus to Claudia. I feel I should give it to you. Yet I have another loyalty now—to Claudia. I feel I cannot open a private letter of hers. But—here it is."

Hannibal took it, turned it over in his long, slender hands, looked at the seal, and handed the letter back to Brecon.

"I can't open it either," he said. Then he laughed and added, "But of course I'm sure what's in it anyway. He's warning her that the Punic Fox will destroy her villa out of particular spite toward him. And for once he's mistaken."

"Yes," Brecon said, "he is, and thank you."

Hannibal nodded and changed the subject.

"Can you tell me something about young Scipio?" he asked.

"I like him," Brecon said. "But he's the only Roman who frightens me."

"Why?"

Brecon told him about Marcus' Fox and Crow verses and repeated them.

"Publius Cornelius kept quoting that last line," he said. "After a while there was a little tune that he sang it to. Oh, I know it was to amuse Marcus, but there was something more to it. He was whistling it the last time he was here, just before he left for Spain. He's not like other Romans. He looked Fabius straight in the eye and told him he ought to attack not you but Carthage. Fabius is angry with him. Most Romans would be afraid of Fabius, but not Publius Cornelius. He's different."

"Not like anyone you've ever seen?" Hannibal asked.

"Yes, cousin. Like you."

Brecon circled widely around Hannibal's camp, cut across scorched fields, and got back on the road again. He had reached the city and was waiting to pass through the gate when a party of Numidians came up behind him. They carried a flag of truce.

One of Hannibal's Iberian trumpeters was with them. He blew a loud blast on his trumpet.

From the wall above the gate a Roman trumpeter replied and, when the notes stopped echoing, bellowed, "State your business, Punic."

The Iberian called out: "I come from Lord Hannibal, commander of the armies of Carthage, son of Hamilcar Barca, called the Thunderbolt. Lord Hannibal sends to Quintus Fabius Maximus and to other noble Romans this message: 'I will sell to any Roman citizen all the shops in the Forum.'"

The soldiers on the wall had been listening quietly. Now they burst into furious shouting. The trumpeter went on and in spite of the tumult completed his message, stating the price in silver, the terms of sale (immediate delivery) and asked, "Is there a purchaser?" Then, hearing only insults and angry yells, he lowered his flag, wrapped it around the staff and rode off toward Hannibal's camp. When the guards looked out at dawn the next day, Hannibal had gone.

CHAPTER 16

FREEDOM

BRECON STOOD leaning against Claudia's loom while she read her brother's letter aloud to him. He was too tired to move across the room to a bench. He might fall before he reached it, he thought.

The letter began with a repeated warning to Claudia to leave the villa, which Hannibal would certainly attack out of personal spite against Marcellus, and take shelter behind the walls of Rome. However, there was much more than that in the letter. It described the many kinds of treasures that were on the way from Syracuse to Rome. There were statues and painted vases from Greece, glass from Egypt, robes of purple and gold from Tyre, carved ivory and ebony, gold and silver goblets, ropes of pearls.

"I am sending to Marcus Cornelius," he wrote, "something that will interest him especially, I think. It is a globe of the world made by Archimedes. For you, Claudia, I send two bowls of bronze and gold. They are of Greek workmanship. They came from the palace of Archimedes.

"I know little of such things, but a young artist of Syracuse, now one of my slaves, says they are very fine. They are wrapped in cloth of Tyrian weaving. It may interest you since you spend so much time at your loom."

The bowls were wrapped in purple cloth with a pattern of gold thread woven into it. Brecon was quite sure how the bowls would look. He felt as if he could see them through the cloth. Yes—there they were with the border of grape leaves and fruit and the procession of gold figures on bronze. The globe too, he knew. He could see Archimedes lift it from its stand and trace with his fingertip the river Nile or point to Gades on the Ocean Sea. The Alps were there too, Brecon knew, and the countries of the East where Alexander marched and the coast of Africa where Phoenicians threw down glass beads and picked up wedges of gold. The globe was gold too, but the metal was thin.

Not worth melting down, he thought bitterly. Not worth wrecking a city for, hardly worth killing an old mathematician for.

He felt suddenly dizzy. Had he felt so all day? He couldn't remember. He knew only that he was burning one minute and shivering the next.

He heard Claudia say, "You look ill, Breconides." She laid her hand on his forehead. "Yes, you have fever. The air of Rome is unhealthy at this time of year. Go to bed. I will send you a healing drink."

Marcus said proudly, "Just lean on my shoulder, Breconides. It's my turn now."

That was the last thing he remembered for a long time.

Days and nights slipped away. They were much the same in his dark room, where mosquitoes buzzed angrily at night and owls called in the cypress trees. Marcus used to tell him the news but it never seemed real, only like part of the bad dream that went on and on in his mind. Sometimes he seemed to know things long before they happened. Sometimes things from the distant past happened where he could see and hear them.

He saw Hannibal, nine years old, standing near an altar and heard him say, "I will never be a friend to the Roman people."

He saw the gates of Capua open and the Romans march in. Many Capuan senators had died or were dying of poison they had taken. The Romans cut off the heads of those who were still alive. They cut off the hands of Numidian javelin throwers. Romans called Hannibal cruel, he remembered. Hannibal at the gates... at the gates... And the spoils of Capua will be rich and beautiful.

He saw Publius Cornelius at New Carthage. He had found out about what tide and offshore wind would do to the lagoon. So one day his main army attacked the city on the land side. While the guards were trying to fight off the Romans on that side, Publius Cornelius led a picked group of men with ladders across the lagoon. Brecon heard them splashing. He tried to warn the city. No one heard. They waded across safely and climbed the ladders (no giant claws, no wall bristling with spears) and... the spoils of New Carthage would be rich and beautiful... "I see that with foxes you have to be foxy."

Then one day Marcus was crying. Because his uncle was dead. Marcellus? Dead? There was a hill. Hannibal was behind it... with Numidians. There was a depression like a sunken roadway... between Marcellus and the hill... Punics... watching. Numidians, dashing in from both sides, caught Romans in the hollow. Speared Marcellus... body burned... ashes sent to his family... Greek jar was... beautiful.

Another day—was this before or after Marcellus died? Brecon could not remember—he knew (he saw this too) Fabius

Maximus seized Tarentum during a feast by treachery (they were eating tarantulas at the feast dipped in batter, fried in olive oil... delicious), and of course the spoils of the city would look beautiful in Rome. Only tarantulas crawled on the wall. He said, "Don't let them bite me," and Hannibal said, "Now Rome has a Hannibal!" He meant Fabius, Brecon knew, but he heard a cold, toneless voice say "Rome has a Hannibal" and a gay young voice whistling a tune and singing "You have to be foxy."

No, Brecon thought, Not Fabius but Publius Cornelius Scipio—twenty-six years old, Hannibal's age when he took command of the army of Spain—he is Rome's Hannibal. I must tell Hannibal.

His fever had not been bad for a day or two but it was worse that night and for a long time afterwards. He did not know how long he had been ill but one day he said to Marcus Cornelius, "This war, almost nine years now," and Marcus had laughed and said, "Almost ten years, Breconides."

When spring came he was well enough to go to the villa with the family, but his fever came back if he walked too far or got chilled or wet. Claudia scolded him, in kindness, he knew. The bad-tasting doses he had to swallow were given in kindness too. He took them but he wished Synhalus were there. Where was he? Brecon wondered.

One thing that made him happy was seeing Marcus walk and even run without a sign of a limp.

Brecon said to Claudia one day, "Marcus Cornelius ought to go to school with other boys. Play games. Learn Roman oratory. He'll be a senator someday. Perhaps a consul."

Claudia said, "But not quite yet. Next year perhaps."

Life at the villa went on that year, the tenth year of the war, without the news Brecon hoped for. He was well enough now, he felt sure, to find his way to Hasdrubal Barca if a message came telling him that Hasdrubal was on his way to cross the Alps. But the message did not come. During his illness Lucius Tarchon had managed the grapevine and still did most of the work. Now the peddlers had begun to visit the villa again. They brought no special news. They said that things were quiet in southern Italy. Hannibal had settled down in the toe of the Italian boot. There was no Roman commander who dared to attack him.

"He has a kingdom there bigger than Carthage," Lucius Tarchon said on one of his visits. "So long as he stays there quietly no one is going to interfere with him."

On his next visit Lucius had a sad piece of news about Hannibal. He had a port now to which galleys came from Carthage. One of them had brought Hannibal a letter from Gisgo. It told him that Imilce and his son Hamilcar had both died of a plague that had run through the city.

Brecon had a return of his fever that night. He woke suddenly, found Marcus sitting beside him.

"You called," Marcus said. "So I came. You've been talking a lot, but not in Greek. I couldn't understand you though you did say 'Athena' several times. The owls were hooting a lot last night—perhaps that's why you thought of Athena and her owl."

"Perhaps," Brecon said.

"There was another Greek name you said. It sounded like 'Sophonisba.'"

"Do I usually talk much when I have fever?" Brecon asked.

"No. I've heard you say 'Athena' before and 'Where is your owl?' and 'Hannibal at the gates!' But everyone in Rome does that. The nurses all frighten children by saying, 'Hannibal is at the gates and will get you if you're not good!'"

"A splendid way to make them sleep well at night!"

Marcus laughed.

"You sound so cross," he said. "You must be better."

He was better. He was always better at the villa than in Rome. He hated the dirty city, where pigs ran around in the streets. The streets were so narrow that if a mule train met a funeral, the drivers would fight with their fists to decide which should back up and let the other pass. Many of the insulae, the apartment houses, were badly built. One night one fell down, killing many of the people in the crowded rooms.

In the Forum, near Philip's barber shop, Brecon heard a high, peevish voice with an Iberian accent say, "What of it if it did fall down. They were beggars anyway. Haven't we got enough beggars?"

This time Brecon met Alain face to face.

"And enough Greek slaves too," Alain added shouldering Brecon aside and swaggering off in a great gust of musk and he-goat and roses.

A voice said quietly, "Better walk on. Don't stand looking like that."

It was Lucius Tarchon. He still worked for the jeweler, who was one of Brecon's men. He had seen the encounter from the shop window. They walked along in silence through the jostling crowd until they reached a quiet place near the city wall where they could talk.

Brecon asked, "Why did he call me a Greek slave?"

"You are dressed like a Greek. Your beard is trimmed in the Greek fashion. You are carrying a schoolboy's satchel and writing tablets. You are a boy's Greek tutor and look like one—as you mean to do. No need to turn crimson with rage and stare after him with your fists clenched."

"I think he knows me," Brecon said. "I think someone has told him how I look, what I do, where I live."

"All the more reason not to let him know you know him."

"You are right, of course, Lucius. Since my fever I find myself growing angry easily. I must do better. Have you news—of the vintage?"

"Yes, I would have come to the villa today if I had not seen you. The grapes are ripe... Turn around. Face me, lean against the wall and smile as if I were telling you about a wrestling match or inviting you to eat oysters with me. There are people a little way off near the wall... *The younger thunderbolt has passed the city with the lagoon and is on his way to the vinegar rock. Set out for...* Forgive me, sir. I did not see you coming... Yes, oysters are in season now and we'll follow them with a roasted piglet two months old..."

"With broccoli," Brecon said, smiling. "Delicious!"

The passers-by were out of earshot now. Brecon added, "Set out for Trebbia? Or Ticino? When?"

"Soon," Lucius said. "We'll go together with the peddler's cart. Meet me in a week's time... more people coming..."

"Yes," Brecon said. "I always enjoy the first oysters. But you must come out to the villa soon. Eat a roasted capon with beans and bacon... They've gone—where shall we meet?"

"At the tomb," Lucius said. "Where we first met. We'd better separate now. Go toward your gate. I'll go back to the Forum."

He was off with a quick wave of his hand. He looked, Brecon thought, rather like one of the dancers on the wall of the Tarquin tomb.

They knew Brecon well at the gate now. The young tutor,

once a slave of the Scipios, now a freedman, came and went often between the villa and the city.

Perhaps, he thought, after the guards had waved him on, I should have gone by another gate. Suppose Alain comes and asks if the Greek tutor of the Scipios has gone through and they say, "Yes, Breconides has just passed"? Why did I take a name so much like my own? Yes, I know Carthalo gave it to me but I could have changed it. Laziness—spies shouldn't be lazy. And I showed anger when he pushed me. I am a fool.

He walked quickly along the road toward the villa. It was crowded with carts coming back from market.

I'll leave the road soon and cut across the fields, he thought. But first I'll sit on that rock and take a stone out of my shoe so these carters will not see me leave the road. Then I'll edge down to the brook.

While the road was empty for a moment he crossed the little stream that ran beside the road, climbed the bank, and hid himself among ferns and young beech trees. Their big leaves, the ferns, and some tangled vines made a good shelter. For a long time he heard only the creaking of wheels and the shouts of drivers urging oxen and donkeys forward. Then from the city came a group of horsemen. One of the riders wore a red-plumed helmet.

Brecon thought, Alain, and then shrugged off the thought by asking himself, Is Alain the only man in Rome with a Roman helmet?

The clatter of hoofs came nearer on the hard road. There was shouting and cursing as the oxcarts moved on in ruts worn in the stone, not making way for the horsemen. At last the riders turned and followed a dusty path along the edge of the road. They came so close to Brecon that he could smell Cream of Roses mixed with the smell of sweating horses.

He recognized not only Alain but also a young man about Alain's age called Cato. "Piggy" Cato they called him in the Forum because of his bristling sandy hair, his light eye lashes and snoutlike nose and his stinginess.

Brecon heard Cato's harsh, grating voice as he rode past. "Yes," he said. "Carthage must be destroyed, I always say."

Alain was agreeing with him as they rode over the hill.

Brecon stayed in his hiding place until the sun began to set. Then he cut across the fields to the villa. Everything was quiet there, but in the lane were the hoof marks of half a dozen horses, going toward the villa and then back to the road.

Claudia was at her loom. The maids were bringing in the supper. He could smell cabbage and beans with bacon and freshly baked bread. There was new honey to put on the bread, green olives, a jug of wine and one of goat's milk. Fowls were simmering in a big kettle.

Claudia left her weaving and asked Brecon to sit down and tell her the results of his visit to the city. He had gone to visit a school Publius Cornelius had recommended for Marcus. Publius wanted Breconides to talk with the master before they decided. Brecon had liked him. He was a Greek, once a slave in the family of Publius Cornelius, now a freedman.

"He seems to teach more by words than by beating," Brecon said. "Oh, there was a rod with birch twigs bound to it in the corner, but it looked rather dry and dusty."

"What were the boys doing?" Claudia asked.

"They were playing games when I was there. They have a good open field near the school. They wrestle and play ball and throw the discus and the javelin. They learn to read and write and to speak well on their feet. They do geometry and recite Homer. The master would like to teach them music but the parents felt that was not Roman so he gave up the idea."

"You feel it is right for Marcus Cornelius?"

"Yes. I showed the schoolmaster, Cleon, things Marcus Cornelius had written and his work in geometry. He says the work is good. I told Cleon I would advise your sending Marcus there. He can ride Starlight, and one of the slaves—I would suggest Alpheus—can ride with him until you move to town for the winter."

"Alpheus?" Claudia said. "You will not go with him yourself?"

"Tomorrow, yes," Brecon said. "But he needs me no longer as a master. And I—would like to travel a little, visit a friend near Placentia. I would like to leave in a week. If my doing so will not trouble you."

Claudia said quietly, "I have known for a long time that the break must come. You have been generous to give us so much of your freedom. Do you know what day this is, Breconides?"

Brecon shook his head.

"It is five years today since you came here and found Marcus sitting helpless in that chair. I promised you your freedom. You earned it and have earned it many times over since that day. Don't think that I would try to stop your using it now. Go—but remember this will always be your home."

Brecon said, "I shall not forget and I thank you for all your kindness, especially when I was ill."

"I would like to give you something from this house," Claudia said. "Will you take one of the bronze bowls that belonged to Archimedes? You said they were the most beautiful you had ever seen."

Brecon shook his head, smiling.

"I thank you. Call one of them mine and I will drink from it when I come again. They are twins, like Castor and Pollux, and should stay together always. I'll carry the picture of it in my mind. And the books of Archimedes—I have them in my mind too. I will leave the rolls for Marcus. Perhaps he will be a great engineer someday. I think he has a talent for it. Indeed, he has many talents. He can choose, and I think Cleon will help him choose right."

Marcus came in just then. He took a long breath and said, "Supper smells wonderful tonight. Is it a special day?"

"Yes," his mother said.

They spent the meal talking about what made this a day to be celebrated, about Brecon's journey, about the school.

It was not until the maids had carried away the dishes that Marcus said, "We had visitors today."

"Anyone I know?" Brecon asked.

"No, but they asked a lot of questions about you. How long you had been here—how long you would stay—where you came from. Piggy Cato was one of them. He came to buy some turnip seed. He said he heard our turnips were very fine and that it was a cheap way to feed slaves. Mother gave him the turnip seed."

"He gave me a great deal of good advice about farming in exchange," Claudia said. "He sniffed when he smelled fowls cooking and told me that it is very extravagant to let the maids have fowls to eat. They ought to eat at a separate table and have turnips with perhaps a little of the broth. Better still, he said, eat only turnips yourself. That's what he always does. I never cared much for turnips myself," she added.

"He gave me some good advice too," Marcus said. "He saw the old Greek brothers. He said they should have been sold long ago. He said, 'Sell a slave as you would a horse—as soon as his best days of work are over.' I told him the Greeks were freedmen and he said that was all the worse. Nothing ruins an estate sooner than a lot of idle freedmen sitting around in the sun, he says.

"But I'm not going to sell the old slaves," Marcus went on, "or turn the Greeks out or sell Starlight, though he said she would soon be too old to ride. He says if you turn old horses out to grass, they eat food the young working ones need and that it's the same with slaves. I hate him. And that other one who smells like a whole barber shop, I hate him too," Marcus said, pounding his fist on the table.

"Don't use up a lot of good hate on them," Brecon said.

"Well, I do hate them. They laughed at your leopard skin."

Brecon felt a pricking icy chill run along his forearms and down his spine.

"How did they happen to see it?" he asked.

"Oh, they asked to see the globe of Archimedes and I took them into my room. They looked into yours first. The big one in the helmet, he's a Spanish prince, an ally of Rome, he said— well, he picked up the skin off your bed and laughed at it. He said to Cato, 'Pretty luxurious place where the slaves sleep on leopard skins. Still, it's about worn out. You can just see the spots. This spot isn't even fur. Looks like an old blood spot,' he said and tossed it down again. I hate him."

"That will do, Marcus Cornelius," Claudia said, "and it's your bedtime. You must be up early to start for school."

Brecon slept badly. Whenever he woke, he was going over and over Alain's visit in his mind. Alain knew who he was, certainly, but did he know that Brecon knew it? Of course Alain had known for years that Brecon was a messenger for Carthalo and for Hannibal. He must have told his Roman friends so.

Only why haven't they chopped off my head long ago? Brecon thought, turning and twisting. I must get away—tomorrow. No, if they don't see me in the city tomorrow they'll find out I've gone and follow me. *I would just be leading them to Hasdrubal! That's what they want...* I see now... when he laughed at the leopard skin, it was to frighten me into running away. What shall I do? What would Carthalo do?

He fell into an uneasy sleep again. When he got up at dawn, he knew only that he must show in no way that he had been frightened by Alain's visit.

Brecon tethered the horses in the field near the school, left Marcus doing geometry, and took his way through narrow streets to the Forum. He had hoped to see Lucius Tarchon, but he was not in the jeweler's shop or near any of the shops into which Brecon went doing errands for Claudia.

He and Lucius had not arranged to meet.

Probably gone already, Brecon thought. And being followed because he was seen talking to me. Perhaps that's where Alain is today.

He shrugged off his fears for Lucius. After all, Lucius was better able than most people to take care of himself.

Not stupid like me, Brecon thought.

He went into the marketplace and ate his dinner at a cook-shop there, not noticing much what he ate. Perhaps, he thought, Lucius will come past, but there was no sign of him. Brecon did not dare ask for him. The less people connected them, the better it would be for Lucius.

He sat for some time watching the cats around the fish sellers' stalls. He had never seen so many cats. There must be fifty. There was one colored like an old piece of tortoiseshell. She was especially clever at pouncing on the scraps thrown away when the fish was cleaned. She would sit on top of an old wine cask in the sunshine, carefully licking her paws and washing her face. She pretended that she was not in the least interested in anything but her own catlike beauty, but when a fish liver was thrown away she was ready to catch it before it struck the ground. He also noticed a honey-colored cat with darker tiger stripes, almost orange in color. Claudia had once said she would like a yellow cat.

He said to the woman at the fish stall where the yellow cat seemed to be on duty, "Could I buy this cat? For a friend?"

The woman shrugged her shoulders, spread out her hands.

"I sell fish," she said, "not cats. Cats belong to themselves. Take a nice piece of tuna. This one is big. I plan to sell him whole but no one comes. I cut him up. Buy a slice. Two slices. What you like."

"Yes, I will take two slices," Brecon said. Then he thought, That wouldn't be enough for the maids. I won't be like Piggy Cato.

"No, I'll take half of it," he said aloud.

"I throw in the cat too," the fish woman said, "but she come back next morning."

"We have lots of mice at the farm," Brecon said.

"You think we have no mice in the market? And you have fish every day at the farm? No, Goldie knows her own place. That's the great thing in life—know who you are and where you belong, isn't it?"

"Yes," Brecon said, "that—must be so."

"Once I send her up the Tiber in a boat with my brother. Next day who you think is here licking juice out of oyster shells?

H'm? Here, sir, let me have your basket. Cabbage leaves, I put in. Then fish. Cover it with more leaves. See? Keep it cool. Here it is."

Brecon did not take the basket.

He thought, I have it. The Tiber. A boat.

The woman said more loudly, "Your basket, sir."

"I ask your pardon," Brecon said. "I was thinking about the Tiber. I've never been up the river in a boat. Where could I find one?"

The woman gave him full directions for finding her brother. He had boats to rent or sell. He would row customers along the river or take them fishing. He had all sizes of boats.

"One big enough to carry elephant when Hannibal at the gates," she added laughing.

"You're not afraid of him?"

"I wish he come again. Never such prices for fish," she said cheerfully, and added, "Brother's name Lartius. Just say Maria send you."

Marcus had had a wonderful day in school.

"I threw the discus. Not far but I learned to hold it right. I hit the very middle of a target with a dart. I have a friend. His name is Verbenna. His family came from near Lake Trasimeno many years ago. He can run faster than I can and throw the discus, but I beat him with the darts. I helped him with his geometry. I showed him my verses about the Fox and the Crow. He thinks they are wonderful. He can throw a ball so it feels as if you picked up a thunderbolt. I'm going to let him ride Starlight tomorrow. Oh, I like school."

"I'm glad," Brecon said.

"Oh, Breconides, I sounded as if I'd forgotten that without you I never would have gone to school at all. I'll never forget, never. I'd still be carried around in a chair if you hadn't come. If I thanked you ten thousand times, it wouldn't be enough."

"What you just said is enough, Marcus," Brecon said. "Now guess what's in the basket. Twenty questions."

"Animal?... Vegetable?... Mineral?"

"Animal."

Marcus had guessed before they reached the villa. He ran in shouting, "Tunafish for supper. Breconides bought it. Tunafish for everyone."

Claudia said, "Tunafish! That's wonderful. Thank you, Breconides. Oh, I have a message for you. A young peddler, I think he's stopped here before, came. He said he had to go north sooner than he had planned and that your belt with the grapevine pattern was not ready. He says it ought to be ready in a day or two and you can pick it up yourself in the shop near the cemetery."

"Thank you," Brecon said. "It doesn't matter. My old one will do. It was good of him to come though."

While the fish was cooking, he thought over the message. It must mean that Hasdrubal Barca was coming sooner than they had expected. The shop near the cemetery must mean the Tarquin tomb. That, at least, he was sure of.

He thought, I will go as far north as the boatman will take me. Then make my way on foot to Clusium.

He said to Claudia, "Since Marcus likes school so much, I think I'll start on my trip tomorrow. I will ride to school with him, but about his getting home—"

"The cart goes into market," Claudia said. "Alpheus can go with it and ride home with Marcus in the afternoon. The cart can carry your baggage. I will start now to see that you have food for your journey."

"You must not take any trouble," Brecon said.

"I will do as I like about that," said Claudia.

Brecon felt sure she would.

Before dawn, she had packed a bag with bread, cheese, almond cakes, a cold fowl, a ham pickled and smoked according to her own rule. It had been hanging from a beam in the kitchen for a year. She had planned to have it last night for supper, but since they had had tunafish, he had better take it along, she said.

"You spoil your slaves—and freedmen," Brecon said. "What would Cato say?"

"That you ought to eat turnips," Claudia said. "But there are none in the bag, I promise you. Now," she said abruptly, "let's not try to say what we would like to say to each other. It's time for you to start and time I went to my loom. A good journey!"

She turned toward the atrium. Marcus had already ridden out of the courtyard. Brecon followed him.

Into a new world, he thought.

He would have liked to look back once more at the villa, but he kept his face turned toward the city.

CHAPTER 17

GULLY AT TREBBIA

THE JOURNEY began well. Brecon felt sure that no one had followed him from the school to the dock. He lay in the bottom of the boat wrapped in his cloak so that no one from the bridges could see his face.

"Up late last night, early this morning. I'll sleep a little," he said to the boatmen.

"I sing you to sleep," Lartius said.

He sang in a voice like a saw cutting an oak plank. Yet Brecon went to sleep. When he woke, they were well beyond the city. He looked back and saw the city and the walls and the towers golden in the morning light. The road north ran close to the Tiber here. A flock of sheep filled the road solidly like a creamy-white river. Hundreds of tiny feet clicked on the stones. Behind them was a great creaking of oxcarts with drivers shouting and goading the pink-eyed white oxen along.

They ate their dinner in the shade of a great willow. It overhung a little stream that ran into the Tiber. Lartius enjoyed the cold fowl.

"Good change from fish," he said.

In fact it was such a good change that he ate most of it and a large chunk of ham. This ham was supposed to be sliced so thin that you could read Aesop's fables through it; but Lartius, Brecon thought, would not be interested in such an exercise. After dinner he was not interested in rowing farther upstream. Brecon paid him and they parted.

"I take you back to city free," Lartius said. "We drift down singing all the way. I sing—you sing."

"Thank you, but I must go on. Which way to Viterbo?"

Lartius gave elaborate directions to which Brecon did not listen, since he was not going to Viterbo. Lartius almost wept as they parted.

"A beautiful friendship," he said, "but too short. My boat is always yours, sir."

He went off singing. Brecon could hear him when he was far down the stream.

The road was almost empty. Brecon walked until he came to a small village. He never knew its name. There he bought an ancient horse and rode along till darkness came on. Then he turned into a grassy meadow, tethered the horse, and slept on his leopard skin under an oak as big as a ship. The dry leaves whispered, crickets chirped, owls hooted.

He thought, Athena, who takes care of you now?

Then he remembered that he had seen Orion the night before. I'm twenty-four years old and she's seventeen, he thought. I keep thinking she's a child. She's married, probably, and is a good sensible fat matron by now. Claudia was married when she was sixteen. And Sophonisba has a prince by this time, no doubt. But I don't believe she's sensible!

He dozed off and woke thinking, Sensible? Have I been sensible? Well, they haven't caught me yet. And slept again.

Lucius was not at the Tarquin tomb. There was a wax tablet lying on the straw mattress. Brecon carried the tablet to the door. In the last fading light, he could just make out the words "Gully at Trebbia" engraved in the wax. He did not light the lamp, so he did not see the Etruscan dancers in their red cloaks or the pale blue horse.

It was at Trebbia that they caught him, Alain and five others. They were hidden in the gully where Mago and his men had hidden on the day of the battle. Brecon had slowed down to look into the gully for Lucius. They plunged out and were around him before he could urge his tired horse forward.

Alain roared with laughter as his men tied Brecon up to a tall poplar tree.

"So, my interesting old friend with that almost Greek name. You found the tablet inviting you to Trebbia. Wasn't it thoughtful of us to leave it for you?"

Brecon said nothing and Alain went on, "Well, as our dear Lord Carthalo used to say, before we caught and killed him at Tarentum, the best way to follow a fool is to go in front of him. So give us your letter, Prince Brecon of the Leopard Skin."

"I—have no letter," Brecon said.

"Search him, men."

They tore off his tunic. They took his money belt and his pouch with Hannibal's flask in it. They hunted through his bag. There was nothing in it but his clothes and his calendar. He had even left the record of his freedom in Claudia's hands. The leopard skin was on his horse's back.

Alain studied the calendar awhile, then threw it on the ground. There was still a small bundle of almond cakes. Alain ate them while his men tore the soles of Brecon's shoes apart.

Brecon watched what they did as if it were happening to someone else. Above Alain's curses he kept hearing the words "before we caught and killed him at Tarentum."

He had not heard from Carthalo for weeks. This must be why—he was dead. The news was meant to grieve and terrify him, and it did. Because it was true. Alain's casual way of telling it convinced him more than any detailed story would have.

At least they shall not see how they have hurt me, he thought. Or learn anything. At least, my Lord Carthalo, I wrote nothing.

What is not written is never read, you used to say. And what I don't know, I can't tell.

Aloud he said, "Have you been doing any wrestling lately, Alain? Prince Alain, I mean."

Bravado, he thought. I'm a fool. Yes—but he shan't see I'm afraid.

Alain had one of the scourges called "scorpions" in his hand. Now he began to beat Brecon with it, not hard at first, not enough to draw blood, asking him questions between strokes.

"What is your message? What is your message for Hasdrubal?... When is he coming?... By what road?... Tell me, or I shall have to crack the whip a little harder."

"I can't—tell you what I—don't know," Brecon said.

He could not help wincing as the sharp metal fangs of the serpent struck him, but he heard Carthalo's voice say, "It's remarkable how much pain a man can bear. And if it becomes too severe nature steps in and makes him faint. So Synhalus says."

He fainted several times, but he told them nothing. Once when he came to, they were taking time off from their work. They had lighted a fire and were sitting around it, passing a wineskin from hand to hand.

Brecon thought about the flask of poison in his pouch. It was still there but they had dropped the pouch on the ground when they had taken the money out of it. Alain had divided the money among the soldiers. They were throwing dice for it now. The much larger sum in the money belt was his, of course. It would not reach around his waist so he wore it looped around his left shoulder.

Blood was trickling down Brecon's arms and legs. He could

feel it drying on his chest. There was a deep cut over his left eye and the eye was shut.

Perhaps I'm blind in that eye, he thought. But so is Hannibal. Look what he does with only one eye.

"Get back to work, men," Alain said. "Put some more wood on the fire. Get some twigs and branches from the gully. We'll need light. And perhaps we ought to warm our friend up a little. It would be a pity if he caught cold."

They piled faggots and brambles from the gully around him.

"The tree will make a fine torch," Alain said. "Now tell me— when is Hasdrubal coming?... where? Oh, your memory's bad is it? *crack... crack...* Better bring some fire, Quintus."

Quintus came forward with a lighted branch, but he moved slowly.

Why, Brecon thought, he doesn't want to light it!

Before Quintus reached the poplar tree, he dropped the branch.

"Prince Alain," he said, "someone's coming. I hear horses."

Brecon heard them too and trumpets, trumpets made of the horns of Gallic bulls.

Alain and his men ran for their horses. They were tethered farther up the road around the shoulder of the hill near where the trumpets were sounding. For a moment Brecon heard Alain shouting louder than the trumpets. Then light from the blazing fire began to flash on Gallic helmets, on shields, long swords, and breastplates. In a moment the Romans were surrounded. Just how long it took to kill them all, Brecon never knew.

It was Lucius Tarchon who had brought the Gauls. He had been watching for Brecon from a hilltop above the gully when he had seen Alain and his men arrive. Lucius had made his way as fast as he could to the nearest Gallic camp and had brought the troops back with him.

He bound up Brecon's wounds and took him back to the camp, where a woman who reminded him of his grandmother washed the wounds and treated them with herbs and magic spells. At first every motion he made was agony, but there must have been something good about the herbs and the spells. Before long he could see out of both eyes and his wounds had healed.

Still Hasdrubal Barca did not cross the Alps. Before he did so Brecon received on the grapevine from Hannibal the word "Come" and the name "Cannae." Lucius received the same order. They started by way of Firenze. There they met one of the peddlers whom Brecon had known in Carthalo's day. He told them that Hasdrubal had crossed the Alps and that many Gauls were joining him as he traveled east along the Po. The news was already on its way to Hannibal. Two Numidians and four Gauls were carrying the message. It told Hannibal where to meet his brother. It did not occur to either Brecon or Lucius that the message was a written one.

They had meant to visit Rome but now they gave up that part of the journey. They stopped at Clusium and spent a night in the tomb. It was a strange place in which to feel at home, but Brecon found that he did. Lucius lighted all the lamps and Brecon lay there gazing at the walls, seeing new things first in one place, then in another. There were borders in red and gold in Greek designs. One of them was called the Greek key. Brecon had seen it in Syracuse. There was a panel where a tall heron stood on one foot and a blue-green fish swam away from him. There was a circle where two owls sat on a pine branch.

Brecon thought of Athena, a sensible matron now, surely,

weaving while her maids carded lamb's wool and spun it into soft creamy thread. He thought of the sound of the loom and the girls singing. He slept better than he had since the last night he had spent there.

In the morning he said to Lucius, "I never saw the walls when I slept here on my way to Trebbia."

"You slept here?" Lucius said. "You never told me that."

"Why, yes. I thought I had told you. I found a waxed tablet here with the words 'Gully at Trebbia' on it. Look, here it is, under my blanket. That's why I came to Trebbia. Alain found it first and left it for me to see."

Lucius looked at the tablet.

"I never left it," he said. "I sent you a message by the jeweler. I wrote nothing. There must be a spy at the jeweler's."

"And waiting to catch you as soon as you come again—lucky we decided not to go to Rome."

When they reached Hannibal's camp near Cannae, the messengers from Hasdrubal had not come. There were rumors that Hasdrubal had met Roman troops in a battle, but no one seemed to know just where or when.

Hannibal, who looked thinner than usual and restless, welcomed them both with his usual kindness.

"Since Carthalo's death and your illness, Brecon," he said, "I can trust very little that comes over the grapevine. I received from you," he said to Lucius, "the word that Hasdrubal has sent messengers to tell me where he will meet me and what road he will follow—I would not be here still if his message had come. I thought that Mago would be with him, that by now we might all be on the road to Rome."

He paced up and down. There was food on the table. He offered it to them but did not eat anything himself.

"A strange rumor has come," he said. "It is that the consul Claudius Nero went north from his camp—it's on the Aufidus, not far from here—that he met Livius the other consul, and that between them they defeated Hasdrubal. They say it was near the Metaurus River. I can't believe it. Nero is in his camp today—that I know. My scouts have seen him. It's more than two hundred miles to the Metaurus. How could he get there and back and fight a battle without my knowing? Tell me, Brecon—how could he? And what shall I do. March north or stay here and attack Nero's camp?"

"I—I don't know, my lord."

"Why should you—if I do not," Hannibal said gently. "We must wait for the news."

The news came that night.

A Roman horseman dashed up to the camp and threw over the outer wall the head of Hasdrubal Barca.

There was a strong family likeness between the Barca brothers. Even in death the strongly arched nose, the curling dark hair, the dark eyes, and the lips curved in a half-smile might have been Hannibal's.

One of the Iberian guards brought the head to Brecon's tent. He was a man who had been with Hannibal for more that twelve years, taking whatever the day brought cheerfully. Now he was sobbing, not trying to stop the tears from running down his cheeks.

"What shall I do?" he sobbed. "I can't tell him—can't show him."

Brecon bit his lip, choked, said quietly, "It's my place, not yours to tell him—since Carthalo is dead. I will go to him. Here take this linen. Wrap up the... his... wrap it up. Is there anything else I should tell him?"

The soldier told him that the Romans had left two African captives in chains near the camp gate.

"They know all about the battle and could tell it if they'd stop howling. Not that they're any worse than I am," he added wiping his eyes on his sleeve.

Hannibal received the news with a dreadful frozen calm, more painful to see than open grief.

They learned from the Africans that Hasdrubal's messengers had been seized. They had a letter written in Phoenician. Someone in Nero's army knew how to read it. Nero had marched quickly north and had joined the other consul.

"They went into the tents of the other army," one of the Africans said. "My Lord Hasdrubal guessed they were there because he heard two trumpeters giving signals. Two trumpeters, two consuls, he thought, and he was right—but it was already too late."

The two men kept up a moaning cry that rose and fell all the time. Against this background they told details of the battle, while Hannibal listened with his hand over his eyes.

"Soon no army," they moaned. "After my Lord Hasdrubal died. Only Gauls going one way. Iberians another. Dead elephants. Prisoners in chains. Horses running wild. No army. No army anymore."

Hannibal thanked the men. He sent them to his own African troops to be fed. He gave them silver. He sent for his officers and, still with that strange calm, ordered them to be ready at first light to break camp and march south to Bruttium.

"Will they not attack us there, now that they know we are so few and they are so many?" asked one of the younger officers.

Hannibal said quietly, "I think they will not provoke me."

As the men left, Brecon heard one of the older men say to

the young officer, "They will not dare attack him. They know the power that is still in this one man."

Brecon repeated this to Hannibal.

"I am glad they still trust me," he said and then added—more as if he were listening to someone else speak than speaking himself—"but I see now the doom of Carthage." No Roman armies came to Bruttium. It was Hannibal's kingdom. Through the ports of Locri and Croton he was in touch with Carthage. When Hannibal sent Brecon to Carthage, it was from Croton that he sailed.

CHAPTER 18

ARTEMIS OR ATHENA

GISGO HAD BEEN badly defeated in Spain by Publius Cornelius Scipio. Now Gisgo was on his way back to Carthage. He had sent a message to Hannibal to say that Scipio was trying to get King Syphax of Numidia and Prince Masinissa of Massyli to become allies of Rome. Masinissa had already turned against Carthage and helped Scipio in Spain. Syphax, however, had not yet sent any of his javelin-throwing horsemen to Scipio.

The message Brecon was carrying to Gisgo was that whatever could be done to stop an alliance between Rome and Syphax must be done. Masinissa, who had been forced out of his Massylian kingdom by Syphax, seemed less important than Syphax, but Hannibal hoped they could both be kept as friends to Carthage.

Brecon had not wanted to leave Italy for Carthage. Since Hasdrubal's death, Hannibal seemed shut away in a dark world of his own. He had never spoken the names of his wife Imilce or of their son or of Hasdrubal. Only once had Brecon heard him speak of Carthalo. Mago, he sometimes mentioned. Mago was supposed to land soon at Genoa, but there would be the whole length of Italy between them.

Hannibal lived as he always had, eating what his soldiers

ate, sleeping wherever he spread his cloak, swimming his horse into the water with them. They loved him, Brecon knew. There were still many among them who had crossed the Alps with him. Brecon could remember their wives trudging behind the army with their babies on their backs and small children holding on to their skirts. Some of the boys were their fathers' shield bearers now. Yet in spite of the loyalty of his soldiers, Hannibal seemed to Brecon the loneliest of men.

Hannibal had seen into Brecon's thought, as he often did— sometimes before Brecon himself knew what they were.

He said, "Yes, I shall miss you, but I have been alone for so long that I have learned not to be lonely. Go to Carthage. You can help me more there than here. Hiram, one of my best captains, is here and will take you. You can trust him with messages. I will send for you if I need you."

He was silent for a while. He was doing some lettering on a piece of parchment. After a little work with a sharpened piece of charcoal, he looked up from his work. "You remember a little Greek girl, Athena? My—your cousin adopted her. She might marry if she had a dowry. Tell Gisgo. He has silver of mine. He can attend to it."

He named a generous sum and added, "If he can find a suitable husband for her, of course. And then there was the boy who had fever and was lame after it. What was his name?"

"Rhodri."

"Of course. I would like to do something for him too. Set him up in business. Or buy him a farm. Speak to Gisgo about it."

He blocked in a few more letters and then asked, "And you, Brecon? What shall I do for you? Would you like a shop or a farm—or a school? I hear you were a good teacher. What would you be if you could choose? If you lived in a world at peace?"

"I'd be a doctor," Brecon said.

The words seemed to be jerked out of him before he knew what he was going to say.

"And why not?" Hannibal asked. "Synhalus is in Carthage. He lives in my house. So does Sosillos. You can study with Synhalus."

"It's late to begin—I'm more than twenty-five years old," Brecon said.

"Nonsense. You began when you were thirteen, helping Rhodri to walk again. You've been healing people ever since. I've seen you. After these battles were fought," he said, showing Brecon the parchment.

"There is a temple near Croton," he went on. "You'll see it when you sail. The Lacinian temple. It looks over the sea. When the rulers of Carthage send for me, I shall have to leave Italy. I have enjoyed Roman hospitality so long that it would seem rude to go without leaving some token of my visit. So this will be cast in bronze and placed in the temple."

TICINO
TREBBIA
TRASIMENO
CALES
CANNAE
TARENTUM

There were many more names. Some of them Brecon had forgotten, some he remembered well—where Gracchus, a consul, died, where Marcellus, the Sword of Rome, was slain.

"The dates," Hannibal pointed out, "are given according to the Roman calendar. It seemed more courteous than using

Carthaginian dates. I would have put down Roman victories too only—I noticed this as I worked—there were none. Not when we were face to face. Did you ever think of that?"

Brecon laughed aloud for the first time in months.

"Who hasn't?" he asked.

"You told me to wake you, Sir Brecon. It's dawn and you can see the Byrsa."

It was Hiram, the young captain of the galley, speaking. Brecon woke out of a deep sleep. He saw something carved in gold against a sky faintly blue and cloudless, rising out of the thin silvery mist.

"The Byrsa," he said. "The temple."

"You've been here before?"

"Yes, about twelve years ago."

"You must have been rather young, sir," Hiram said respectfully. He was only twenty himself. Brecon naturally appeared quite venerable.

Brecon said, "I suppose I was young but I felt older than I do now. I was about fourteen and I had all the cares of the world on my shoulders. For one thing, I was personally responsible for getting Hannibal's army safely across the Alps."

"You were, sir?"

"No," Brecon said, laughing, "but I thought so. No elephant could take a step without my worrying about it! Now I've come home for a holiday."

"Home, sir? Forgive my asking—you speak Phoenician well but not exactly like a Carthaginian, sir."

"As much of a home as I have," Brecon said.

He had tried many times to get news of his grandmother. Not long ago he had received it. She had died after a short illness. She had sent Brecon a message. She hoped he would come back to Spain and take his place as Chief of the tribe. Romans, she said, were not so bad when you got used to them. One of them, a chief named Scipio, had come to her for a medicine to prevent baldness. He was a well-mannered young man and she had given him some of her special lotion.

The man who brought the message had been one of Carthalo's men. He was also one of Brecon's tribesmen.

"A grand old lady she was," he said to Brecon. "She'll be missed indeed. I wish you could have seen her rubbing that magic mud of hers into Publius Cornelius' scalp. If that wouldn't make the hairs jump up on end and grow, nothing will. Will you be going back and fight your cousin to be Chief?"

"No," Brecon said.

Let my cousin, he thought, be Chief and have the stone house and the cave with the magic paintings. I have no friends there.

But in Carthage, he thought, looking up at the Byrsa, quite close now, he had friends—Sosillos and Synhalus, Rhodri and Athena. Perhaps Rhodri would like to marry her now she would have a dowry and Hannibal would buy them a farm. Or a shop with things in it from all over the world. And Sophonisba, he thought, would be nearby in her father's palace. Brecon wondered how old she was calling herself now.

The city had changed very little. There were many galleys in the outer harbor. The inner harbor was still the same—the island with its high signal tower, the small boats dashing back and forth, the white marble wall where they moored their ship.

Brecon thanked Hiram and gave him silver. He said he could find his way without help, would carry his own bag. He walked through the marketplace looking into shops. Boys were taking down the shutters and the morning light sparkled on Egyptian glass and painted wine jars from Greece. In one window a man was stringing pearls.

It had been foolish, Brecon realized, to bring presents from Italy. Probably he could buy something in any little shop in Carthage better than the earrings he had brought for Athena and Sophonisba. He had bought them with money he had earned as a tutor. He had planned to send them when a chance came but it had never come. They were still tucked into his money belt.

He had thought of them when he had seen the belt looped around Alain's arm that day at Trebbia. Later Lucius had brought him the belt, his pouch, and his calendar. It had been trampled into the mud during the fight. For some time there had been no room left to add new records of the moon's changes. Like Hannibal, he used the Roman calendar now. Spain would do so too before long, probably, and his tribe would speak Latin—only with a Spanish twang, of course. The calendar was no longer useful. Still, he kept it, and the shabby leopard skin.

Besides the earrings in his belt he had books for Sosillos and Synhalus and a belt with bronze and gold ornaments for Rhodri. That was all he had besides his few clothes. The bag was not heavy to carry.

Carthaginian matrons were already coming into the market to buy the freshest fish and eggs and fowls. Many of them, Brecon noticed, wore wigs. The most fashionable color was a shade of red, rather like his own hair when he had crossed the Alps.

I could sell that hair if I could only grow it now, he thought, but no one would buy this old brown color.

There was a shop full of wigs. They were various shades—red, yellow, golden bronze, and black. Among them was a mirror of polished silver.

So you can see how much you need new hair, Brecon thought as he caught sight of himself in the mirror.

He decided to have his beard shaved off and his hair trimmed.

I might not look more than seventy-five then, he thought, remembering the young captain's respect for his years.

A tall and beautiful girl, followed by three slaves with empty baskets on their heads, passed the shop as he came out again, trimmed and shaven. The girl's hair, a gently waving light brown, looked strange among the frizzy wigs of red and brassy gold color of the older women.

In Syracuse Brecon had seen a statue of Artemis that reminded him of this tall girl. Yes, this was how Apollo's twin sister would look and move, swiftly, smoothly, without hurry. Only of course Artemis would not be out marketing, but guarding forest animals from harm or visiting women in sickness. The street was crowded now but she made her way along it without jostling anyone. A path opened before her. Both men and women stood aside and bowed as she passed by.

He left the market and climbed the hill toward Hannibal's palace. He remembered the curving road, the terraced gardens, the blossoming almond trees. There were the pink ones, whose nuts Imilce used in honey cakes, and the white ones, which produced the bitter, deadly poison still in his pouch.

If I could have reached it that day, he thought, I would have used it. I never would have breathed this sunshine, this soft spring air.

Someone left Hannibal's palace and came running down along the road toward Brecon. He was a slender young man who moved with only a very slight unevenness in his gait.

He slowed down as he saw the stranger and said politely, "May I carry your bag for you, sir?"

"Yes, Rhodri—you carry the bag. I'll carry you on my back," Brecon said.

Rhodri opened his brown eyes and his mouth and at last stammered, "But it can't be—but it is—Brecon! Brecon! You've come home."

It was home from that moment. Sosillos and Synhalus were sitting in the big room with the floor that looked like pink marble, a room looking down on the harbor. They were both gray-haired men but they were putting plenty of energy into the discussion they were having. Brecon had listened less than a minute when he knew that they were talking about whether the spirit and the body were two things or one. He also knew what they had said and what they were going to say. Sosillos believed they were two. Synhalus believed that—he was just going to say what he believed when a voice behind him said, "One but seeming like two that work on each other in a most complicated way of which we know little—perhaps we'll learn something in two or three thousand years."

Both men spun around.

"Are you a doctor, sir?" Synhalus asked.

"No, Synhalus—a student, if you'll have me."

He smiled, and they knew him and said, as Rhodri had, "Brecon, you've come home."

At the loom a girl was weaving purple cloth. Her back was to the room and she did not notice what was going on in it. She wove so rapidly that there was a good deal of noise from the loom. She was a brown-haired short girl with plump arms.

Brecon said to Rhodri, "Is that Athena?"

Rhodri stared at him, then laughed, and said, "You've been gone a long time, Brecon! No, that's Charmian, Synhalus' niece. She helps Athena with the housekeeping."

"Athena's not married, then?"

"No, of course not."

"You mean she has no dowry, I suppose. But she will have a generous one. We must find her a good man. And you are to have a farm, Rhodri, if you'd like it—or a shop. So you can marry too. I thought perhaps you and Athena—"

Rhodri ran over to the girl at the loom.

"Charmian," he said, "Charmian! We can be married. We can have a farm. Or a shop. Which would you like? This is Brecon. You remember all about Brecon, don't you? He's come with a magic bag. He can pull anything we like out of it. Just say!"

She was a pretty, dark-eyed, laughing girl.

"You know it's a shop, Rhodri," she said, "with things from Egypt and Greece and Tyre in it. And we'll live right here and help Athena. But you are joking. What did he really bring?"

"I brought him a belt," Brecon said, "from Syracuse. The shop is a gift from Hannibal."

Rhodri began to call out names and the big room filled with people. Brecon remembered many of them—the old steward, almost blind now, soldiers of Hannibal's with a leg or an arm missing, women who had been servants of Imilce's. There were boys and girls Brecon had never seen before. They were led up to him and he was told "This is my grandson... daughter... niece...." as the case might be.

Each time a new girl came in he looked to see if it might be Athena, but she did not appear.

At last he said to Rhodri, "But where's Athena?"

"Gone to market," Rhodri said. "You know it takes a lot of food to feed such a family. Some comes in from the villa but there are always things to buy from the market." He looked out across the terrace. "Here she comes up the path. No, you can't see her now—the path twists."

"I'll go and meet her," Brecon said.

There were three women with baskets on their heads. Behind them came a tall figure in white linen. She stooped and picked up a young fluttering bird just before a black cat pounced on it. She put the bird into a flowering almond tree and watched it until it tried its wings once more and flew safely from a pink

tree to a white one. She was holding the cat, tickling her behind the ears and talking to her.

"You'll have fish for dinner," Brecon heard her say.

He thought, Yes, Apollo's twin sister, protector of animals—but Athena too.

Then she saw him and came running toward him saying, "Brecon, Brecon! We've waited so long, so long!"

He said, "No one else knew me at first. But you did, Athena."

Rhodri and Charmian now came running down the path.

Rhodri said, "Athena, such news—Charmian and I are going to be married! Hannibal is giving us a shop and giving you a dowry. Brecon's going to find some good hard-working young man to marry you."

Brecon said hastily, "I've changed my mind."

Rhodri laughed.

"I don't believe you have," he said. "I always knew you liked her best. I told her so every time Sophonisba used to say you were in love with *her*." Then he added, "Athena has a good head for arithmetic. Why don't you go into the almond grove and have a good practical talk with her? About the dowry, you know, and living on a farm and making cheese from camel's milk?"

Brecon and Athena spent the rest of the morning in the almond grove. Neither of them ever told whether they had mentioned the dowry or camel's milk cheese. Everyone seemed pleased but not much surprised when they announced that they were going to be married.

"Because, after all," Athena said, "what else have I been waiting for?"

CHAPTER 19

ROYAL DINNER

SOPHONISBA CAME with her father the next day. She did ot recognize Brecon. If he had not seen her with Gisgo he would not have known her. She was a head shorter than Athena and looked younger. Her hair was dyed the most fashionable and expensive shade of red. It had a drop of Tyrian crimson in it. She had so many emeralds on her fingers, around her neck and wrists that Brecon hardly dared to offer her the pearl earrings he had brought for her. Athena already had hers on. She was also wearing the bracelet and the gold chain that had once fastened the owl to her wrist. He had flown out one night long ago and had never returned.

Sophonisba received her earrings politely. She did not put them on but she looked at Brecon several times afterwards. She did not look straight at anyone, but sidewise out of her long green eyes.

As if, Brecon thought, she was never quite sure what is going to crawl out of the bushes.

Brecon gave Gisgo Hannibal's message about King Syphax.

"He said to do whatever is necessary to keep Syphax from helping Rome. To pay him his price, whatever it is."

"Well," Gisgo said, "we have a chance to learn his price soon. He has invited me to a dinner. A very special dinner. It will be given on the seacoast, not far from Cirta—that's his city, you know. There's a point—Siga, it's called—west of here, with a small harbor. He will have an important guest. And he wants me to bring an interpreter, one who speaks Greek and Latin and can talk with Phoenicians and Numidians too. I told him that I knew just the man."

Sophonisba said, "And we'll all go. Athena and Rhodri and Charmian. It's just the season for a little sail, isn't it, Father?"

"No!" Gisgo roared. "You might be captured by Romans. Dragged through streets in a Roman triumph. We have to take a fighting galley, not some pretty little pleasure boat."

"A swift galley and an escort of fighting ships," Sophonisba said. "We'll be in no more danger from Rome than we are in Carthage every day."

After Gisgo had said no about seven times he said yes. They would all go—Synhalus, Sosillos, Rhodri and Charmian, Sophonisba, Brecon as interpreter. And Athena, of course.

Sophonisba added as an afterthought, "Oh and there's a young prince—what's his name? Masinissa. He came to see you, Father, one day but you were not there. He lives somewhere near Cirta. We could take him too. Save him a dusty ride. They say he might become an ally of Rome. You might persuade him not to."

"Not a bad idea," Gisgo said.

Sophonisba had produced the idea so casually that Brecon was quite sure it was not a new one—to her. He remembered how, in New Carthage, she had got him into the wrestling match with Alain.

Her thoughts must have followed the same path as Brecon's.

She asked suddenly, "How is the fat prince—what was his name? Alidor? Aldus? Or was it Alain?"

Brecon said, "He left Hannibal and joined Rome. He was killed in a skirmish with some Gauls, I heard."

"Oh, really," Sophonisba said and nothing more was said about Alain.

Rhodri and Charmian, Brecon and Athena had been married more than two weeks the day seven Carthaginian galleys set out for Siga. Not long after they had anchored, two Roman galleys rounded Siga Point. They could probably have been sunk or captured, but Gisgo ordered his captains not to attack them.

"They have a safe conduct from King Syphax," he said.

They let the Romans pass and tie up their galleys at the quay even though all but one of the Carthaginian galleys were fully armed. Gisgo and Brecon were landed at the quay soon afterwards. They walked along the shore toward the tent King Syphax had ordered set up near the harbor. The rest of the party, by Gisgo's orders, stayed on board their galley, that is, except for Prince Masinissa. He sullenly refused to speak to Syphax or go near his tent. His horse had been carried on one of the war galleys. He and the horse had both been landed and Masinissa had ridden off before the Roman galleys arrived. He had hardly spoken during the voyage but had stared at Sophonisba like—Like a tiger charmed by a snake, Brecon thought.

Sophonisba had tried to wheedle Gisgo into taking her to the King's tent, but for once he was firm.

"This is a business matter," he said. "Women have no place

at such a meeting. King Syphax would never allow his wives to be present."

"Suppose the Romans decide to carry us off!" Sophonisba sobbed.

"Rhodri and two hundred men will take care of you," Gisgo said.

Brecon did not envy Rhodri or Charmian. Sophonisba was already beginning to tell Rhodri how handsome and brave he was. However, Athena had given Brecon a look that said "Don't worry. Everything will be all right," and with Athena there, of course it would be, he knew.

King Syphax's guest had already landed. He was a handsome young Roman a little older than Brecon. He was dressed not like a soldier but like a Roman proconsul, in a spotless white toga with the folds as carefully draped as if they were carved out of marble. He was clean-shaven. His hair, Brecon noticed, was growing a little thin on top.

He must have used up all the lotion my grandmother gave him, Brecon thought.

It was hard to tell whether Gisgo or Scipio, who had last met each other in a fierce battle, was the more surprised. However, they said nothing but kept their eyes on the King, who was speaking in his own tongue and making gestures of hospitality. During the speech, Scipio did glance once at the harbor. To see if our galleys have moved, Brecon thought.

When Syphax had finished speaking, Gisgo said to him in Phoenician, "The interpreter is here, your Highness."

Syphax waved Brecon into the tent. He had been standing in the doorway. Scipio could have seen him only as a dark shape against the light. Now he looked puzzled as Brecon came forward.

"Haven't we met before?" he asked.

"Yes, Publius Cornelius. I was your nephew's tutor. This is my first chance to thank you for arranging about my freedom."

Scipio said, "Why, of course. Breconides! I did not recognize you without the red beard. You deserved your freedom—but what are you doing with it? Besides interpreting, I mean. Or does that keep you busy?"

"No—that is just for the day," Brecon said. "I am married. I live at Carthage. I am studying medicine with Synhalus, a famous Egyptian doctor."

"I remember. You told me about him. I would like to hear more, but you must introduce me to these noble gentlemen."

King Syphax repeated some of his phrases of welcome. He said he was proud to have the great commanders of the war in Spain to dine peacefully under his humble roof, to eat his bread and salt.

There was a good deal more to the meal than that, Brecon noticed. He wished they had not seasoned the stuffing of the roasted lamb with rose water. Gisgo ate heartily, praising everything. Scipio was too busy talking to eat much. He explained with all his charm the advantages of becoming friends of Rome. Since Romulus first founded the city, he said, Rome had made allies, first of her neighbors, then of people farther away. By standing together they could keep peace all over the Middle Sea, in its islands and on the shores around it.

"This is a good time to make peace with Carthage," King Syphax said. "Lord Gisgo would be only too happy to be your friend, I know."

"I am happy indeed to meet him here," Scipio said. "He is a delightful companion. I feel only friendship for him."

"How proud I would be," Syphax said, "if you would agree on terms of peace here—in my tent."

Scipio turned to Brecon.

"Say to the King that peace terms are decided upon only by the Senate and the Roman people. I am under their orders. Be sure they understand that I hope peace will come soon—that they will both be friends of Rome."

Brecon told King Syphax what Scipio had said. Then he added, to Scipio, "I would like to ask about some Roman friends of mine—the Lady Claudia and Marcellus."

"Well and happy and grateful to you for their happiness," Scipio said. "They would like to send you messages of friendship, I know. Marcus does well in his studies; but he will never make a soldier, I think. He designs bridges—such bridges as no one ever saw. They seem to fly from one bank to the other. Aqueducts big enough for elephants to walk in and great towers that vanish in the clouds. But he knows the books of Archimedes by heart; so, someday I think he'll build something that will stand firm, and you'll be proud of him."

"I think so, too," Brecon said. "Please tell him so."

Before Scipio left he visited Gisgo's galley. King Syphax came with him. Both wished to pay their respects to the ladies, they said. Scipio spoke Greek during the visit. He talked to Sosillos about Plato and to Synhalus about surgery. He told Athena how Brecon had made his nephew walk again and how Marcus was now the best discus thrower in his school. He congratulated Rhodri on being the first patient of a man who would be a great physician. He also congratulated him on his beautiful wife and praised her weaving. He admired Sophonisba's emeralds. It was hard to tell which sparkled more, the stones or her eyes, he said. He added pleasant remarks about Gisgo's galley.

Gisgo in turn admired the Roman quinqueremes.

Brecon translated all these compliments to King Syphax, who sat in silence staring at Sophonisba. To Scipio's renewed praise of the galley Brecon added a remark of his own.

"You know something interesting about those ships of yours, Publius Cornelius?"

"No, what is it?"

"Why with all those oars and five rowers to an oar, there's not a single man in them called Gisgo."

Gisgo gave a choked laugh which he disguised not very successfully as a cough.

Scipio simply raised his handsome eyebrows and said, "Really?"

Then there was a silence in which everyone thought of the name no one spoke aloud—Hannibal.

Scipio broke the silence by reminding King Syphax that he hoped he would always be a friend of Rome. Syphax said he had always been one and would be forever. Then they embraced each other and Scipio started back to Spain.

Gisgo said gloomily, "It's more dangerous to meet that young Roman in a tent and listen to him than it is to fight him on a battlefield."

King Syphax now began to speak, but not about Scipio. He spoke to Sophonisba. He said he would send her a white mare with a bridle trimmed with gold, a bit of silver, and a saddle of purple leather. Unless she would like emeralds better. Sophonisba said she would like both.

Syphax then said he must go ashore. He added, to Gisgo, that he had always been a friend of Carthage. He would prefer to continue to be one. After all, Scipio had only offered to buy horses and javelin throwers from him. He could always find a purchaser. He had sold many thousands to Hannibal.

Gisgo went ashore with the King. When he came back to the galley he knew the price Syphax asked. It was Sophonisba.

CHAPTER 20

SOPHONISBA

A YEAR LATER Lucius Tarchon came to Carthage. He brought news from Rome and Sicily.

Scipio, he said, had not been allowed a triumph when he returned from Spain. He was only a proconsul, so a triumph would not have been legal. However, the whole Senate welcomed him outside the city walls and he was allowed to march through the streets as a private citizen. His veterans and his captives followed him. Carts full of silver from the Spanish mines went ahead of him. Captured Carthaginian banners of purple waved. Trumpets sounded. Thirty white oxen were driven ahead and sacrificed at the Temple of Jupiter.

It looked rather like a triumph, Lucius said. The Roman people hailed him as a victor and cheered when he told them, "This war is just begun—I shall finish it. Carthage has waged war against Rome. I shall wage war against Carthage."

Fabius spoke against Scipio. Yet Scipio was elected Consul and was sent to Sicily. No legions went with him but he had permission to raise an army and cross to Africa if he thought the crossing would be to the advantage of the state. He was now raising and training an army in Sicily. In charge of his finances was Marcus Porcius Cato.

Cato thought—and said—that Carthage must be destroyed, but he also thought Scipio was spending too much money. He sent an unfavorable report to the Senate. Scipio, he said, was un-Roman. He read books. Greek books, of course. Since there were no Roman ones. He wore Greek dress. He—a Roman commander—had been seen at a Greek banquet with a wreath of ivy and parsley on his head, drinking with Greeks out of Greek wine bowls and reciting Homer. He listened to flute players. He threw the discus. He walked about the gymnasium in a flimsy Greek cloak and slippers.

The Senate sent a committee to look into these serious charges. It reported to the Senate that Scipio had well-drilled legions, well-equipped galleys.

"How long before he attacks?" Gisgo asked.

"Perhaps a year. He is short on cavalry. He sent one of his officers to ask Masinissa for horsemen but got only promises. He counts on Syphax for help."

"Syphax will soon be my son-in-law," Gisgo said. "Hannibal will be glad to hear that."

It had been difficult to arrange the marriage. Sophonisba had seen Masinissa again. She would persuade him, not to join Scipio, she said. He was much younger and handsomer than King Syphax. And if, she said, her father would only help Masinissa get his throne away from his rascal of a cousin, Masinissa would have as many horsemen as Syphax.

"Syphax has them now," Gisgo pointed out, "and you would be a queen."

"One of half a dozen," Sophonisba said. "Masinissa has only

two wives. And I know he would be more help to Carthage than Syphax would."

Sophonisba had a real love for her city. She was a different person when she spoke of it, Brecon had always noticed. However, Masinissa vanished into the desert. Syphax was at hand with gifts of horses and jewels. One day he gave her a kidskin pouch full of old-fashioned silver coins. He said she could buy something beautiful with them if she could find something more beautiful than the coins. The coins were more than a hundred years old. On one side of them was a lion and a palm tree. On the other was what King Syphax said was a portrait of Sophonisba.

The goddess on the coins did look a little like Sophonisba. She had the same large eyes, beautiful straight nose and softly curved lips. Her waving hair fell down from under a cap fluted and twisted like a shell. She wore earrings rather like those Brecon had brought from Rome. Perhaps it was being thought as beautiful as the goddess that made Sophonisba agree to marry King Syphax. They were married a little more than a year after Athena and Brecon were married. Their son—Athena told Brecon—smiled for the first time that day.

Brecon was not at Sophonisba's wedding. He went in Gisgo's galley with a group of Numidians to Scipio as their interpreter. Scipio was at Lilybaeum in Sicily. He was almost ready for the crossing to Africa. He had forty ships of war, four hundred transports, and almost twenty thousand men. He had only a few horsemen. He counted on getting these from King Syphax and from Masinissa. Everything was ready. Cooked provisions for two weeks were being loaded onto special ships. Water and provisions for two months were already on board.

The message from Syphax must have been a blow to Scipio,

but he received the envoys with his usual courtesy. He showed no sign of being troubled. Sophonisba had persuaded her husband that he must tell Scipio that he must not rely on any aid from Syphax.

"I must hold," the King said, "to my ancient friendship for Carthage."

Scipio's answer was to thank the envoys and to tell them that they might return to Africa in safety. He did everything possible to speed their journey. He did not run any chance of delaying his own by telling even his officers what Syphax had said. Soldiers were embarking in the transports when Gisgo's galley left the harbor.

Carthage had always felt safe behind her walls while Hannibal was in Italy. The news that Scipio was on his way to Africa roused the city. Men watched from the Byrsa for the Roman fleet. Galleys were ready to defend the city from it. However, it came not to Carthage but to Utica, a day's march away. Scipio expected that Utica, which was more Greek than Phoenician, would quickly become a friend of Rome. Then he would have a base from which to attack Carthage. Utica, however, did not welcome Roman friendship. It shut its gates against Scipio. He besieged the city and laid waste to the country around it. He still tried to persuade Syphax to send him horsemen, but Sophonisba kept the King true to Carthage.

Although Masinissa came with horsemen there were only two hundred of them. In order to slip safely around Carthage with his men, Masinissa spread a rumor abroad that he was dead. It sped along ahead of him as he dashed past the city, riding his horse like a figure molded in bronze. He was with Scipio to laugh at the news just after it reached the Roman camp.

When the winter storms began, Scipio was in a fortified camp near Utica. Like Hannibal, he was almost his own prisoner in a foreign country. Like Hannibal, too, he set traps for his enemies. An army from Carthage marched to a spot where they were sure they could surround Scipio and defeat him. Masinissa was waiting in a concealed gully as the Numidians had waited at Trebbia. This time the Carthaginians were defeated.

Scipio sent messengers to Syphax's camp to discuss possible peace terms. With the envoys went a number of Scipio's officers disguised as slaves. While the peace talks were going on, the spies learned all about the camp. They reported that it consisted chiefly of huts, close together and covered with mats of woven reeds. The best weapon to use against it, they told Scipio, was fire.

One night Scipio's galleys sailed with siege engines for Carthage. The troops began the attack by seizing a hill outside the city. While the attention of the troops was on this hill, Roman soldiers crept up to Syphax's camp and set it on fire in several places. At first the fire seemed accidental, spread by the wind. While the Numidians were trying to put it out, Scipio attacked the camp from one direction, Masinissa from another. Gisgo, Syphax, and Sophonisba escaped with some troops, but forty thousand men were slain or burned to death. Yet Sophonisba persuaded Syphax to keep fighting for her city rather than to give up. He raised a new army. With Masinissa's help, Scipio defeated it.

To Syphax this was the end. He was Scipio's prisoner, in chains, to be sent to Rome, to be shown on the streets like a lion in a cage. Sophonisba, however, was not beaten yet. In her own way she still fought for Carthage. Masinissa had blazed through the land from which he had been disinherited. Its people joined him by thousands. It was an easy matter to seize Cirta, Syphax's capital.

Yet at the palace he was conquered. Sophonisba was there. She begged him not to let her, a Carthaginian, become a Roman slave. Masinissa fell madly in love with her. She would never be a slave, he said. He would be hers and she would be his wife.

Syphax had already divorced Sophonisba. He told Scipio that she had used magic spells on him, blinded and charmed him so that he had foolishly turned against Rome. She was a witch and no longer his wife. If Scipio would set him free, not send him to Rome, he would bring him many horsemen. It was too late now. Syphax was sent to Rome in chains. Sophonisba become Masinissa's wife.

They were happy together for a few days. Then Scipio sent for Masinissa. Scipio knew that Sophonisba had turned Syphax against him. Now that Masinissa ruled his people again, it might mean disaster for Rome if she bewitched him as she had Syphax. Scipio remembered her beauty, her charm, the look in her strange green eyes.

"She's more danger to Rome than ten thousand horsemen," Scipio said.

When Masinissa came to Scipio's camp, Scipio received him not in anger but with kindness and calmness.

"Once, Masinissa," he said, "you came to me in Spain. You offered me your friendship if I would help you regain your country. I promised to do so, and I kept my promise. You will soon be called King. I think you must have seen some qualities in me that you valued or you would not have trusted all your hopes to me. Now you have sometimes spoken kindly of my virtues. If I have one it is to be temperate, to control my passions. I hope that Rome—and I—will not lose your friendship; that you will not betray us, as Syphax did."

Masinissa burst into tears and went into his tent.

The next day he sent by one of his servants to Sophonisba a cup with poison to put in it and a message.

It said: "Masinissa cannot be a husband to Sophonisba but he keeps his promise that she shall not come alive into Roman power."

Sophonisba held the cup in her hand while she dictated a short letter: "I accept Masinissa's gift. It is welcome since it is all my husband can give me. I would, however, have died more gladly if I had not married so near my death."

She wrote her name on the paper, drank the poison, and died.

Brecon and Rhodri had heard that Masinissa had left her. They rode fast across the desert to take her home, but came too late.

Masinissa told Scipio he was going to take poison too. Scipio, sensible as always, begged him not to make the affair more tragic than necessary by a rash action. So Masinissa tried on his new gold crown and a splendid robe embroidered with gold in which he looked very handsome. He also sat in his royal chair of gold and ivory and was called King and friend of Rome by Scipio.

Gisgo, however, did not take his daughter's death so reasonably. Grieving for her death, despondent over his defeat by Scipio, he too drank poison and died.

ZAMA

CARTHAGE NOW ASKED for peace terms. Scipio announced them. Prisoners must be restored to Rome. Hannibal and his armies must leave Italy. Mago Barca had landed at Genoa. He must leave too. Carthage must give up all the islands in the Mediterranean. Masinissa must be acknowledged as of Massaesyli, formerly the kingdom of Syphax.

All these things were told to Hannibal by Brecon, who went with other Carthaginians to call Hannibal home.

It was almost sixteen years since Hannibal had crossed the Alps. In all those years he had never been defeated by a Roman army in battle. In all those years the city of Carthage had been safe from Rome.

Hannibal managed to slip out of Croton with his army—only about twelve thousand men now—without being seen by any of the Roman fleets between him and Carthage. He made a wide circle around Sicily and landed many miles south and east of Carthage. No one was looking for him there. He moved north to Hadrumentum. It was there he heard that his brother Mago had been wounded in a battle in northern Italy and had died of his wounds on his way to Carthage. Some of Mago's troops managed to join Hannibal. The blow of Mago's death was hard for him to bear.

When the news reached Rome that Hannibal had left Italy, the Romans did not know whether to shout with joy because he had gone or shake with fear because he now faced Scipio in Africa, his own country. They did both. Fabius Maximus had died. Some of his last words were that Hannibal would be a more dangerous enemy in Africa than in Italy.

The Romans knew well that he still had with him men who had crossed the Alps with him, that these men had lived in Italian cities—Capua, Tarentum, Syracuse. Some of these men had killed Roman consuls with their own hands. They had fought at Cannae, a name still terrible in Roman ears. Hannibal might have had more fasces, fasces captured in battle, carried before him than all the magistrates of Rome. His troops could have carried eagles of the Roman legions too. Nurses still said "Hannibal at the gates" to frighten children, though, strangely, Hannibal (Annibal) was a name now given to Italian boys.

Scipio's whole plan of war had been to fight Hannibal in Africa rather than in Italy. Yet now that Hannibal was only a few days' march away there were difficulties. One was that the Roman senate was arguing over the peace terms. Another was that Utica had never surrendered. Then Laelius, one of his best officers, had taken King Syphax to Rome and had never returned. Also, Masinissa had gone to Rome. He enjoyed being called King by the Romans. He enjoyed even more seeing Syphax in chains dragged through the streets. Scipio began to wonder whether Masinissa—King Masinissa—would ever come back to Africa and bring his thousands of horsemen against Hannibal.

Winter storms came. Scipio was still in his corner of Africa, but not feeling so safe as when Hannibal was across the sea. Some Roman transports got through to Scipio with provisions; others were driven ashore near Carthage. People in Carthage were hungry that winter, for Scipio had cut off many of their sources of supply. Ships left the harbors of Carthage and seized the wrecked Roman galleys. The truce was broken.

Masinissa came home at last. He was very busy seizing towns that had once belonged to Syphax. The sons of Syphax resented the new king's behavior. Some of them were visited by Brecon. They agreed to help Hannibal.

Would Hannibal's forces keep getting stronger? Scipio decided not to wait for time to answer that question. He left his camp near Utica and marched up the Bagradas River, burning villages, making slaves of their people.

Brecon brought the news of Scipio's march to Hannibal, and men began to pour out of Hannibal's camp. They were men Brecon knew—Gauls, Libyans, Balearic slingers, Bruttians and Apulians from the south of Italy, Iberians who had crossed the Alps sixteen years before. Eighty young African elephants flapped their big ears and curled their trunks and trumpeted as they followed the troops. One of Syphax's sons sent word that he would come soon with many horsemen. Masinissa had not joined Scipio yet, he said.

The country Hannibal crossed was more strange to him than Italy. He had left it thirty-six years before. The town near where he camped was called Zama.

Zama was five days' march west of Carthage. It stood on a plain with a ridge east of it. Hannibal sent a scouting party to explore the land near Scipio's camp. Three of them went too close to the camp and were captured. The others returned to Zama, bringing this bad news, but within a short time the captives appeared.

Scipio, instead of putting them in chains, killing them, or cutting off their hands, had greeted them politely and then sent them on a tour of the camp. He told his officers to show them everything they wished to see. They saw more than they could possibly remember and then were led back to Scipio, who asked them whether there was anything else they would like to inspect. When the bewildered scouts said no, Scipio ordered them to be given a good dinner and then sent back to Zama.

"He wants me to attack him now," Hannibal said to Brecon. "Even without cavalry he's sure of victory." He was silent a moment and then said, "I am sorry the truce was broken. Perhaps Scipio, like me, really wants peace. Go to him, Brecon, tell him I would be honored if he would meet me between our camps for a talk."

When Brecon was brought to Scipio's tent, Scipio smiled kindly at him and said, "I thought when they said a messenger had come that it might be you. How do your studies progress? And your family, how are they?"

"Not badly," Brecon said. "But not so well as if there were peace in the world. My wife is well," he added. 'We have a daughter now, and a boy, older."

"Their names?"

"The boy is called Hannibal," Brecon said.

"And the girl?"

"Sophonisba."

Scipio did not exactly gasp but he drew his breath more deeply than usual. At last he said, taking pains, Brecon thought, to speak casually, "But didn't they say you had a message for me?"

Brecon repeated it.

"It will be an honor to meet him," Scipio said courteously. "You will act as interpreter, I hope. My Greek is not polished enough for such an occasion. Though no doubt your master's Latin is excellent—after so long in Italy."

"I think he would prefer to speak Greek and have an interpreter," Brecon said.

"I shall move my camp to Naragarra so that the meeting place may not be too far from the camp," Scipio said, and added "Until we meet again," and went back to the Greek book he was reading. He was dressed in Greek clothes too. What, thought Brecon, would Piggy Cato say?

Brecon was escorted out of the camp by its eastern gate. He did not know that, while he had been talking with Scipio, Masinissa and the first of his Numidians had ridden in from the west.

Scipio's new camp was on a slope, a javelin's throw away from the river. Hannibal moved and camped four miles away. He was farther from the water. The hot African sun made it thirsty weather for men and horses. That afternoon men rode out with flags of truce from both camps. They stopped a hundred yards apart. Scipio from the Roman party, Hannibal and Brecon from the Carthaginian troops dismounted and walked toward each other.

They stood in silence for a long time, Scipio gazing at Hannibal, Hannibal at Scipio. At last Hannibal began to speak.

"I wish that neither of our countries had ever coveted the possessions of the other. There was room for us to live at pcacc as we were. But we went to war, first for Sicily, then for Spain. Your native land has been in great danger. Now ours is. Can we not end this quarrel? Fortune is fickle. She plays with us as if we were children."

He spoke slowly, pausing between sentences for Brecon to put them into Latin words.

"Once—after Cannae," he said, "I was master of most of Italy. Now here I am in Africa, trying to find safety for my city. I beg you—do not be overproud of the great things you have done for Rome. Try, like an ordinary man, to choose the most good, the least evil. If you conquer you will add little to your fame. If you suffer defeat you will darken your shining past."

Still Scipio did not reply. Hannibal, speaking through Brecon, made his proposals for peace. They were that Sicily, Sardinia, Spain, and all islands between Italy and Africa should belong to Rome and that Carthage would never make war on Rome because of any of these countries.

Scipio then said, "Carthage has already accepted terms less favorable than those you offer and since has broken the truce. If Rome agreed to your offer we would be rewarding you for treachery, teaching you that it pays to betray us. I regret that I see no use in our talking longer. Either yield to our mercy or fight us and conquer."

He made a stiff Roman bow, turned, and rode back to his camp.

Nothing Greek about you today, Publius Cornelius, Brecon thought.

It was still dark next morning when both camps began to stir. By daylight both armies were drawn up on the plain of Zama. Hannibal, with his Bruttian soldiers around him, stood on top of a little rise in the ground. Brecon was near him, ready to carry his messages to soldiers from many lands, speaking many tongues. As the light grew stronger, Brecon could see a large group of Numidians on Scipio's right wing. He could see Masinissa. On the left wing Laelius, back from Rome in time, led the Italian cavalry.

Brecon asked, "Are not the maniples of footsoldiers arranged in a new way?"

"Yes," Hannibal said. "There are clear lanes between them instead of the third maniple being behind the first and the fourth behind the second."

His own troops were also drawn up in a new way. As usual, the elephants were in front, but behind them were what amounted to three separate armies. The first was made up of Ligurians, Gauls, Balearic slingers, and other light troops. Behind them, at a distance, were Africans and Carthaginians. Still farther in the rear, the veterans of his Italian campaigns were drawn up around him. On his left Numidian horsemen faced Masinissa. Carthaginian horsemen on his right faced Laelius.

When he gave the signal, the elephants charged. As they started their swinging rush across the open ground, a great blast of sound came from the Roman war trumpets and there were loud shouts from the Roman soldiers. The elephants had never been in battle before. Some turned and rushed back, killing their own men. Others ran away in panic. Some of them ran straight down the open lanes between the Roman maniples and passed harmlessly through to the rear of Scipio's army. Others swung right and trampled a path through the Carthaginian cavalry. Laelius' men charged on the frightened horsemen and completed the disaster. Masinissa took advantage of the confusion to attack Hannibal's Numidians. They broke and fled, though still fighting, across the plain.

Hannibal placed great trust in his second group, the Africans. They fought well, but without cavalry on their flanks they were soon surrounded by the Romans, killed or made prisoners.

Now the Romans faced the old guard, Hannibal's veterans under his own command. They stood firm and their line was longer than the Roman line. Here Scipio showed his genius. Trusting in the perfect discipline of his footsoldiers, he sounded the call to retreat. His men did so in spite of the advancing enemy. Then, at the shouts of their centurions, they formed a long line with no gaps between the maniples. The line was solid, unbroken, longer than Hannibal's line.

Hannibal's men fought well. They might have won if Masinissa and Laelius had not returned in time. Now there was a new Cannae—only this time Hannibal's men were encircled. He fought his way out of the trap, many of his veterans followed him. Twenty thousand men died before the sun set that day. Almost as many were prisoners. Hannibal and a small troop at last left the field.

The battle of Zama was over.

CHAPTER 22

PEACE IN CARTHAGE

FROM HADRUMENTUM Hannibal sent Brecon to carry a warning to the Council and Shofets of Carthage. It said, "We have lost not only a battle but the war. Accept the terms of peace offered to you."

Brecon did not stay to hear the Council argue about the peace terms. He went back to Hadrumentum, taking Synhalus with him. They did what they could for the wounded men who straggled into the camp. On his way he learned that the sons of Syphax had come to Hannibal's aid—but too late. He also heard the terms of peace. They were naturally more severe than the earlier ones. Carthage must surrender all but ten of her war galleys and all her elephants. She must agree never to make war in Africa without Rome's consent. In the next fifty years she must pay Rome ten thousand talents of silver.

Hannibal had not been in the city of Carthage since he was nine years old. When he rode into it after the battle of Zama, it was like a foreign city to him. Yet even though he came to it defeated, people cheered him as if he came in triumph and tried to come close enough to him to touch his shabby cloak. He was a legend, a legend that had suddenly come alive.

In Rome the people welcomed Scipio but the Senate distrusted him. There were murmurs that he might try to make himself a king. Cato's party felt that he should have destroyed Carthage. Somewhat grudgingly they added the title "Africanus" to his name.

In Carthage Hannibal was made a member of the Council. He found its long meetings tiresome. Once, when the peace terms were being discussed, a young noble—not one of those who had faced Scipio at Zama—made a speech calling on the Carthaginians to arm themselves, to man the city walls to save their war galleys and their elephants. Hannibal stood this nonsense as long as he could. Then he stepped forward and pulled the young orator off the dais. There were shouts of disapproval.

Hannibal spoke from where he stood.

"I ask your pardon," he said. "I was nine when I left Carthage. Now I am forty-five. I know a little about camps, not much about council chambers. I will try to learn your rules. Please let me say this. Italy has also suffered. If fortune had allowed me to seize Rome, what terms would you have given her? A few days ago most of you feared disaster and destruction with a Roman proconsul ruling over us. These terms are the best you can hope for. Accept them."

The Council accepted them, but there was anger among the rich men of the city at being taxed to pay the indemnity. One wept in the Council chamber and said the hardship was too heavy to endure.

He saw Hannibal smile and he cried out, "So it amuses Hannibal Barca, son of Hamilcar, to see the tears we shed, to see us suffer under the troubles he has brought down on us!"

Hannibal stood up and said, "I am amused not by hardships but to see you weeping over the least of them. You did not weep over the loss of our army, our fleet, the honor and power of our city, but only when you are going to lose some of your money!"

Yet he did what he could to help this man and others like him. He traveled through the outer suburbs, farms, and other possessions of Carthage investigating methods of raising taxes. When he came back, he told the Council that with honest methods of collection the silver could be paid to Rome without extra taxes. He was made Shofet and given power to make reforms. Carthage was honestly governed.

He worked at this task for seven years. They were some of the happiest of his life. His household, managed by Athena, ran smoothly. He had his old friends Synhalus and Sosillos and some of his old soldiers with him. He loved Brecon's and Rhodri's children as if they were his own. Rhodri and Charmian had three boys. Brecon and Athena, two boys and two girls. The great moment for them all was when Hannibal came home from one of his journeys and they found out what was in his bag.

When he was staying in the palace, he used to ride out to his villa every afternoon. He had a swift black Numidian horse he was fond of. The children—his grandchildren he called them—took turns riding a gentle bay mare he had bought for them. In the evenings before they went to bed, he would play knucklebones with them or show them how to make patterns with string or tell them stories.

Brecon was one of the best doctors in Carthage now. He was often late in coming home because a patient had sent for him. One evening he looked from the terrace into the big room with the pink floor. Hannibal was sitting on the floor with little Athena in his arms and the others in a circle around him. It was a warm evening, with the scent of roses mixed with the smell of the sea. It was so still that Brecon could hear sailors singing on the decks of trading galleys below in the harbor.

One of the boys was saying, "It's my turn to choose. Tell about the elephant, the elephant who forgot."

A contented "A-a-ah!" rose from the children. Brecon stayed on the terrace in the shadows and heard Hannibal tell the story.

"This little elephant," he said, "was being trained to do a dance with other elephants. He was going to appear in a very fine show with his mother and his father, his brothers and his sisters, and with all his cousins and his aunts."

"No uncles?" asked Sophie.

"No uncles. They were all in the army. Now one of the great things about being in the show was that the little elephant and all the others would be beautifully dressed. He kept thinking how grand he would look with a purple and gold saddlecloth and a little ivory tower on his back and his toenails all painted white and a beautiful wreath of violets and roses around his neck."

"And earrings," said young Brecon, who was Rhodri's son. "You forgot the earrings—like emeralds, only of Egyptian glass."

"Yes, earrings, of course. Now the steps of the dance were quite hard to learn. First they marched in, each holding the next one's tail with his trunk, and then they made a circle. Next they all dropped the tails and sat up and waved their feet. Then they did trumpeting."

"Toot-toot—*toot*!" said young Rhodri, who was Brecon's son.

"And then they danced, two steps to the left, two to the right, and turned."

"*All* the way around!" said Hannibal, son of Brecon.

"Right! Well, you see it was complicated, but they all did their parts well; only the youngest elephant kept forgetting. He would dance two steps to the right when the others danced left and that mixed everyone up. After the third time the trainer whipped the little elephant."

"Hard?" asked Sophie.

"Not very hard. The trainer said, 'This hurts me more than it does you,' but it made the little elephant so ashamed that he cried large tears. They ran right down his trunk, right down into the bowl of bread and milk and chopped hay that was his supper.

"The elephants all had stalls where they slept at night. They were the same size, so the little elephant had plenty of room in his. Their trainer was on guard that night. Someone always had to be on guard because someone might steal an elephant. Or a mouse might frighten one. An elephant always thinks a mouse might run up his trunk and tickle him. This would be no laughing matter.

"It was a bright moonlight night. The guard was eating some dates and some elephant's milk cheese when he heard a noise. He got up and walked along the stalls. All the elephants were asleep—"

"Except one!" said Hannibal, son of Rhodri.

"Except one. The moonlight shone right into the stall. The little elephant was—he was *practicing.* Two steps to the left, two to the right and turn. And he did it again. And again. And after that—"

"He never made another mistake!" everyone said together, "and he wore his beautiful wreath and his ivory tower and danced better than anyone!"

It was bedtime now. Nurses came in—("Say thank you to my Lord Hannibal"... "Thank you, Grandfather Hannibal. Thank you. *Thank* you...") and soon they were all gone.

Hannibal said to Brecon, "This was a happy day. One of many."

"I hope there will be many more like it," Brecon said.

"Not the same, I'm afraid," said Hannibal.

"What is it, my lord?"

"Our city has become too prosperous. It's been honestly governed. Trade is good. Rome is beginning to fear us again. I have just had word that Cato says I am getting ready to attack Rome."

"With what?"

"Exactly! Without either soldiers, ships, elephants, or cavalry! It's ridiculous, but to me it is dangerous. Cato is Consul. He has persuaded the Senate to demand that Carthage surrender me to Roman commissioners who will arrive tomorrow. Their orders are to take me to Rome. Lucius sent the message."

"I can't believe in such treachery," Brecon said indignantly.

"Yes, every time I got them in a trap, the Romans used to groan about Punic Faith. This, I suppose, is Roman Faith. But they will not catch me easily. Tomorrow I shall go for my afternoon ride as usual. It is young Rhodri's turn to ride with me. Come with us, Brecon, so you can take him safely home when I leave you. Hiram has my swiftest galley waiting for me on the coast below Hadrumentum. I have gold, silver, a crew I can trust. I'll be in Tyre before Cato is on my trail. Or—if they catch me—well, I'll never be a prisoner dragged through the streets of Rome. You know that, I think."

"Let me come with you," Brecon said.

"No. Stay here where you have your family and the work you

have always wanted to do. Perhaps I can come back someday. Thank Athena and Rhodri and Charmian for all their kindness. Tell no one I have gone until two days have passed."

The commissioners came to Carthage early the next morning. Hannibal was on the island in the inner harbor when their galley arrived. He greeted them and was among their escorts to a palace prepared for them on the Byrsa. Then he went to the market. He bought toys for the children. He went into Rhodri's shop and looked at an old Etruscan wine jar.

"A real antique," Rhodri told him. "None of those clever copies they make in Greece now. It even has its own lid. The lids are often missing."

"I like it," Hannibal said.

It was a strange design. Part of it was cut into the clay, part was painted. There were two staring eyes and, twisting around them, two black snakes spotted with white. Between the snakes a dolphin swam happily along.

"Do you think Athena would like it?" Hannibal asked.

Rhodri said she had not seen it but that Brecon liked it. He had seen one something like it in an Etruscan tomb once. Athena liked a Greek vase with a procession of Athena painted on it.

"Not so rare as this," Charmian said.

"I'll take both," Hannibal said. "It's my birthday in a few days. I can't remember other people's birthdays so I give presents on my own. Sorry I can't buy yours here—it's my favorite shop."

He wrote messages on pieces of parchment and left them with the presents in his room when he rode away that afternoon. The guard at the gate on the land side of the city waved to him as casually as if this were any evening when Lord Hannibal

Barca and some of his family were riding out for a breath of fresh air.

Young Rhodri rode ahead, Brecon and Hannibal side by side. They did not talk a great deal except about some business Brecon would take care of. About other things there was too much to say and too few words.

At last Brecon said, "If you ever need me, will you send for me?"

"Yes," Hannibal said. "I promise, but I'll be a wanderer, hard to find perhaps."

He was a wanderer for thirteen years.

CHAPTER 23

LAST VICTORY

LETTERS CAME from him sometimes. The first one was from Tyre. Hiram, the captain of the galley, brought it to Brecon.

Hannibal wrote:

Cato had a good chance to catch me. The harbor where we put in the first night was full of traders, in ships from Tyre mostly. The captains knew me. I told them I was going to Tyre on a visit and that to celebrate our meeting they must all dine with me on the beach. It was steaming hot. I suggested that we needed awnings and that sails made the best ones. So while I was buying food for the dinner, they brought sails and spars and made a shady place for us to eat. I gave them plenty of good Greek wine. They were still drinking when the stars began to shine. One by one they dropped asleep on the sand. I sailed before dawn.

I'm afraid they were late getting to Carthage with the news that they had dined with me. It must have taken some time to put the spars and sails back.

Hannibal was at the courts of many monarchs during those years. Sometimes one would consult him about plans for conquering Rome. He used to give his advice but, as they did not follow it, little came of it.

One of these kings, Antiochus of Syria, called himself the successor of Alexander the Great. He had marched over much of the ground Alexander had covered and he too came back with elephants, Parthian horses, silks, and jewels. There the resemblance ended. Antiochus—"the Great" as he called himself—loved parades.

During one of them he said to Hannibal, "There go enough men for the Romans, eh?"

Hannibal, who had a habit of saying what he thought, replied, "Enough for a good mouthful even if they're hungry—yes!"

Antiochus had a philosopher at his court who liked to lecture on the art of war to anyone who would listen. One evening Hannibal was one of the listeners. He made no comment until someone asked him what he thought of the lecture.

"I've heard plenty of foolish talk in my life but nothing to equal this," he said.

Flattery was something Antiochus liked and in which Hannibal had no practice. He was passed over by the King when important decisions were made, blamed when the plans did not succeed. At last Scipio Africanus conquered Antiochus. Scipio offered fair terms of peace to Antiochus but the Roman senate, led by Cato, said the terms were too mild, that the King must pay more, give up his fleet and his elephants, and surrender Hannibal to the Romans.

Cato also had charges made against Scipio. These were the old ones—that he was un-Roman, read books, and wore slippers. There was also a new charge—that Scipio had taken money that should have gone into the Roman treasury. Scipio met this envious attack in his own way. He brought his account books into the Senate, tore them to pieces, and scattered the scraps on the floor.

"You may look for proof there," he said. "And I hope your own records show who brought fifteen thousand talents of silver into your treasury, freed Italy from Hannibal, and made Rome master of Spain, Africa, and Asia."

It was Scipio's last speech in the Roman senate. He left Rome as a poor man and never returned. He gave instructions that at his death, his body should not be buried on Roman soil.

Antiochus did not turn Hannibal over to the Romans because he could not find him. He was on the island of Crete, whose people were called pirates by the Romans. Hannibal lived near a temple at Gortyna. Brecon found him there. Hannibal had not sent for Brecon but Brecon had talked with Hiram, the captain of Hannibal's galley. He was leaving Carthage for Crete the next day. Brecon went with him.

As he walked up through an olive grove Brecon knew he was near the right house because of some bronze statues of Phoenician gods he saw along the path and in the garden. As usual, it was as if he and Hannibal had seen each other a week or two ago.

Brecon explained how he happened to come. He could stay only a day, he said. Unless Hannibal needed him.

"I would like to say yes," Hannibal said, "but will not—yet. How did you know the house?"

"By the statues," Brecon said.

Hannibal began to laugh.

"If I tell you something, I do not much think you will tell it to the priests at the temple, will you?" he asked.

"I doubt if I'll see them," Brecon said.

"You had better know this," Hannibal said, "because you are one of my heirs and I have named you in my will to manage my estate for the others. If Cato catches me," he went on, "take those statues home with you. All my gold and silver are hidden in them."

"Is that safe?" Brecon asked.

"No one notices them," Hannibal said. "When I came here, I brought them with me. I also had some bronze jars filled with lead with a few layers of silver and gold coins on top. The priests are taking care of them for me in the temple. It's quite easy to loosen the lids, see the coins, and then seal them up with a little hot wax again. They take *great* care of them."

This time it was Brecon who laughed. He was pleased with the idea of the priests, who had signed a receipt for the jars, taking so much trouble to get a look at the coins.

"You couldn't have fooled Archimedes that way," he said.

"There was only one Archimedes," Hannibal said.

"Yes, and one Hannibal."

The Cretan pirates, if they were pirates, did not interfere with Brecon's voyage. He returned safely to Carthage. Some months later Hiram visited him. A Roman, a member of the Fabian family, had attacked Crete, perhaps to punish the pirates, perhaps to rescue Roman soldiers enslaved by the Cretans, certainly to capture Hannibal. However, Hannibal had gone, bronze statues and all, Hiram said. Brecon wondered what Fabius and the priests said when they opened the jars. Somehow he felt that no one said, "A body wholly or partly immersed in water loses..."

At last, after thirteen years, the summons came to Brecon. Hannibal was in Bithynia, Hiram said, on the Sea of Marmora as guest of King Prusias. Scipio knew where he was but he kept the secret. Scipio and Hannibal had met once at Ephesus. They had a long talk, Hiram said. Scipio asked Hannibal whom he considered the greatest soldier of all time.

"Alexander the Great," Hannibal said promptly, "because with a small army he defeated enormous ones and conquered the remotest regions of the world."

"And second?"

"King Pyrrhus. He taught us how to make camps properly. He showed good judgment in choosing his ground and placing his troops."

By this time Scipio sounded a little impatient.

"The third—who's the third?"

"Why," said Hannibal, "myself. Unquestionably."

Scipio laughed.

"What would you have said if you had defeated me?"

"Oh then," said Hannibal, smiling, "I would have placed myself above Alexander and Pyrrhus and all other commanders of all time."

When Scipio went away, he said, "I am sorry you have spent all these years wandering from one place to another. I'm afraid you must be homesick sometimes—as I am."

"Yes," Hannibal said, "as you are, so am I—for Italy."

The house was in a fishing village called Libyssa. There was a snow-topped peak Hannibal liked to look at. Some homesick Greek had named it Mount Olympus.

King Prusias used to send for Hannibal to ask his advice about governing his country. The King could not read and write. However, he was interested in the fact that Hannibal was writing a book, a history of Rhodes. Prusias was pleased with the idea that he had an author at his court.

Prusias warned Hannibal that Flaminius, a Roman consul, had asked him where Hannibal was. He would have to leave again, Hannibal knew. He sent for Hiram and told him to come and to bring Brecon with him.

The journey had been a long one.

When at last they reached the inlet, the captain said, "I won't go right to the village. It must not be known that he plans to escape—as I suppose he does. We thought he could always stay here. It seemed so peaceful when I was here before. But Rome has long arms, sharp claws. Climb up that path and you'll find the house. You'll know it by some old bronze statues. I will be here, ready to start at once if he comes."

It was not a large house but it had six doors, with Phoenician statues beside them all. Hannibal was watching the path from a window. Brecon could hear his quick footsteps as he came to the door and unbarred it.

"I can see your path and the one to the village too," he said.

It was extraordinary how little he had changed. His hair was still thick and curly, though touched with gray. The lid of his blind eye drooped a little more than Brecon remembered, but he still had his old look of seeing into and through things. He was smoothly shaven. His clothes were clean but plain. A gardener or a shepherd might have worn them, but, Brecon thought, no one was going to mistake Hannibal for either.

"Shall we go?" Brecon asked.

"Not before dark," Hannibal said. "No chance now of getting past the city and out of the harbor. Flaminius' men are there. I have just heard that they told poor Prusias to seize me and hand me over. Prusias said, 'He's my guest friend—I won't do it.' That's a pretty brave thing to say to a Roman consul. He's a good little king, not brilliant, but a good companion. He told the Romans, 'Look out for Hannibal. He's dangerous when cornered.'"

He asked Brecon about his family and Rhodri's. He remembered all the children's names and how they looked. Brecon must buy presents for them all.

"Give them their hearts' desires," he added.

He was silent for a moment, listening, walked to the win-

dow and looked out, turned back, and asked, "Can you tell me anything about Scipio Africanus?"

"I'm sorry—yes," Brecon said. "He died a few weeks ago."

"Rich and happy and back in Rome?"

"No. Poor and in exile," Brecon said.

Hannibal said, 'We should have been wanderers together. We were always more like brothers than enemies. I am glad his exile is over."

Just then he heard something. He looked out of the window.

"There are guards at the gate," he said, "but I don't think they saw me. Can you go and look out all the other windows and see if all the doors are guarded? They are all barred. Try to look without being seen. There are curtains. Look from the edge, not the center."

Brecon made the rounds quickly.

"There are guards everywhere except at the kitchen door," he said.

"We might get out that way through the little gate in the garden wall," Hannibal said. "Come."

The garden gate was guarded too. They could hear a man outside say, "I wish Flaminius and his lot would come. I want to go down to the village and get a drink."

"They're coming up the hill from the village now," said another voice.

Hannibal and Brecon went back to the house. The servants had gathered in the kitchen, the only room of which the windows were hidden by the garden wall.

The men servants looked gloomy and frightened. The cook was sobbing.

"Those Romans will kill us all," she said.

Hannibal said gently, "They will not harm you. Thank you,

all of you, for your kindness to me. This is Sir Brecon, my—my adopted son. He will see that your wages are paid. Be patient a few days. You are servants of my friend the King, not of mine. Tell them so," he said to the steward, "when they come. When they knock, bid them welcome in the name of Hannibal, son of Hamilcar, who announces to them his last victory over Rome."

He added to Brecon, "I had to see Carthage bow to Rome, but my other promise I can keep."

He pulled from his pouch a small flask and took off its wrapping.

"The time has now come," he said, "to put an end to the anxiety of the Roman people, who have grown weary, waiting for the death of a tired old man. Some wine, please," he said to the steward.

The man brought it in a bronze and gold bowl. Hannibal tasted the wine and set the bowl down.

He smiled at Brecon and said, "Keep the bowl, Brecon."

He unsealed the flask and put it to his lips. The smell of bitter almonds filled the room. He fell into Brecon's arms. Brecon was still holding him when the heavy raps came on the door.

AUTHOR'S NOTE

THE ROMAN HISTORIANS Livy (Titus Livius) and Polybius mention most of the characters in this story. Among them are the three Barca brothers—Hannibal, Hasdrubal, and Mago—Hasdrubal Gisgo, Maharbal, and Carthalo. Bog, the astrologer, Synhalus, the Egyptian physician, and Sosillos, Hannibal's Greek tutor, are also mentioned. Syphax, Masinissa, and Sophonisba all existed. Fabius Maximus, Marcellus, Minucius, Flaminius, Varro, the Scipios—father and son—are all well known in Roman history. Philemenus and Nico, the young Tarentines, were real people as, of course, was Archimedes.

One of the striking things about Hannibal is that we know him only through the eyes of his enemies. There are no Carthaginian accounts of his life. He was a writer himself, but none of his books survived him. Yet even Livy, who wrote his Annals as a monument to the greatness of Rome, cannot hide the greatness of Hannibal. He calls Hannibal cruel, perfidious, and eager for money. Yet nothing he tells us about Hannibal is so savagely cruel as the Roman treatment of Hasdrubal Barca's dead body. Romans broke treaties with Carthage when it suited them to do so. Hannibal needed money to carry on the war that Rome had chosen to fight against Carthage. Since Carthage did not supply enough money, Hannibal used his own. From Livy we learn that Hannibal never asked his men to go where he would not go himself, that he ate little, dressed simply, slept" on his cloak on the ground near the sentries. Although his troops were of many races, none ever mutinied against him.

Certainly the men who followed him loyally for sixteen years did not think of him as cruel, unworthy of trust, or ungenerous. His army was always smaller than the Roman army it faced, but Hannibal's presence gave each man a confidence that doubled his strength.

Livy was not born until more than a hundred years after Hannibal died. He got his information from earlier writers, whose works have now vanished. Luckily we have Polybius's history. Livy probably used it, though his praise of it is faint— "not untrustworthy" and "not contemptible" are some of the compliments he pays Polybius. The latter is not so interesting a writer as Livy, but he is more trustworthy for several reasons.

One is that he was actually alive during the last part of Hannibal's life. Another is that in Greece, his native country, he was himself a soldier and a statesman. He understood what he was writing about. After he was enslaved by the Romans, he became a tutor to Publius Cornelius Scipio Africanus the Younger, the adopted grandson of Scipio Africanus. Polybius was present at the final destruction of Carthage. When he began work on his History, the Scipio family helped him in his research by making family papers available to him. He traveled widely in Africa, Spain, and Asia Minor, and even made a crossing of the Alps to see the obstacles Hannibal encountered.

As I had no translation of Livy, I had to read it in Latin. I had not used my Latin much for about fifty years, and it was a little rusty. I was luckier with Polybius. The book was in Greek, but there was English on the opposite page. The Kellogg-Hubbard Library found the Livy for me, and the Brookline (Massachusetts) Public Library made it possible for me to use the Polybius. I am grateful to them both. Anyone who becomes interested in Hannibal will enjoy reading Harold Lamb's and Leonard Cottrell's books about him. Cottrell, like Polybius, had the enthusiasm to follow much of Hannibal's probable route in the Alpine crossing. De Beer in *Alps and Elephants* convinced me that he had identified the route correctly. F. A. Dodge's *Great Captains: Hannibal*, an old book, is still one of the most interesting accounts of Hannibal's military genius.

The name of Hannibal's son is not given in any of the books I read. I am responsible for thinking that Hannibal, who was devoted to the memory of his father, may have called him Hamilcar. The date of his death and that of his mother are uncertain. We know only that Hannibal never saw them again after he left New Carthage for Italy.

I hope that some of my readers will feel, as I did, that reading about Hannibal makes them wish to learn more about the great change that took place when the Roman Republic became the Roman Empire. The war with Carthage was one of the causes for that change.

Some of the books I read were John Buchan's *Augustus*, Robert Graves's *I, Claudius*, Edith Hamilton's *The Roman Way*, Elizabeth Bowen's *A Time in Rome*. One thing led to another; and I found myself reading Cowell's *Cicero and the Roman Republic, The Complete Works of Horace, The Poems of Catullus, The Satires of Juvenal*, Gibbon's *Decline and Fall of the Roman Empire*, Carcopino's *Daily Life in Ancient Rome*, Shakespeare's *Antony and Cleopatra*, Shaw's *Caesar and Cleopatra*, Fowler's *Social Life at Rome*, Plutarch's *Lives*—in other words, everything I came across that had any bearing on the subject.

I suppose I got ideas from all of them. The story about the Elephant Who Forgot is over two thousand years old; so, it seems as if Hannibal, who was interested in elephants, may have known it. Like the elephant, I am forgetful, too; and I can't remember to which book I am grateful for it.

Any mistakes are original: I made them myself.